Boys in Blue

Leipfold Mysteries
by Dane Cobain

Driven

The Tower Hill Terror

The Leipfold Files

Boys in Blue

Boys in Blue

Leipfold Mysteries • Book 4

Dane Cobain

Encircle Publications
Farmington, Maine, U.S.A.

Encircle editor: Cynthia Brackett-Vincent

Cover design: Christopher Wait
Cover photographs © Getty Images

Published by:

Encircle Publications
PO Box 187
Farmington, ME 04938

info@encirclepub.com
http://encirclepub.com

To every James Leipfold,
Maile O'Hara, and Jack Cholmondeley.

A Note on the Text

MAILE AND LEIPFOLD LIVE in a London that's similar to, but not identical to, our own. It's a London where the villains are straight from the pages of a comic book, where the heroes are unusual (but normal) people, struggling to do the best they can in the knowledge that life doesn't always turn out like it does in the storybooks.

Because of that, not all of the city's geography is one hundred percent accurate. If you walk along Balcombe Street, you won't be able to follow it down an alleyway, up the stairs and into Leipfold's office. You won't be able to visit Cholmondeley at the Old Vic, either.

Likewise, all of the characters are creatures of the imagination. Any similarities with real people—living or dead, fictional or otherwise—are purely coincidental.

If you ever find yourself falling through a rabbit hole and resurfacing in Leipfold's London, be sure to buy him a lemonade from me. And if he's riding Camilla, give her a pat on the handlebars.

Chapter One:
Gardening Leave

SERGEANT GARY MOGFORD WAS in a bit of a tizzy. His mind was like a sports car racing loops around a circuit, and he couldn't catch up with it no matter how hard he tried. It had been that kind of night. He'd been about to knock off for the evening when the call had come in.

Mogford had blood on his hands, as well as on his cheek and his forehead. It wasn't metaphorical. The paramedics, when they'd finally arrived, had tried to wipe it off him, but he'd fought against them and worn the blood like a badge of honour as the ambulance had wound its way through the city.

Constable Groves and Sergeant Mogford had responded to a routine bulletin about a couple of suspicious youths, maybe half a mile away from the underground prison where Kat Cotteril had been held hostage. The case still weighed on Mogford's mind. While he'd belatedly realised that he'd miss the old man, he was secretly glad that Cholmondeley had taken the fall for failing to crack it.

The kids—because that was what they were if his quick visual was anything to go by—had resisted arrest. Three of them had rushed the two coppers, and the fourth had pulled out a firearm and discharged it during the commotion. At first, Mogford thought it had been a warning shot. Then, as the kids broke away like waves on the shore, he'd seen the blood blooming on Groves' breast, and she'd slumped meekly to the floor before Mogford had been able to catch her.

The fourth kid, the one who'd taken the shot, had lurked a little longer than the others.

"Take that, pig!" he'd jeered. "Tell your bosses that this was a gift for old man Cholmondeley."

Then he'd tucked the gun, a snub-nosed pistol that looked like a relic from the Second World War, into the belt of his jeans, before zipping his coat to hide it and setting off in pursuit of his cronies. Mogford had already taken a half dozen steps after him before he remembered his fallen comrade. He'd stopped himself, cursed and then returned to her side.

Groves was conscious but badly wounded, and Mogford had taken a couple of seconds to check her over before reaching for his radio and calling it in.

"Attention, all units!" he'd shouted. "I need backup on West End Street. Officer down. Repeat, officer down. Send me a goddamn ambulance. Groves has been hit!"

The dispatcher had sent Mogford a quick reply to ask for information, and Mogford had obediently explained how Groves had taken a bullet. Then he'd given a brief description of the assailants and explained their current trajectory. There were no cruisers in the area, but dispatch had said that they'd have feet on the ground within six minutes. An ambulance was already on its way.

"Tell them to get a move on," Mogford had growled. "It's bad. It's real bad. We need to get her to a hospital."

"Roger that."

Mogford had signed off the discussion and thrown his radio down, then kneeled on the floor in a pool of blood to staunch the flow of blood and to keep Groves talking until the medics arrived. He knew from unpleasant experience that if she lost consciousness, she might not find it again. Worse, the initial shot was only part of the problem—without immediate medical attention, she could have bled out on the pavement or gone into shock. So he'd talked to her about nothing and everything, about the future, the past and the present.

And, while he'd waited for the ambulance to arrive, he'd found himself offering up a prayer for the first time since he'd been a child and had accidentally killed a pigeon with his slingshot.

Don't let her die, he'd thought. *Don't let her die, don't let her die, don't let her die.*

* * *

It was the following day, and Sergeant Gary Mogford was in Superintendent Isabelle Richards' office. It was much nicer than Cholmondeley's old office, which was bare and bleak and which smelled faintly of eau de cologne.

Richards' office was kitted out with oak panelling and family photographs printed onto fabric and hanging from the walls like little tapestries. It had a neutral smell, with a hint of freshness from the open window. It was cold in there, mostly because the room had been empty all day.

Richards nodded at Mogford and gestured for him to take a seat. Her own chair was old, an antique. She'd bought it herself and brought it in, then swiftly promised vengeance on anyone who tried to take it. But the visitors' chair was sculpted from blue plastic, the same type of chair that they had sitting in the waiting rooms. Mogford wondered whether it was some sort of metaphor for the trappings of power, but he suspected it was more of a shrewd, calculated move to make visitors to her office feel conspicuous and out of place.

Once they were both sitting down, and after Mogford had plopped his notebook onto his lap and flicked through it to find a clean page, she said, "Thanks for coming, Sergeant."

"My pleasure, ma'am," he replied. He snapped off a brisk salute that looked more comical than he'd intended, then smiled bashfully across at her. "What can I help you with?"

"Constable Groves," she said. "How is she?"

"Tough to tell, ma'am. I went to see her last night, but she's not looking good. She's lost a lot of blood and fallen into a coma, although the doctors say her condition has stabilised. Now it's just a waiting game. Want to know what I think?"

"Why not?"

Mogford leaned forward conspiratorially and said, "I think she's bloody lucky to be alive, if you'll pardon my French."

"Your what?"

"Never mind," Mogford said.

Superintendent Richards looked at him as though he was a piece of shit on her shoe.

"Indeed," she said. "Well, anyway. I have a favour to ask of you."

Mogford shrugged and said, "If I can help, I'll help."

"Excellent." The superintendent clasped her hands together. She looked like a cross between a supervillain in a bad comic book and a frazzled nun at prayer, and Mogford suspected that she was actually a bit of both.

"Ma'am?"

"I need your help, Sergeant," she said, unclasping her fingers and letting her hands drop to the desk. "I have a proposition to make."

She paused and looked him up and down again.

"I have a problem," she said. "You see, now that Jack Cholmondeley's gone, I need a new detective inspector to take his place. Any ideas?"

"Well," Mogford began, "there's Sergeant Riggs from the forensic team. He's quite–"

"I'm not talking about Riggs, Sergeant Mogford," Richards interrupted. "I'm talking about you, you silly sod. How do you fancy a promotion?"

"Me?" Mogford's mouth hung agape, and he dropped his pen to the floor, then tried to style it out by pretending that nothing had happened.

"Yes, you," Richards said. "I'm offering you a promotion."

Mogford gasped, and the colour drained from his face and melted away. He'd known this moment would come someday, and he'd been preparing himself just in case. He liked being a sergeant. But he also had no choice.

"It'd be an honour," he said, eventually.

"Good," Richards replied. "There'll be no change to your title, of course. Not yet at least. But it's worth a couple extra grand a year if you play your cards right. Speaking of which..."

Mogford groaned inwardly and asked, "What is it?"

"I need you to track down Jack Cholmondeley," Richards said. "I need you to bring him in."

"Ma'am?" Mogford looked confused, like a puppy who'd been kicked in the face by a stranger.

"For questioning," Richards added. "Let's see what he has to say for himself."

"Ma'am."

Mogford saluted again and froze in position. Richards stared at him from across the desk. "Is there anything else I can help you with?"

"No, ma'am."

"Good," she said. She smiled softly. "Now pick that bloody pen up and get out of my office. I've got a police force to run."

*   *   *

When the policemen came for him—two of his own lads, good boys that he'd trained himself—Detective Inspector Jack Cholmondeley was in a dark, dark place. He was also at the bottom of a bottle.

Several days earlier, after his men had cracked the case of the Tower Hill Terror, Cholmondeley's wife had asked him for a divorce. The detective inspector was married to his job, like all good policemen, but he'd been married to Mary Cholmondeley for just as long. When he wrapped things up at the office after a long day of dealing with murderers, rapists and the ilk, Mary was his one constant, the only thing that kept him going. Of course, her obsession with ceramic garden gnomes—and, more recently, tacky plastic flamingos—could be difficult to deal with, but she made up for it by always making sure that there was a hot meal on the table.

And now she was gone, or at least she was going. She'd announced her intention to divorce him, packed a couple of his cases with his most vital belongings and then shipped him off to pastures new.

Which meant that Detective Inspector Jack Cholmondeley was living in a rented room on the outskirts of Camberwell. It was a spit-and-sawdust shithouse that belonged to a bygone era. The rooms were so scummy that they could be rented by the night, as long as cash was provided up front.

Cholmondeley had driven there in his Beemer after spotting the to-let ad in *The Tribune*'s classifieds, and he'd taken one quick look around before deciding that he didn't want to leave his car outside in case he never saw it again. And so hesitantly, reluctantly, he'd parked it by James Leipfold's office in Balcombe Street.

That had been on the Friday night. On Saturday, he'd received word from the station that he was being placed on gardening leave pending an internal investigation, and on Sunday, he'd bought himself a 700ml bottle of Jack Daniel's.

Cholmondeley looked around the room, his eyes settling on the wall-mounted clock that was hanging from a nail on an old corkboard. It said that it was 2:18, with no indication of whether it was the morning or the afternoon. It didn't matter much to Jack Cholmondeley.

His room came with an uncomfortable mattress on a cast-iron bedframe, a chipped basin with a small light above it and a built-in wardrobe, which he'd filled with his clothes. His suitcases were stacked side-by-side in one corner of the room with a copy of *The Sunday Times* folded up on top of them.

He poured out another glass of whiskey on the rocks, minus the rocks because the room had no fridge or freezer. His rent covered the use of a communal kitchen and bathroom, but he was yet to use the first and he'd only used the second when he'd had to.

There was a knock at the door, and he cursed quietly to himself. Then he stood up slowly, narrowly avoiding bashing his head across the eaves, and walked over to the sink. He splashed a little water across his face and examined his reflection in the mirror. The bags under his eyes were bigger than normal and his greying temples were more accentuated, but he didn't think he looked too bad.

The real problem was his clothing. He'd never felt comfortable out of uniform, even before he'd been a copper. As a kid, he'd been more at ease in his school uniform than in his Sunday best, and he hadn't owned any casual clothes.

His mother had been of the old school, a fearsome Irish Catholic with a tongue fierce enough to lick the paint off a radiator. He'd wanted for nothing, but only because he hadn't been allowed to want things. He'd been taught instead to thank God for what little he had. Not that he'd ever been anything more than a lazy agnostic.

All of that practice was coming in useful now, with his marriage falling apart and his professional life on hold. It was hard to be grateful about living in a shit-heap, but he had to start somewhere.

Jack Cholmondeley forced a smile onto his face and opened the door. Two uniformed officers were standing outside in the foyer.

"Ah, Constable Cohen," he said. "It's good to see you. Can I tempt you with a cup of coffee? I don't have a kettle here, I'm afraid, but there's a wonderful Café Nero just—"

"I'm afraid not, sir," Constable Cohen replied. He was one of the younger coppers, a British Asian with a Jewish surname who'd started out on reception. The only gay copper in a world of latent homophobes, he'd struggled to make headway at the Old Vic until Cholmondeley had taken him under his wing. In return, he'd always displayed a remarkable amount of loyalty towards the old man. Cholmondeley could see from the expression on Cohen's face that he wasn't happy to be there.

"Please," he said. "I'm on gardening leave. You can call me Mr. Cholmondeley. You can even call me Jack, if you'd like."

"I'd rather not, if you don't mind, sir," Cohen replied, his ears reddening. "Could you accompany us to the station, please?"

"Am I under arrest?" Cholmondeley asked.

"Not at the moment, sir."

"And do I have a choice?"

"Not really, sir, no," Cohen said. "Sorry, sir."

*   *   *

On the other side of the city in Balcombe Street, times were brisk for Leipfold Investigations. Just a couple of months ago, the lack of clients and the high rent had almost put Leipfold out of business.

But ever since he'd hired Maile O'Hara, his tech-savvy assistant and metaphorical partner-in-crime, business had been booming. It probably helped that, unlike Leipfold, she knew her way around the social networks. She also had an eye for a story. While she'd only been working on their website for a couple of months, enquiries were up 300 percent and there was more than enough work to go around. They were snowed under.

"We're going to need to hire someone else," Maile said.

She was leaning into her brand-new standing desk and tapping away at her keyboard. Leipfold had finally caved and signed off on the budget for the desk after the culmination of their last case. She'd set the desk up as soon as it had arrived. It hadn't taken her long to develop the disconcerting habit of looking down at

Leipfold from across the room, like some sapient CCTV camera with bat tattoos and a dark sense of humour. It was adjustable too, which meant that when she was working late, she could lower it down and scooch across to it in a chair.

"We can't afford it," Leipfold said lazily, turning his attention back to *The Tribune*. He was scanning the local news and looking out for anything unusual, an activity that took him as long as it took him to drink a cup of tea and eat a handful of ginger biscuits.

"I'm not so sure about that," Maile told him. "I've been working on the finances, remember? Cash flow is looking pretty good."

"We need to hold some back for the future," Leipfold replied. "And besides, those ads you're running are costing a fortune."

"They're working, aren't they?"

"Point taken."

"Anyway," Maile pressed, "we can afford a cleaner."

That was true, at least. The cleaner they'd hired was a young woman called Jowie Frankowska, a contact they'd made through an earlier investigation. She'd reluctantly agreed to clean the office at a discount rate as a half-arsed thank you to the agency.

Since Frankowska had started cleaning the place, the office had become almost unrecognisable. She'd tackled everything from the spider webs and the dust on Leipfold's old files to the big, opaque windows, which had turned out to be clear beneath the grime. After a good amount of cleaning and polishing, they lit up with sunlight in the mornings and transformed the room.

"She was a good hire," Leipfold agreed, thinking back to his morning cuppa. She'd even cleaned the limescale out of the kettle and managed to bleach out the stains inside Leipfold's favourite mug. "I guess we could use the help, if we can make it work financially. What did you have in mind?"

"Someone to do the paperwork," Maile said. "Someone to do the boring stuff so I can focus on bringing in more work and helping you out with the cases."

"And someone who'll work for national minimum wage," Leipfold said.

"I don't know about that," Maile replied. "You had me here on an unpaid internship."

"But where will I find someone as foolish as you?"

"I've got a few ideas about that," Maile said. "You leave it with me."

"Fine," Leipfold said, folding up his newspaper and climbing abruptly to his feet. "Draft up a job description and work some of your magic. I'll take a look when I get back."

"Where are you going?"

"Camilla's calling my name," Leipfold replied, talking over his shoulder as he rummaged around for his leathers. "I'm off to see an old friend of ours to see how he's holding up. I'm going to visit Jack Cholmondeley."

*   *   *

But when he pulled up outside Cholmondeley's new digs on his motorbike, he found himself just in time to watch the old man being ushered into the back of a police car.

For Jack Cholmondeley, that wasn't so unusual. If anything, it was part of the job. But something about it made Leipfold uneasy. The old copper wasn't wearing handcuffs, but he did have his head bowed and even from a distance, Leipfold could see the look of pained regret in his subordinates. Something was amiss.

Chapter Two:
Whiskey

IN ONE OF THE dingy investigation rooms somewhere below ground at the Old Vic, Jack Cholmondeley was on the receiving end of his own advanced interrogation techniques. Several years earlier, the top brass had sent him on a four-day course in Harrogate, and he'd brought back his notes and imparted his newfound wisdom to the younger recruits.

Unfortunately, it didn't work. In fact, it was just a spin on the old good cop/bad cop routine, only the good cop was Constable Cohen and the bad cop was Sergeant Mogford. He couldn't fault them for playing to their strengths, but their hearts weren't in it. It didn't take him long to find out why.

"Shot?" he exclaimed, when they told him what had happened. "But when? And why?"

"Can't tell you that, boss," Cohen said. "I've been told—"

"Now listen here," Mogford interrupted, leaning in a little and putting his not inconsiderable weight behind the movement. Cholmondeley was the taller of the two men and he was also in better shape, but Mogford was meaner, though not vindictive. "Whether we like the situation or not, it is what it is. We've had orders from the top that while you're on gardening leave, we're not to share any information about active cases."

"You know, gardening leave is a strange term," Cholmondeley murmured. "Especially when you no longer have a garden."

"Constable Groves was involved in a serious incident," Mogford continued. "You know as well as I do that you're duty bound to help us to investigate an attack on one of our own."

"Yes indeed," Cholmondeley replied. "Duty bound by my conscience, if nothing else. But I don't understand, Gary. Why am I here?"

"Before they fled the scene," Constable Cohen said, "the assailants said something we were hoping you could shed some light on."

"What might that be, son?"

"'Tell your bosses that this is for old man Cholmondeley,'" Mogford quoted. "Strange, don't you think?"

"Probably just some old con with a grudge against me," Cholmondeley replied. "I can give you a list of names if you think it would help. I must warn you, though. I've made my fair share of enemies."

"Hmm." Mogford paused for a moment to consult the notes in front of him. "If you could do that before you leave here, that would be great."

Cholmondeley looked around the room, squinting at the two-way glass as though he was trying to see who was on the other side. He had a pretty good idea of who might be there.

"You know," he said, leaning forward and lowering his voice, though he knew it would still be picked up by the microphones. "It seems to me as though there's an agenda here. I think someone's out to get me."

"Yes, sir," Cohen replied. "You should watch your back out there. If these hooligans were willing to attack Constable Groves in broad daylight, they'll be willing to take a shot at you, too."

"Oh, I doubt that," Cholmondeley said, thoughtfully. "If they wanted to attack me, they could have. But they didn't. Why is that, do you think?"

"You tell us," Mogford growled.

"I'm still working on it," Cholmondeley replied. "Why attack Groves instead of just going for me? To send me a message?"

"You're close to her," Mogford said. "You always have been. It's no secret that she's your protégé. You've been grooming her to climb the ranks."

"She has a lot of spunk," Cholmondeley replied. "She reminds me of myself when I was younger."

"They probably thought it'd hurt you more if they shot her than, say, me."

"You might be right there, Gary," Cholmondeley said. "No offence meant, of course."

"None taken."

"Groves is a good cop," Cohen said. "I suppose I should be thankful that they chose her and not me."

"Or Mary," Cholmondeley mused. "Why didn't they target her?"

"She's not a cop," Mogford said. "Perhaps they don't want to involve a civilian. Problem is, guv, I get that they shot Groves to send you a message. But what was the message?"

Cholmondeley just shook his head and asked for a glass of water.

* * *

"Do me a favour, Maile," Leipfold said. "Run some research for me on a private client."

Maile looked up from her computer screen, where she was in the middle of confirming that she wasn't a robot. The boss had been in a strange mood ever since he'd visited Jack Cholmondeley, and he hadn't said a word to her since he'd walked back into the office. He'd grunted his assent when she'd asked if he wanted a cuppa, but that was about it.

"Sure," she said. "What do you need?"

"It's Jack Cholmondeley," Leipfold replied. "The man's in a bind.

You know what happened with his wife, right?”

“You mean when she showed up on a dating app, he confronted her, and she kicked him out of their house?” Maile asked. “Poor guy. He always seemed so…well, *nice*.”

“He’s not dead, Maile,” Leipfold reminded her. “He’s just down on his luck, that’s all. I know what that’s like. I’d like to help him if I can.”

“And you think that prying into his marriage is a good way to do that?”

“I don’t know much about romance,” Leipfold said, “but I do know that the Cholmondeleys had something special. Why would Mary risk it all?”

Maile sighed, then reached into her bag and pulled out a stick of gum. She tossed it into her mouth and started chewing.

“What exactly do you want me to do, boss?” she asked. “I’m kind of busy right now. I wasn’t joking when I said we need some help. Do you want me to chase ghosts or do you want me to make money?”

“I want you to do both,” Leipfold replied. “I’ve got one of my hunches. I think someone’s out to get Jack Cholmondeley.”

“So why do you want me to look into Mary?”

“He loves that woman,” Leipfold said. “God knows why, but he does. If someone wanted to hurt Jack Cholmondeley, Mary would be the obvious target.”

*　*　*

Jack Cholmondeley was back at his bedsit after helping the police with their enquiries and being released without charge. Constable Cohen had offered to drop him home, but Sergeant Mogford had overruled him, ordering him instead to spend the morning digitising files from the evidence room so that they could clear out some space.

Cholmondeley said he didn't mind because he wanted to walk.

It was nearly four miles back to his apartment, and his pace wasn't as brisk as it used to be, so it took him the best part of an hour and a half. Back when he'd first joined the force, that pace would have been too slow and would have excluded him from walking the beat. But as he kept on reminding himself, he was no longer a police officer.

And so he took it slowly, enjoying the feel of the city's streets beneath his feet, occasionally taking the long way round if it meant seeing more of the scenery. Some people thought London was ugly, but Jack Cholmondeley had always found a subtle beauty in her streets, even when he was walking through the back alleys.

He was so lost in his thoughts, he found himself absentmindedly walking back towards the sprawling townhouse that he'd shared with Mary, and then he cursed as his brain processed an order and his feet turned themselves around. They marched themselves into an off-license on the way back, too.

By the time that he got back to his bedsit, his feet were tired and his legs ached, but the perpetual, critical voices in his head had quietened down. He thought he might even get some sleep if his noisy neighbours ever quietened down.

He'd been living in the bedsit for the best part of a week, but he was yet to meet any of the other tenants. That all changed when he got back from his walk and started fumbling with his keys at the main entrance. He'd just found the right one when a young woman walked up from behind him and slipped her key in the lock.

"Allow me," she said.

"Thank you, young lady," Cholmondeley replied. "I've never got the hang of these things."

"Tell me about it," the woman replied. "I keep losing them."

"You should change the locks."

"With a landlord like mine?" she scoffed. Then she softened. "But you're living here too now, aren't you?"

"Yes, indeed," he said. "My name's Jack Cholmondeley. What's yours?"

"Natasha Raynor," she replied. "I live at number four."

Cholmondeley nodded. He lived at number five, which meant that her apartment backed on to his. Most of the noise came from the floor above, and so he ticked her off his mental list of suspects.

Despite being on gardening leave, his instincts were still intact. Natasha Raynor made for an interesting specimen. In her early twenties, her conservative outfit screamed PhD student, but Cholmondeley was old-fashioned and the main thing he noticed was her skin tone. He guessed she was British Asian, though perhaps only on her mother's side, which would explain the name. She was pretty, but not in a striking way, and her eyes sparkled mischievously as though she saw the world in a different light, as though life itself was just an in-joke.

"Have you been here long?" he asked weakly, hoping that his awkwardness wasn't shining through, or worse—that he was coming across as an old pervert. "I mean to say, I'm new here. I'm still working things out."

"What's to work out?" Raynor replied. "You get what you pay for. No one lives here by choice. I'll see you around, Mr. Chumnumberly."

"See you around," he replied. Jack Cholmondeley was old school, and so he held the door open and tipped his hat to her before following her into the building and returning to his apartment.

That evening, he ate beans on toast in front of the TV, watching reruns of old American detective shows in his Y-fronts. He poured himself a whiskey on the rocks, demolished it, and then poured out another but without the ice. Soon, he was swigging directly from the bottle.

Mary didn't call him that night, though he wasn't expecting her to. Ever since she'd kicked him out, she'd been giving him the cold shoulder. Unfortunately for Jack Cholmondeley, his job was his life and his life was his job, and that didn't leave much time for socialising. Mary had always been the only person who ever called him, other than his colleagues. But his colleagues only had his work number and he'd had to turn his phone in, and Mary was leaving him to stew it out. And so his phone remained silent.

Other than a battered copy of *The Brothers Karamazov* that Leipfold had lent him, his phone was the only personal item that he had with him. He didn't even have his police badge, which had been turned in alongside his work phone.

He sighed and took another swig of whiskey. He'd long since given up on pouring it out into a glass.

*   *   *

At the Old Vic, Constable Cohen was in the middle of an uncomfortable conversation with Superintendent Richards. She was so far up the hierarchy that he wasn't normally on her radar, but she was taking an unusually close interest in Cholmondeley's gardening leave, and Cohen had resigned himself to her micromanagement. Most young cops would have relished the opportunity to work so closely with a superior officer. For Constable Cohen, it was just inconvenient.

"Don't you think everything's running more smoothly since we got rid of Jack?" Superintendent Richards asked.

"You mean Detective Inspector Cholmondeley?" Cohen replied, a lick of colour seeping into his cheeks at the loaded question.

"Perhaps not for much longer," Richards said.

"What do you mean?"

"Oh, nothing," she murmured. "But you have to admit, Sergeant Mogford is doing a wonderful job."

"Well, he's certainly doing something," Cohen said. That was about as far as he was willing to go. Mogford was good at what he did, when he wanted to be, but he was also an old-school copper with a short temper. "It's just a lot of change, that's all. I'm sure we'll all get used to it."

There was an awkward silence as they realised that the only thing they had in common was the job they shared. And even that wasn't accurate, because they didn't share a job, they shared an employer. Superintendent Richards was as far away from a beat cop as it was possible to be, while Cohen had zero interest in politics and was only there because he liked to help people.

"How's Constable Groves?" Richards asked, breaking the silence with a voice so terse it could have had troublesome schoolboys scuttling back to their desks with their tails between their legs. "Have you seen her?"

"She's at St. Thomas'," Cohen replied. "I saw her before my shift. She's still sedated, but she's conscious. The doctors say she'll live."

"That's wonderful news," Richards replied, smiling sweetly at him. "Were you two close?"

"We *are* close, ma'am," Cohen said. "No news on a discharge date, but it can only be a matter of time."

"Good," Richards said, clapping her hands together suddenly and giving Cohen a nasty shock. If they'd been walking the corridors instead of sitting down in the canteen, he would have dropped his cup of coffee. "I'll have Sergeant Riggs and his forensics team run some tests on the bullet that the doctors removed. We'll see if we can figure out what kind of weapon was used. Perhaps the firearm was used somewhere else and we'll be able to find a match."

"Yes, ma'am."

"We'll have her back on the beat in no time."

"If you say so, ma'am," Constable Cohen replied.

* * *

It was a typical gloomy Thursday evening in the middle of March, and Jack Cholmondeley was alone in his bedsit with another bottle of whiskey. He'd been buying the expensive stuff, the aged scotch that he usually drank, but it was starting to cost him a small fortune. He was still being paid by the Met Police, but only until his contract ran out. Then he'd be switching over to his pension, and he'd worked too hard to drink it all away in his one-room hell-hole.

He sighed and checked his phone again, but there were no new messages. He'd caved and called Mary a few times, but they had caller ID and she knew his number, so she hadn't answered. But he wasn't ready to confront her in person. Not yet.

Cholmondeley opened up his contacts and scrolled down to the first of the two names that were stored there. Then he called James Leipfold.

"Hello?" he said, once the call connected. "James?"

"Jack!" Leipfold said. The call quality was terrible and there was music playing in the background. Leipfold was raising his voice to make himself heard above it. "How are you, buddy?"

"Not so good, James," Cholmondeley said. "Not so good."

"Trouble at the station?" Leipfold asked. "I saw you getting escorted into the back of a cop car."

"Nothing I can't handle," Cholmondeley replied. "Are you busy tonight?"

"Not with anything I can't postpone." There was a burst of crunchy feedback, and then Leipfold came back on the line. The music in the background was quieter, though still audible. "What's up?"

"I need someone to drink with," Cholmondeley said. "I can't stand drinking alone."

"I don't drink, Jack," Leipfold reminded him.

"I'll get you a lemonade," Cholmondeley replied. "What do you say, James?"

Leipfold sighed, and now that the music had quietened down, it carried clearly.

"I'll be over in an hour," he said. "Make sure that my lemonade has ice in it."

*   *   *

As he cruised away from the bar on the back of Camilla, Leipfold had to admit that sobriety had its perks. Being able to drive home was one of them, though he'd have to take a detour to see Jack Cholmondeley first.

Maile had wanted to go with him, but Leipfold had put his foot down. She'd already had two drinks herself and was due to meet her housemate, Kat Cotteril. And so he'd driven to Cholmondeley's alone, basking in the loneliness of the night. The rain had kept most people inside, leaving the roads empty and the city's streets his for the taking. It reminded him of the night several months ago when Donna Thompson had been mown down by a car. The streets had been empty then, too.

His thoughts drifted as he rode, but he still kept his eyes on the road. When he reached Cholmondeley's place, he chained the bike to the railings outside the corner shop a couple of doors down. It was partly lit by the glow of a street lamp and the shop had cameras. Leipfold suspected that they weren't turned on, but they would at least act as a deterrent to anyone thinking about taking Camilla for a late-night joyride.

The intercom to the building didn't work, and so Leipfold did as requested and called Cholmondeley to let him in. The old man greeted him at the door in a mothballed tweed suit that looked like it belonged in a charity shop, then led him through the harshly lit hallways and into his apartment.

Leipfold watched as Cholmondeley poured a glass of whiskey and took a slug from it. The old man winced at the taste and then, seeming to remember that he had a visitor, he rifled through a carrier bag and came out with a can of Schweppes.

"I don't have a fridge, I'm afraid," he said, apologetically.

"It'll do just fine," Leipfold replied, taking the can and cracking it open. He took a sip from it. "To more salubrious surroundings."

"To more salubrious surroundings."

A momentary silence descended as Cholmondeley knocked back another slug of whiskey. They could hear a woman moaning and the banging of a distant headboard, as well as a loud television set that seemed to be screening some sort of crime show.

"Are you going to talk to me, Jack?" Leipfold asked, swirling the lemonade around in its aluminum can. "You know, about Mary? About what happened?"

"There's not much to tell," Cholmondeley replied, gloomily. "You already know most of it. Mary had a profile on that damned dating app, so I confronted her about it. I gave her a chance to explain herself. You know, in case there was an innocent explanation. Perhaps someone was just using her photographs."

Leipfold maintained a neutral expression, though privately he found it unlikely that anyone would pretend to look like Mary Cholmondeley.

"Anyway," Jack continued, "she isn't talking to me, so I have no way of knowing. If I could just talk to her, perhaps I—"

"If she wants to talk to you, she'll call you," Leipfold said, firmly. "Though I'll admit that I don't know much about relationships, Jack. Truth be told, I don't like people."

"And the pope wears a pointy hat."

"Indeed," Leipfold said. He paused to take another sip from his lemonade. The banging headboards had intensified, and the moaning woman was screaming the name Joe. She was either climaxing or she was an impressive actress. It was a sound that neither man had heard for several years, at least in person.

"Sorry about the neighbours," Cholmondeley said, as though he was remarking on the weather. "I'm hoping not to stay here too long. They let me pay by the week."

Leipfold didn't bother to reply to that. He was living somewhere similar himself.

"You need to pick yourself up and get back on your feet, Jack," Leipfold said. "This is no time to give up and let life walk all over you. You've got to seize the day, old friend. *Carpe diem* and all that."

"*Carpe potum*," Cholmondeley replied, taking another hit of his whiskey. Leipfold watched him wince as the sharp liquor hit his throat. "If it's all the same to you, James, I'd quite like to sit around in my underpants until Mary sees sense."

"You'll never win her back with that attitude," Leipfold said. "Jesus, Jack, I remember a time when the tables were turned and it was you who helped me. Now it's my turn to return the favour. You've got to stop drinking. You're going to kill yourself."

"Maybe tomorrow," Cholmondeley said.

Abruptly, James Leipfold launched himself off his seat and grabbed the bottle from the old man's bedside table. Before Cholmondeley could stop him, Leipfold had perched over the little sink in the corner and was pouring the stuff down the drain.

"Hey," Cholmondeley said, "that's twenty quid a bottle."

"Exactly, Jack," Leipfold said. "It's a waste of money."

Cholmondeley lunged at him, but Leipfold was too fast and he snatched the bottle away. Then Cholmondeley rushed him again, but he was drunk and the older of the two. He had no chance.

"Jack!" Leipfold shouted, as he pinned Cholmondeley's arms behind his back and pushed him against the wall. "Jack, this isn't you! Get your shit together!"

"I can't, James," Cholmondeley replied. "I don't know how."

Then he burst into tears.

*   *   *

It took James Leipfold the best part of half an hour to get

Cholmondeley to settle down again, as well as at least three chipped mugs full of water from the sink and half a tube of toothpaste. It didn't sober him up completely, but it also didn't do any harm.

Cholmondeley asked to go to the bathroom. While he was in there, Leipfold let himself into the poky shared kitchen and brewed a pot of coffee. He met a lovely young woman called Natasha while he was in there. She said she was from number four and was kind enough to show him where everything was.

"Are you entertaining?" Leipfold asked, nodding at the five cups of tea she was pouring out.

"Oh, you know," Natasha replied. "I have some uh…friends over."

"The world would be a better place if more people were friends," Leipfold said. Then he nodded at her and returned to Jack Cholmondeley, who was sitting on his bed with his head in his hands and his elbows on his knees. There was a strong acidic smell in the air, and Leipfold surmised that he'd emptied his guts. But that was arguably a good thing because it would help to clear his body of the alcohol that had been wreaking its havoc on him for the last few weeks.

"You've got to get it together, Jack," Leipfold said, for the umpteenth time that evening. "You hear me?"

"Will you stay with me tonight, James?"

"Of course," Leipfold said, quietly resigning himself to a night without sleep. Even if Cholmondeley dozed off, there wasn't much room in there. There was a chair he could sit on, but there wasn't enough space for him to lie down, even on the floor.

"You're a good man," Cholmondeley said. "A good friend, too."

"Nobody's ever said either of those things to me before," Leipfold replied, but he was smiling and there was a twinkle in his eye. "Listen, Jack. I'll stay with you tonight if you promise to do something for me."

"What is it?"

"I want you to go to the station tomorrow and demand to talk to Superintendent Richards," Leipfold said. "Have a word with her and find out what's happening. If you're not going back to the police force, you need to know now."

"What about Mary?"

"Mary needs time," Leipfold said. "She needs some space too, for that matter. But you need to talk to Richards."

"Ugh," Cholmondeley groaned. "I think I'm going to be sick again."

Chapter Three:
Minimum Wage

IT WAS A LONG night for Jack Cholmondeley. The coffee worked wonders at sobering him up, but it also made his heart race dangerously until he could hear it beating in his temples. It also kept him up for most of the night, but that was nothing new.

Leipfold fell asleep in the chair.

In the morning, when the sun had risen and the first sounds of activity from the neighbouring apartments had leaked through the paper-thin walls, he woke James Leipfold, and the two of them shared a cup of coffee. Then Leipfold climbed on Camilla and rode off towards his office. The man looked as fresh as a bead of dew on a spring daisy.

For his part, Cholmondeley felt like death. He envied Leipfold for his clear head and wished he didn't still feel the tell-tale throb of last night's alcohol in his veins. For a moment, he thought about supping on the hair of the dog. Just one drink, just *one*.

But instead, he dragged himself into the shower and did the best he could to soak away his aches and pains before donning a fresh shirt and pair of trousers and climbing back into his jacket. He spritzed himself with Old Spice, looked in the mirror and gave himself a C-, then left the apartment, shutting the door behind him.

He hoped he was legal to drive.

The journey to the Old Vic was surreal, mostly because he had to pick his car up from Leipfold's office and wasn't used to approaching the station from that side of town. He also wasn't used to the visitor's car park, but they'd taken his pass away along with his badge. And it wasn't like he had much choice.

He also had to put up with waiting in reception until Richards could clear a window in her schedule for him to see her. It took two hours, during which Constable Cohen brought him three cups of tea. When Richards finally deigned to see him, she had him escorted into one of their poky interview rooms as though he was a common criminal.

"What do you want, Jack?" she asked, as soon as they'd sat down on the uncomfortable plastic seats.

"Closure," Cholmondeley replied. "A good friend of mine suggested it. I've given my life to the police force. I think it owes me an explanation."

Richards sighed and then looked around, as though making sure that they weren't being overheard. It was ironic, Cholmondeley thought, considering there was enough recording equipment in the walls alone to power a small studio.

"Listen, Jack," she began. She was putting on her professional voice, but it didn't work on him. He was used to dealing with the liars and the petty crooks on the street, and they were better at the art of deception than Richards would ever be. "It's like this."

"I'm listening."

"I'm under a lot of pressure from top brass," Richards said. "The fact of the matter is, Jack, you're being pensioned off. It's a budgetary thing, you know how it is. Some algorithm somewhere flagged you up as a waste of money."

"Cutting salaries and pensioning off cops won't help to keep peace on the streets," Cholmondeley said.

"You know that, and I know that," Richards replied, nodding absentmindedly. "But try telling that to the pen-pushers in charge of the coffers. Besides, let's face it. You're getting old."

"Charming," Cholmondeley said. He tried to push a smile on to his face, but it felt more like a grimace. "I'm not much older than you."

"But I've moved with the times, Jack," she replied, that creepy, unnatural smile still plastered across her features. "You're a relic, a fossil. There's no call for cops like you in a modern police force."

"We'll see about that."

"We already have," Richards said. "I'm sorry, Jack. It is what it is. We just don't need you around here. After you finish your gardening leave, you'll be eligible to start your pension. It's up to you whether you take it or not. Either way, your days as an active policeman are over. Now, I've got a rather important meeting and I can't afford to waste any more time here. Are we done? You can show yourself out, I'm sure."

*   *   *

"…so you see how it is, James," Cholmondeley concluded. "I'm being pensioned off."

"But you're the best cop on the force," Leipfold said, pinching the bridge of his nose and looking exasperatedly across at Jack Cholmondeley. They were sitting in the office's reception area, where the plastic chairs had recently been replaced by a couple of sofas that Maile had found going for free on an online marketplace.

"I'm old news, James," Cholmondeley said, his hands trembling noticeably as he took careful sips from a cup of coffee that was far too hot for human consumption. "I've had it."

"There must be something you can do," Leipfold replied, his mind already wandering. Jack Cholmondeley had been taking up a lot of his time of late, but he didn't want to turn the man away. He'd just have to work a ton of overtime to stay on top of the new cases and clients that kept coming in.

"Well," Cholmondeley said. "About that."

He paused for a moment, and Leipfold could already tell what was coming. He was going to ask for a favour, and judging from the length of the pause, it was going to be a biggie. It went on for so long that eventually the silence became too much.

"What is it?" Leipfold asked. "Spit it out, man."

"I thought I might try pulling a Leipfold," Cholmondeley said. He took another sip from the piping hot cuppa and winced when the liquid hit his tongue. "It's what we called it at the Vic when someone took on a case outside the official team and then beat them to the punch."

"I'm honoured," Leipfold replied, though he didn't feel it. "So it sounds like you need to find yourself a case."

"I've already got one," Cholmondeley replied, a shadow passing across his face. "Someone shot Constable Groves and said it was a message for me. I intend to find out who shot her."

"Before your pals on the force?" Leipfold asked. "Be careful, Jack. Without your badge, you're nothing. They could bust you for getting in the way of an active investigation."

"They won't."

"What makes you so sure?"

"We never busted you, did we?" Cholmondeley replied. He smiled, and while it was a thin half-grimace, it was as though a ray of warmth had settled over him. "No, don't worry about me, James. I know what I'm doing."

"You sure about that?"

That came from Maile O'Hara, who sounded as chipper as always. She'd wandered over from her desk and was eyeing Jack Cholmondeley with a look that Leipfold couldn't read.

"I'm nipping out to the shops," she said. "Do you need anything?"

"A bottle of scotch," Cholmondeley said.

"Ignore him," Leipfold told her. "Take a fiver out of the petty cash and get us some biscuits. The ones I like, you know, the—"

"The ginger biscuits," Maile said. "Yeah, I know. Back in ten."

"Where were we?" Leipfold asked, once Maile had let herself out and left the two of them in peace.

"You were about to offer me a job."

"I was?" Leipfold asked. "That doesn't sound like me. But you've caught me at a good time, Jack. I'm hiring. How does national minimum wage suit you?"

"It suits me just fine," Cholmondeley replied. "When do I start?"

"Today," Leipfold said. "Why do you think I asked Maile to get more biscuits?"

*   *   *

When Maile re-entered the office, Leipfold and Cholmondeley were embracing. She felt as though she'd walked in on a scene from some PG movie with a moral to it.

"Oh, sorry, boys," she said, backing out of the door and into the hallway. "I'll come back later."

"Don't be silly, Maile," Leipfold said. "Come on in. You can say hello to our new employee."

"New employee?" she replied, raising her eyebrow. "You mean Jack's joining us."

"I have nothing else to do," Cholmondeley said, flashing her a charming smile as he and Leipfold broke off their embrace.

"Could be a problem," Maile said, re-entering the room and setting a pack of biscuits down on Leipfold's desk before returning to her own and sitting down in front of her machine. "We've got some interviews booked."

"Then cancel them."

"They're booked for today, boss," Maile replied, reproachfully. "It's too late to cancel them."

"Then go to the pub and interview them there," he told her. "We can stretch to that."

"But what if I find someone good?" she asked. "Can we afford to take them on if Jack's joining the team?"

"I am *here*, you know."

"I don't think Jack will be here for long," Leipfold said. "He'll be back on the streets before we know it."

"Good," Maile said. She looked over at Cholmondeley, who was back to sitting on the sofa with his cuppa. "No offence, Jack. I like having you around the place. It's just that I'd feel a hell of a lot safer if I knew you were out there, busting bad guys."

"I mostly do desk work now," he replied.

"Whatever," Maile said. She flashed her hands across her computer keyboard and logged into her machine, then booted up her emails. She'd been gone for less than twenty minutes and she'd had three new enquiries while she was away. "Jeez, we've got a lot to do."

"Times have changed since you used to get your cases from *The Tribune*, eh, James?"

"I still do that too," Leipfold said. "And sometimes they just sort of show up. You know, life has this—"

He was interrupted by a buzzing sound, and Maile watched laconically as the two men looked around for the source of the noise before Cholmondeley patted down his suit and came out holding a mobile phone. Maile was unsurprised to see that it was an old Nokia flip phone, a model that hadn't been popular for at least ten years. She only knew one other person who used one, and that was Kat's weed dealer.

"Speak of the devil," Leipfold said.

"It's an unknown number," Cholmondeley said. "Who could it be?"

"There's only one way to find out," Leipfold replied. "Go ahead and answer the damn thing."

"Put it on speakerphone," Maile added. "So we can hear it."

"How *do* I do that?"

"I'll show you," she said, rolling her eyes and trying not to think about her emails. She hopped up from her chair and rushed across to him, then answered the call and switched the call to the speakers.

"Hello?" Cholmondeley said.

"Detective Inspector? Is that you? It's me, Constable Cohen. I need to speak to you, sir. It's urgent."

Chapter Four:
The Dark Web

JACK CHOLMONDELEY HAD ASKED for some company, but
Leipfold and Maile were busy with clients and so his first job for the
agency was an unofficial task for his own investigation. But then, if
even half the stories were true, Leipfold spent more time sticking his
nose into speculative cases than he did on paying the bills.

And so he went to see Constable Cohen alone, agreeing to meet
him at a trendy Soho coffee bar where the two of them could fade
into the background and where none of their colleagues was likely
to stop by for a caffeine fix. It wasn't just out of the way; it was on
the other side of town.

Cholmondeley didn't think much of the place. It was too hip
and trendy for his liking, and he would have been more at ease at a
Costa Coffee. Still, the place was abuzz with conversation, and he
couldn't fault it as a destination for a discrete chinwag.

Constable Cohen ordered a macchiato while Cholmondeley
stuck with a flat white. The young copper picked up the bill, and
Cholmondeley wondered whether the funds were coming from
his own pocket or from the petty cash tin at the Old Vic. They sat
down at a two-seater table in one of the corners, facing each other
beneath the eaves of a set of old stairs that led to a second floor.

"It's good to see you, boss," Cohen said.

"The feeling's mutual," Cholmondeley replied. "Thanks for the
coffee. You wanted to see me?"

"Well, it's like this," Cohen said, looking uneasily around the room. Cholmondeley considered it a rookie mistake. It attracted unnecessary attention and was more trouble than it was worth. "Things at the station are…well…"

"Well?"

"Sergeant Mogford's in charge," Cohen said. "He's not a bad guy, but he's not cut out for it. Then we have Superintendent Richards watching everything we do like a hawk with a bad sense of humour. We're not getting anything done. Some of us—not all of us, mind you, but enough of us—want you back."

"It's not my place to interfere," Cholmondeley said. "Why shouldn't I just enjoy a quiet retirement? I've done enough."

Cohen shook his head.

"With respect, sir," he replied, "you don't understand what it's like. Mogford is on a power trip, and he's taking it out on me. Richards is on the warpath and is cracking down with a vengeance. It's like she's trying to erase every record of your existence. She even threw your old mugs out."

"So what would you have me do?"

"This is off the record, right?"

"Of course," Cholmondeley replied. "Why so nervous? It's only me."

"You don't understand," Cohen repeated, his eyes performing another automatic sweep of the room. "If Richards finds out I've been talking to you, she'll have my badge. She's ordered us all to cut off any communications and to report to her if you try to establish contact."

"And yet you're here anyway," Cholmondeley mused. He smiled. "Loyalty is a fine thing, is it not?"

"Yes, sir," Cohen replied. "We want you back."

"We?"

"You know I can't give you any names, sir," Cohen said, reproachfully. "Officially, this conversation doesn't exist."

"So what would you have me do?"

"I think you should find out who shot Constable Groves, so we can nail the bastard."

"I do feel somewhat responsible," Cholmondeley admitted. "How is she, by the way?"

"She's on the mend," Cohen said. "But she's not out of the woods yet."

"It's a start," Cholmondeley replied. He sipped from his flat white and smiled as he felt the magic bean juice hit the back of his throat. He paused for a moment and then sighed. "To tell you the truth, I'd been thinking of looking into it. For Jenny, you know? But what about you? Surely, you're investigating the attack with all the resources you can throw at it."

"We are," Cohen said. "But something smells fishy to me. I don't think the top brass want to hear about it. Oh, they're letting us investigate, but they're also throwing every piece of red tape that they can at us. I've spent more time filling out forms than I've spent talking to witnesses, and truth be told, none of the witnesses are any good. We've hit a dead end. We're stuck up shit creek without a paddle. We need your help, boss. So what do you say?"

Cholmondeley noticed that Cohen hadn't swept the room for a couple of minutes, and he smiled. Good. That meant he was in control of his nerves.

"I'm in," Cholmondeley said. "But I'm going to need something from you. It won't be easy."

"What is it?"

"I need you to be my man on the inside," Cholmondeley replied. "Nothing illegal, of course, and all off the record. I just need a little information. And maybe the odd favour."

"I'll do what I can, sir," Cohen said. "But I'm not sure if I'll be much help."

"Oh, you will," Cholmondeley said. "And besides. If you want me to pull a Leipfold, I'm going to need you to pull a Cholmondeley."

*   *   *

When Cholmondeley got back to his flat that night, he was so preoccupied with his thoughts that he didn't notice the young woman on the stairs until he bumped into her. She was standing outside the door of number four and fumbling with a set of keys. Cholmondeley nudged up against her with his head down and sent them tumbling to the floor.

"Sorry about that," he said. "Here, let me get those for you."

"Thanks," she replied, as he bent down to retrieve the keys, grunting at the pain in his lower back. "You're a gentleman. There aren't many of you around these days."

"Oh, I try," Cholmondeley said, vaguely. "I see you live with Natasha."

"Who?"

"Natasha," Cholmondeley repeated. "I was talking to her just the other day."

"I'm sorry," she replied. "I don't know what you're talking about. Who are you, if you don't mind me asking?"

"I'm Jack Cholmondeley," he said. "I'm staying at number five."

"Then I guess that makes us neighbours," the woman said. She turned her back on him and slipped her key into the Yale, then twisted it in the lock and let herself in. "I'm Inga. It was nice to meet you. I'll see you around, Mr. Cholmondeley."

Then she entered the flat and closed the door behind her. Cholmondeley had just enough time to catch a glimpse of whitewashed wall and an empty coat rack in the hallway.

"Weird," Cholmondeley murmured, and then he slowly shook his head to clear it and walked on down the hallway to his flat. By the time that he let himself in, his thoughts had returned to Mary, their quaint suburban garden with her collection of plastic flamingos and the cushy job that he'd left behind half a lifetime ago.

Had it really been just a couple of weeks?

His hands shook and his body ached for a drink, just one to take the edge off, but he couldn't. He had work in the morning. He was due in at Leipfold Investigations.

And so he settled down for a takeaway curry and a rerun of an old episode of *MasterChef.*

* * *

The next day, at Leipfold's office in Balcombe Street, Maile O'Hara was the only one with a hangover. But that was okay because it made things much more interesting.

The boss had the radio on, and he was listening to the Home Secretary—a bland, forgettable man called Roger Gough—deliver a speech about technology. He'd promised to invest heavily in cybersecurity to protect the country from terrorists, but Maile knew that what he really meant was that he was sending more money to MI5 so they could spy on citizens. This latest campaign of his was all that her hacker friends were talking about.

It wasn't helping her hangover.

It was a Saturday, which theoretically meant that she was only working from eleven to three, but she usually showed up at ten and stayed until the early evening anyway. She didn't want to miss anything.

Even though she was the one with the pounding head and the dry mouth, she thought that Jack Cholmondeley looked a hell of a lot worse. The poor guy looked haunted, but at least he sounded okay. He was waffling on about his neighbours while Leipfold had his head down and his eyes on page thirty-seven of *The Tribune.*

"So, James," he said, once Leipfold had finished his crossword and was ready to brief him. "What have you got for me?"

"I've got nothing, Jack," Leipfold replied. He shrugged. "Sorry, old friend. I wasn't expecting you to come in today. Ask Maile, maybe she has something."

Maile's heart sank. She *did* have something. She just wasn't convinced that Jack Cholmondeley was the best person to deal with it.

"First thing's first," she said. "I think it's your turn to make a cuppa."

Leipfold snorted from his desk and then immediately started coughing.

"Sorry," he spluttered. "My water went down the wrong hole."

While Cholmondeley busied himself in the kitchen, Maile fired off a couple of emails and ran a sweep across their social media profiles to see if anything new had come in. There were no new enquiries since the night before, but in many ways, that was a relief. They already had enough to go around.

"Here's the deal," Maile said, once Cholmondeley had returned with a round of drinks, including her usual order of a builder's tea in a Hello Kitty mug. "We've got a private enquiry. All very hush-hush. James, has Jack signed the NDA?"

"Not yet."

"I'll print a copy," Maile said, returning her attention to Cholmondeley. She noticed he was wearing a new shirt, but he was still in the same tweed suit that she'd come to associate him with since his departure from the police force. Not for the first time, she thought about how something as simple as a wardrobe could define a person. "Give me a couple of minutes. Come to think of it, aren't we running out of biscuits?"

"We're always running out of biscuits."

"Exactly," Maile said, trying not to chuckle when Leipfold tipped her a wink before going back to his computer. "Off you go, Jack."

When he got back from the newsagents, Maile had the contract ready for him to sign and a black biro for him to use. He scrawled his John Hancock across the bottom and returned the forms, and Maile scanned them in and added them to the company's digital repository.

"Now what?" Cholmondeley asked.

"Grab your notebook and scooch over here," Maile said. "It's time for me to brief you."

"How exciting."

"You just wait," Maile said. "Okay, so here's the deal. We've been contracted by a private firm to look into a network of spammers. They've been trying to swing the results of a few elections."

"Who's the client?" Cholmondeley asked.

"James?"

"We don't know," Leipfold supplied. With Maile's help, he'd mastered the skill of talking while tapping away at the keyboard. "He used a pseudonym and got in touch with Maile over the whatjamacallit."

"The dark web," Maile said. "It's all fully anonymous. He pays in bitcoin."

"In whatcoin?"

"It doesn't matter," Maile said. "I need you to go through a list of IP addresses and look for matches. I'd do it myself, but I don't have time. If you find a match, flag it up with me and I'll take a closer look. Make sense?"

"Sure," Cholmondeley said. "I've just got one question."

"Yes?"

"What's a spammer?"

"Christ, Jack," Maile replied, pursing her lips and glaring at him like an unamused schoolteacher. "I hope you're joking."

* * *

While Maile was walking Cholmondeley through a laborious, complicated-looking process involving formulae on an Excel spreadsheet, Leipfold was pulling on his leathers and getting ready to head out.

The weather was temperate and the conditions were good. While the roads were thronged with tourists and weekend travellers, it was a pleasant enough ride. It was what would happen at the end of it that cast a shadow over his day, but Leipfold had always believed in getting the worst jobs done first so that the rest of the day would be relatively smooth sailing.

He wound his way north through the city and then parked Camilla on an expansive gravel drive outside a pleasantly-proportioned semi-detached house in an affluent neighbourhood. The garden was littered with pink flamingos. There were at least two dozen of them, and some were three or four feet tall. He shuddered and turned slightly so that he wouldn't have to look at the things as they stared back at him with their lifeless eyes. He felt like he'd been driving through a safari park in the Twilight Zone and someone had kicked him out of the car.

The Cholmondeleys didn't have a knocker; they had an antique doorbell with a rope pull. Leipfold grimaced and pulled at the rope. A bell tingled from somewhere within the house.

When the door opened, he was greeted by an apparition in blue. Mary Cholmondeley was so overdressed that she looked like she'd just walked down the catwalk at a fashion show.

"James?" she said. "James Leipfold, is that you?"

"It's me," Leipfold replied. "Sorry about that."

"What are you doing here?" Mary asked. "Did Jack send you?"

Leipfold shook his head. "I'm here of my own free will," he said. "Jack loves you, Mary. God knows why, but he does. Do you really need this many flamingos?"

"I like them," she replied defensively, folding her arms across her ample bosom and causing a sound like a pair of curtains being drawn across a bay window. "What can I do for you?"

"Can I come in?"

"No."

"I thought as much," Leipfold said. "It's a good job I brought my own coffee."

"I'll give you twenty seconds to tell me why you're here," Mary replied. "Get talking."

"What are you going to do, Mary?" Leipfold asked. "Call the cops?"

"You're here about Jack, aren't you?"

"Got it in one," Leipfold said. "His heart's breaking, Mary. You should speak to him."

"I have nothing to say."

"Why are you doing this?" Leipfold asked. "The old man is devastated."

"I just don't love him anymore," Mary said. "It's that simple. Not that it's any of your business."

"But you used to love him," Leipfold replied. "What changed?"

"It's complicated," Mary said. She sighed. "He's too dedicated to his job. He loves the police force more than he loves me."

"He loves you both, Mary," Leipfold said. "People are complex. They can love multiple things at once, even people. His love for his job doesn't detract from his love for you. And besides…"

"Besides what?"

"You haven't heard?" Leipfold asked. "Jack isn't with the cops anymore. They're pensioning him off. He's got a new job."

"Who's he working for?" Mary asked.

"He's working for me."

Mary paused for a moment. Then she sighed again.

"I'm not sure if that's a good thing or a bad thing," she said. "Perhaps you'll be a positive influence. Perhaps not. But it doesn't change anything, James. If I'm honest, I'm enjoying my newfound freedom."

"There must be something that Jack can do to win you back."

"I'm not a prize that can be won or lost, James," Mary replied, pursing her lips. "There's nothing that Jack can do to change my mind. I'm moving on with my life. Now, is there anything else?"

"Well, there is *one* thing," Leipfold said. He paused, and tension passed between the two of them like electricity on a power line. "Constable Groves has been shot."

"Who?"

"One of Jack's coppers," Leipfold said. "He thinks it was to send him a message. Do you know of anyone who might want to hurt him?"

"Is this a joke?"

"I'm deadly serious, Mary."

"Then no."

"Worth a try," Leipfold said. "Look after yourself, okay? If someone wants to hurt Jack, you'd be an obvious target."

"Jack has always loved his job more than he loved me," Mary said. "If you ask me, it sounds as though whoever's behind all this knew that. Now if you don't mind, I've got housework to do. I think you've darkened my doorstep for long enough."

Chapter Five:
A Screwdriver, a Hammer, and a Pile of Wood

JACK CHOLMONDELEY FELT LONELY.

It was Sunday evening, and he'd always found them unpleasant at the best of times. It was the arse end of the week. Nothing good ever happened on a Sunday. And he was all alone in his tiny apartment.

He'd tried to settle down with a good book, but there was too much noise leaking in through the walls and so he'd switched the radio on instead. He still hadn't bought himself a TV, and so he'd made a mental note to track one down in the second-hand shops. Then he'd settled back down to read while listening to Classic FM.

It felt like he was being productive, but he wasn't, not really. He'd had a decent enough first few days at Leipfold Investigations, even though the work had been tedious and repetitive, but he hadn't made any progress on his investigation into who shot Constable Groves. But then, that was unsurprising because he didn't have any leads. He'd have to go and see her once she was discharged from hospital.

The guy from upstairs was screaming again. Cholmondeley still hadn't met him, and he sometimes whiled the evenings away in contemplation, telling himself stories about who the old guy was and what he was up to. In most of the stories, he was just a sad and lonely old man with nothing left to live for. A little like Jack Cholmondeley.

He put his book down and strolled into the kitchen, where he made himself a Pot Noodle. Cheap and cheerful, he'd bought two dozen of the things to sustain himself. He'd been thinking about buying a kettle for the room so that he wouldn't have to go into the kitchen.

In the evenings, the little kitchen was almost always empty, especially after 9 PM once the soaps had finished. But for once, Jack Cholmondeley found himself with a little company while he was waiting for the kettle to boil.

"The water here is terrible," the woman said. "How do you put up with it?"

"Reluctantly," Cholmondeley replied, thinking about the filter that Mary had always insisted on. "The name's Jack Cholmondeley. And you are?"

"Angelique," she replied.

"I'm at number five," Cholmondeley said. "What about you? You don't live with the old guy who screams all night, do you?"

"Yeah," Angelique replied. "He's my dad."

Cholmondeley stared silently at her for a moment or two and then she laughed.

"Only joking," she said. "I'm at number four."

"With Natasha and Inga?"

"I don't know about that," she replied, shaking her head. "I'm still new here. I don't really know anyone. It was nice meeting you, Mr. Cholmondeley."

The kettle reached the boil and switched itself off. Jack Cholmondeley turned to look at the sound. When he looked back, the girl had gone, taking a glass of squash and a handful of paracetamol with her.

*   *   *

"I almost forgot," Leipfold said. "How did the interviews go?"

"It was a shambles, really," Maile replied.

"Good," Leipfold said. "Then we won't have to hire anyone."

"Well, I wouldn't go that far."

Maile flashed Leipfold a winning smile and then winked at Jack Cholmondeley, who had his hands busy with a screwdriver, a hammer and a pile of wood. Leipfold had finally caved and signed off on the budget for a new desk, but only on the condition that the old man made it himself.

"What do you mean?" Leipfold asked.

"Well, what does it sound like?" Maile replied. "Most of them sucked, but not all of them. There's one guy in particular that I think you should meet."

"Yeah?" Leipfold said. He didn't seem too pleased by the thought. "Well, I guess you'd better bring him in."

"Oh, we couldn't do that, boss," Maile replied. "Not yet, at least."

"If we do hire this guy, he'd better pull his weight," Leipfold said. "Speaking of which, how are you getting on over there, Jack?"

Jack Cholmondeley paused in the middle of putting a drawer together and said, "Smashing, thanks. Of course, the instructions are useless, but there's an art to these things. It'll come together eventually."

"Good," Maile said. "Perhaps once you've finished, you can finish off my spreadsheet."

"Of course."

"Have you made any progress on the Groves case?" Leipfold asked.

"Not yet," Cholmondeley said. "But I'm working on it. Say, James, I think I have another mystery for us. There's something odd going on at number four."

"Come again?"

"The place next door to mine," Cholmondeley said. "Call it my copper's hunch."

"Then investigate, Jack," Leipfold replied. "But do me a favour, okay? Don't work the case on my time."

"Of course," Cholmondeley replied. He sighed and moved on to the next step of the desk's assembly. "You know, James, I'm learning a lot here."

"Such as?"

"Maile here has been teaching me about algorithms," Cholmondeley said. "She's a very capable young woman."

"Just don't get any ideas about poaching her."

"I am here, you know," Maile said. She'd always hated being talked about, but at least it was all positive. For now, at least. "Anyway, Jack, you're a good student. You want to learn."

"The day I stop learning will be the day I die," Cholmondeley replied. "And besides, I've got a good teacher. What's the next lesson?"

"Reverse engineering," Maile said. "I took the data you parsed for me and checked the IP addresses. Looks like they're being routed through London."

"I thought you said these spammers were Russians," Cholmondeley replied.

"That's what the client said," Leipfold explained. "But the client isn't always right."

"But in this case, perhaps they are," Maile countered. "We're looking at an amateur job, here. Maybe *too* amateur. They haven't tried to cover their tracks at all."

"You've lost me," Cholmondeley said.

"The Russian government has access to some of the best hackers on the planet," Maile said. "There are two possibilities. Either this network is run by amateurs out of London, or it's run by skilled professionals who want it to *look* like it's coming out of London."

"The Russians?"

"Could be," Maile said. "But maybe not. And what if it's the Brits trying to make it look like the Russians tried to make it look like the Brits?"

"I hate politics," Leipfold said.

"Me too," Maile replied. "But don't worry about it. I've got an idea."

*   *   *

Maile and Leipfold left Cholmondeley to man the office and climbed on the back of Camilla with Maile riding pillion. Leipfold was hunched low over the handlebars, more focused on leaning into the corners than on Maile's arms around his waist, at least until he shot through a red light and she pressed her arms against him, crushing the air from his lungs.

"Oi," Leipfold said. "Watch it."

But he had no idea whether she heard him.

They were following up on the Russian hackers, heading towards the industrial estate they'd tracked the IP address to. Before they'd left the office, Maile had parsed through the data and discovered a web address. After running a WHOIS on the domain, she'd pinpointed the address it was registered to, as well as a company called Christie Exports.

A Google search had brought up nothing, and the warehouses were part of one of the dozens of new developments that had sprung up over the last couple of years, so it wasn't on Google Streetview, either. That was why they were winding their way through the streets towards Aldgate.

They found the address all right, though there was no sign of a company. It just looked like an empty storage unit.

"This brings back memories," Leipfold said. "We seem to deal with more shell companies than legit ones."

"What should we do?" Maile asked. "Should we try and force our way in?"

"Let's knock on the door first," Leipfold replied. "No point breaking any laws until we have to, especially with Jack Cholmondeley around."

"Fair does."

The main entrance to the unit was a huge set of steel shutters, which gave the place the appearance of a defunct aircraft hangar. There was something disquieting about it, and it reminded Leipfold of the feeling he got when he looked at photos of 112 Ocean Avenue. He didn't believe in the supernatural, but sometimes it felt as though places had long memories, as though the ghosts of the past lived on in the subconscious memories of the present.

Leipfold and Maile followed the unit along and found themselves strolling down an alley that led to the rear entrances. The doors were unmarked and most of the windows were covered with steel blinds, bars and anti-vandal paint. This was the kind of place where no one shouted their name from the rooftops. It was all about anonymity.

They counted the doors as they walked until they reached the one that corresponded with the lockup, and then Leipfold knocked on it with a gloved fist. He'd left his helmet with Camilla, but he was still wearing his leathers.

There was no response.

Leipfold knocked again, but still no dice, and then he knocked a third time before leading Maile further along the alleyway to where it hit a dead end against a bank of earth.

"Hmm," he said. "Perhaps we—"

"Can I help you?"

Leipfold and Maile turned as one to see a well-dressed man in his early forties emerging from the warehouse door. He looked like the kind of guy who'd unironically wear a monocle. And he looked out of place in the middle of the working-class industrial estate.

"Perhaps," Leipfold said, cautiously. "That depends. Who are you?"

"You know my name," the man replied, and suddenly Leipfold did.

"You're the client," Leipfold said. "You're Mike Croft. I spoke to you on the phone."

"And I sent you a small fortune to see if you were up to the challenge," Croft replied. "Yes, I remember it well."

"Did we pass?" Maile asked.

"In a manner of speaking," Croft said. "You don't seem too surprised."

"We're used to it," Leipfold said. He shrugged. "A lot of people send us on a trial job before they tell us what they actually want. Speaking of which…"

"Let's go inside," Croft replied. "We don't want to be overheard."

Croft led them in through the security door and directed them to take a seat. The huge room was empty, except for a small metal table and four chairs positioned around it. They talked quietly so that their voices wouldn't carry.

"I thought you might be bringing your new employee," Croft said.

"You know a lot about us," Leipfold said. "Why?"

"I make it my business to know who I'm working with," Croft replied. "This Jack Cholmondeley chap. Who is he and where did you find him?"

"He's a cop," Leipfold replied. "Or at least, he used to be."

"Do you trust him?"

"I'd trust Jack Cholmondeley with my life," Leipfold replied, with no hint of exaggeration. "Why do you ask?"

Mike Croft laughed, but there was no humour in it. To Leipfold, the expression on his face looked more like a grimace, especially in his eyes.

"That's a funny story," Croft said. "And in many ways, that's why you're here. Let me begin at the beginning."

"That usually helps," Maile observed.

"Yes, well," Croft said, momentarily taken aback. "You see, I work for a low-profile arm of the government and—"

"Let me see your ID."

"I'm sorry, young lady, but it doesn't quite work like that," Croft replied. "You could say that we're *extremely* low profile. We're so low profile that officially we don't exist. And that's why we're talking to you."

"Go on," Leipfold said, cautiously. Croft had piqued his interest, but he was also aware that whether the man was telling the truth or not, it likely spelled trouble either way. Trouble was good for business, but it was also a pain in the backside.

"You could say I'm a sort of ombudsman," Croft continued. "You know that old saying, *quis custodiet ipsos custodes?*"

"Who will watch the watchers?" Leipfold translated.

"Exactly," Croft said. "I do. It's my job to investigate accusations of corruption within the police force."

"Which is why you asked me about Jack Cholmondeley."

"If he's on the take, he could compromise the investigation before it's begun," Croft said. "But if he's an honest cop and he'll help us to root out the bad apples, he could be a valuable ally."

"We can trust him," Leipfold said. "But what would you have us do?"

"I've got a couple of names to get you started," Croft said. "People we suspect of corruption. I want you to look into them, online and off, and build me profiles on what they get up to and whether there's any evidence of them being paid off."

"By who?" Maile asked.

"By anyone," Croft replied.

Leipfold whistled softly through his teeth. "You're asking us to look for a needle in a haystack," he said.

"Of course," Croft replied. "But like I said, we've been watching you. If anyone can get the job done, you can."

"Thanks for the vote of confidence," Leipfold replied. "So where do we start?"

"With the first name on the list," Croft said. "Ever heard of a copper called Isabelle Richards?"

*   *   *

Jack Cholmondeley's head was spinning, but at least it wasn't from the booze.

When Maile and Leipfold had returned from their mission, they'd found him serving drinks to two women from a haberdashery company who wanted Leipfold to carry out some corporate espionage. They'd got back at just the right time, because Cholmondeley was beginning to panic. He knew how to interview suspects, but he'd never had to interview a potential client before. He didn't know what the process was or what Leipfold would have wanted him to do.

And so when the two of them returned to the office, Leipfold took charge of the interview while Cholmondeley sat in. For her part, Maile O'Hara was standing at her desk, occasionally chipping in whenever the women had a technical question or Leipfold struggled to express himself. The meeting went well and ended with the client signing a retainer and the case being assigned to Jack Cholmondeley.

Then Leipfold had taken Cholmondeley aside and briefed him on his meeting with Mike Croft and the investigation into the police force.

"Jesus, James," Cholmondeley had said. "Don't you think you're in over your head?"

"It's how I work best," Leipfold had replied. "Are you going to help us or not?"

And so of course, Cholmondeley had acquiesced and agreed to play his part in the investigation. His first task was to write a list of all of the cops he thought could be compromised, an unforgiving task at the best of times. As an old-school cop, Cholmondeley had an intense sense of honour, which made him a lot like the bad guys he was chasing. It also meant that he didn't like dobbing people in. But if there was one thing that he hated more than snitching, it was bent cops.

On his way back home, Cholmondeley stopped off at a stationery shop and bought himself a bunch of plastic wallets and ring binders with petty cash. Thus armed, he spent his Monday evening working on dossiers for each of his officers. He wrote down everything he could think of, from their fashion sense to their next of kin, and he also did what he could to track down some photos.

But there was a problem, and that problem's name was Mary Cholmondeley. He couldn't stop thinking about her, and about what he'd lost. And so he did what he always did when the thoughts got too much for him: he bought himself a bottle of whiskey.

On his way back from the shops, carrying his scotch in a blue plastic bag, he bumped into Angelique from number four, who was smoking a cigarette outside and staring absentmindedly along the street.

Cholmondeley nodded at her, and she smiled back at him. Then he went into his room and popped the top off his bottle of mind bleach.

*   *   *

Three and a half hours later, Jack Cholmondeley was standing uncertainly outside his old house and looking at the windows. The lights were out in the living room and the dining room, but it looked like there was a lamp on in the bedroom as well as the big light in the upstairs bathroom.

He checked his watch and it read 1:10 AM.

Cholmondeley walked up to Big Beaky, one of the biggest and baddest of his wife's pink flamingos, and then he kicked it in the face with a heavy boot. Big Beaky lifted up out of the grass and caught a little airtime, soaring in an ungraceful arc and landing in the dirt. Cholmondeley looked at it for a moment or two, and that was all it took to make him feel bad for the bird, even though it was made out of plastic.

He walked over to it and picked it up, then planted it back in the soil.

"Mary!" he bellowed. "Mary, my love! It's me, Jack!"

Then he thought about it some more and remembered the doorbell. He pressed it a couple of times and shouted Mary's name again as the bell echoed throughout the house. The main light snapped on in the master bedroom above him and when the bell finally stopped ringing, he could hear the heavy tread of feet on the hardwood stairs.

"Mary!" he shouted again.

The downstairs light clicked on and then the front door opened, but it wasn't Mary. It was a young man, probably half his own age, and he was only wearing a pair of Calvin Klein boxer shorts.

"Can I help—" the man began, but that was as far as he got before Cholmondeley's fist swung through the air, narrowly missing his chin. He would have connected if he'd been sober—or if he'd been ten years younger.

"Jesus Christ!" the man exclaimed, backing into the house and swinging the door closed as he went. It bashed off Cholmondeley's arm and rebounded into the wall. "Mary, call the police!"

"I *am* the police," Cholmondeley roared.

Chapter Six:
Superintendent Richards' House

"WHERE THE HELL IS Jack?" Leipfold asked. "I need that dossier he's been working on."

It was 11:15 AM on a Tuesday morning, and the old man hadn't shown up to work. Leipfold had made some progress on a couple of other investigations, renegotiated a higher rate with Mr. Croft and finished the crossword in just over eight and a half minutes, but now he was ready for his third cup of coffee and he wanted to crack on with the case.

"Are you asking me?" Maile replied, glancing over at him from her desk before turning her attention back to her monitors. "Why would I know? He's your friend."

"He's *our* friend now, Maile," Leipfold said. "And friends take care of each other. We need to check up on him. He's been struggling without Mary."

"Have you called him?"

"I hadn't thought of that," Leipfold admitted. "I'll give it a go."

Cholmondeley didn't answer, but he did at least show up for work just after Maile had headed outside for her lunch break. He looked terrible and he smelled even worse.

"Jesus Christ, Jack," Leipfold said. "What gives? Have you smelled yourself today?"

"I haven't had time to go home for a shower," Cholmondeley replied. "Sorry, James."

"Where were you?"

"I was in the cells," Cholmondeley said.

"*What?*"

"I think you'd better put the kettle on."

Leipfold did so and made them both a cup of coffee, cracking open a fresh pack of ginger snaps to go with it. Then they both sat down on the sofa and started dipping their biscuits while Cholmondeley brought Leipfold up to speed. When Maile returned from her lunch break, he'd just got to the point where he swung the punch, and she sat down on her office chair and rolled it along the floor towards them to catch the tail end of the conversation.

"I talked to Mary," Cholmondeley said. "She came down in her nightdress. I thought we'd be able to make some sense of this mess and patch things up. Turns out that she'd called the Old Bill and was just stalling for time. They showed up, they read me my rights and then they carted me off to the station."

"At least they let you off," Leipfold said.

"*Pfft*," Cholmondeley scoffed. "They let me *out*, but there's a difference. I'm waiting on a date for the magistrate's court."

"Wait, what?" Maile asked. "What happened?"

"You'd better start from the beginning, Jack," Leipfold said.

* * *

It was a couple of hours later, and if anything, Jack Cholmondeley felt worse than he had when he'd woken up on the uncomfortable cot in the cells of the Old Vic. He'd had a couple of hours' sleep at best, enough to sober up but not enough for the hangover to kick in. Now that the day had worn on, it was starting to hit him at full force.

He'd already excused himself to buy a toothbrush and some toothpaste from the corner shop, but all the toothpaste in the world wouldn't have been enough to cover the fumes that leaked out of him through his pores and on his breath. Eventually, the reek of it had been enough to push Leipfold over the edge.

"Jesus, Jack," Leipfold said. "You smell like a yeast infection."

"Okay," Maile murmured. "So that's gross."

"I'm sorry, James," Cholmondeley said. "I can't help it, I—"

"I don't trust you to get behind the wheel," Leipfold interrupted. "So I'm going to have to send you out on foot. I've got a job for you."

"But my head feels like it's under attack by a plague of locusts."

"You've been reading the Bible too much," Leipfold said. "In my experience, it's much more like having an angry hummingbird trying to break out of your skull from the inside."

"You know, you're right!" Cholmondeley exclaimed. "Does it ever stop?"

"Give it a couple of days," Leipfold said. "Maybe dose up on paracetamol until then. And drink a ton of water. To be honest, Jack, I don't really care what you do. I have no sympathy."

"But you were a drunk!"

"Yes, I was," Leipfold replied. "And that's why I have no sympathy. I was a drunk, Jack. But you're not, it's not you. Now go on, I have a job for you to do."

"What is it?"

"I want you to tail your old boss," Leipfold said. "I want you to follow Superintendent Richards."

"Can't Maile do it?"

"I'm busy," she said. "Soz. We've got a private genealogy case, and I'm the only one who can handle it."

"But what if I get caught?"

"Don't," Leipfold said, as though it was as simple as that.

But Jack Cholmondeley was an awkward, ungainly man, and while he didn't have much trouble getting to the Old Vic and finding Superintendent Richards as she left for the day, he was spotted almost immediately. He tried to duck behind one of the riot vans, but he was too slow.

"Jack?" she said. "Jack Cholmondeley, is that you?"

"Uh…"

"Come on out where I can see you."

Jack Cholmondeley did as he was told, almost reflexively. He'd spent too much in time in meetings with her when she was his active superior.

"What are you doing here?" Richards asked. "Are you here for revenge, is that it?"

"I—" Cholmondeley began, but that was as far as he got. He'd started talking automatically, because a question demanded an answer, but then his brain cut out and left him hanging. He took a couple of steps towards her, holding his hands up in a gesture of peace, and he tried to smile. He hoped it didn't look as forced as it felt.

"I'm not the one you should be looking for," Richards protested. "Please, Jack. They made me do it. It was out of my hands."

Cholmondeley paused and just stood there, looking at her. He'd interviewed more petty criminals than he could count, and that had given him what his fellow officers referred to as *the knack*. He had a better than average success rate when it came to spotting truths from lies, and he was pretty sure she was being honest. He just didn't know what she was being honest about.

"Go on," he said.

He tried to keep his voice level, because the last thing he needed was for her to press charges on him for threatening her. Unlike the night before, when he'd been ruled by passion, he was letting his brain do the work. He knew that the confrontation would be caught on CCTV, and so it was imperative that he played it by the book. At the same time, though, he wanted her to talk. It was a delicate balancing act.

"It came down from above," Richards said. "From the Boys in Blue."

The response took Cholmondeley aback and he found himself choking back a laugh.

"They don't exist," he said.

"That's what they want people to think," Richards replied. She looked around at the open car park and seemed to arrive at a decision. "We'd better go somewhere more private."

* * *

In the end, after the superintendent vetoed Cholmondeley's suggestions of a coffee shop or a library as being too public, he took her to the only place he could think of.

He took her back to his shitty little bedsit.

There was something surreal about the meeting. The two of them were dressed in civvies because Cholmondeley no longer had the right to wear his uniform and Richards worked a desk. She was wearing a fashionable suit with a pair of expensive Louboutins. They both looked out of place in their squalid surroundings, and the superintendent was visibly ill-at-ease when Cholmondeley went into the room first to stash his used clothes at the bottom of his wardrobe.

"It's not much," Cholmondeley said, sheepishly. "But it's home."

"It's a shithole, Jack," Richards said. "It makes me want to put plastic bags over my feet."

"It's not a crime scene."

"Not yet, at least."

"Just watch your step and you'll be fine," he said. "You can sit on the bed."

"I think I'd rather stand," she replied, glaring around the room as though expecting something to climb out of the walls. "Actually, Jack, I have a better idea. Let's go to my place."

"Well," Cholmondeley said. "If you're sure."

They hopped in the back of Richards' Daimler, the superintendent flashing sidelong glances at Cholmondeley as she wound through the streets towards her house.

It was an old Georgian affair, a masterpiece of architecture that stood imposingly over the street like the Eye of Sauron. When Cholmondeley saw the façade, he whistled softly under his breath. The Cholmondeley residence—the one he was currently banned from being within three hundred yards of—had cost over half a million back in the early 2000s. This place, if it went on the market for a quick sale, would bag ten times that.

The inside was even more luxurious, with mahogany panelling and expensive artwork on the walls. Superintendent Richards led him out from the grand hallway with its spiral staircase and into a small study, which was lined with vintage books on panelled bookcases. Cholmondeley noticed that they were arranged by the Dewey decimal system and not alphabetically by author or scattered higgledy-piggledy. She had a stunning first edition of *The Hound of the Baskervilles* that must have set her back a pretty penny.

"Sit down, Jack," Richards said, gesturing towards a leather chaise longue. She herself sat in an antique armchair, leaning forwards with her hands pressed together like a villain from a Bond movie.

Cholmondeley obliged.

"Where do I even begin?" she murmured. Then she sighed and looked across at Jack Cholmondeley. "Perhaps it's best if we start with you. Tell me everything you know about the Boys in Blue."

"Just that they're a legend," Cholmondeley said, shrugging his shoulders. "The cop Illuminati. A secret society of bigwigs in the forces."

"That's about the size of it," Richards replied. "If only they really were a legend. The Boys in Blue are all too real, Jack. And they're gunning for you."

"We'll soon see about that," Cholmondeley replied. "I plan to investigate."

"No, Jack, don't," Richards said. "You don't understand who you're dealing with. These are powerful people. We're talking privately educated, high-ranking military officers, top cops from across the board. And they won't hesitate to kill to keep their secrets."

She paused for a moment and leaned back in her chair. Then she looked across at Jack Cholmondeley and met his bloodshot eyes.

"Who do you think shot Constable Groves?"

Chapter Seven:
Abraham Shakespeare

JAMES LEIPFOLD, MAILE O'HARA, and Jack Cholmondeley were in the office, sharing a first brew of the day while attacking a pack of ginger snaps. Leipfold was sitting at his desk, timing himself as he tackled the latest crossword in *The Tribune*, while Cholmondeley was sitting on the sofa, scribbling furiously away in his notebook. Maile O'Hara was at her own desk, working her way through the incessant stream of emails that kept appearing in her inbox.

Business was brisk. They were scaling up so quickly that their success rate was taking a hit, purely because they were taking on new cases twice as quickly as they were closing the existing ones. It was a nice problem to have, but it also felt like stretching a balloon past its bursting point.

Maile wondered what would happen when it popped.

Cholmondeley had already briefed them on his conversation with Richards, and so Maile had started searching for information online. Despite her initial scepticism, she'd found more than she could ever hope to parse, and so she'd taken instead to dipping into hyperlinks at random to get an overall feel for what people were saying.

Cholmondeley had told her that the Boys in Blue were just an old folk tale, but it turned out that they were also popular fodder on the myriad conspiracy sites that littered the web like discarded tinfoil hats.

"So what do we do next?" Cholmondeley asked.

"You seem fresh today," Leipfold said. "No two-day hangover?"

"Like you wouldn't believe," Cholmondeley replied. "But I've been drinking water like there's no tomorrow, and I got a good night's sleep once the terrors wore off."

Leipfold grunted and filled out the last couple of letters in his crossword, then paused the timer and said, "Nine minutes, twenty-seven seconds. Not my best."

"It's not your worst, either," Maile said. "Hey, listen to this. There's an ex-army guy on Reddit who was recruited by the Boys in Blue back in the Falklands. He says he spent twelve years in the government before they kicked him out for voting the wrong way on a piece of legislation. Now he's all about peace and love, apparently. He's doing an AMA."

"Sounds more like MDMA," Leipfold replied. "What's an AMA?"

"Ask me anything," Maile and Cholmondeley chorused. Leipfold looked up curiously, and Maile blushed.

"I've been giving him some lessons," Maile explained. "He's a good student. Unlike some people."

"Yes, well," Leipfold said, clearing his throat theatrically. "Back to the business at hand. Now, I think—"

But what Leipfold thought would have to wait because he was interrupted mid-sentence by the shrill sound of the intercom. It had already gone off twice that morning—once for the mailman and once for someone who needed directions—and it was showing all the signs of being one of those days.

"Don't everyone get it at once," Leipfold grumbled.

"I'll answer it," Cholmondeley said, lifting himself up from the sofa and shambling towards the door. "I've not had a chance to do it, yet. How do you work this thing?"

"Just pick up the phone and see who it is," Maile said. "Then you can press the button when you're ready to buzz them in."

"As easy as that, huh?"

Cholmondeley reached the phone, picked it up and said hello, then frowned as he listened to the response. Maile watched with rapt fascination, looking at him in the same way that a photojournalist might look at a new-born barbary macaque.

"I see," Cholmondeley said. "Hold on a moment."

He covered the mouthpiece with his hand and looked at Leipfold and Maile.

"It's Shakespeare," Cholmondeley said.

"William?" Leipfold asked.

"Abraham," Cholmondeley replied. "He says he's here for an interview. But there's a problem."

Maile O'Hara burst out laughing and the two older men both turned to look at her. She'd booked this meeting and then forgotten all about it. Now that it had rolled around, she knew exactly what the problem was.

"I think we'd better go downstairs," she said.

*   *   *

"Ah," Leipfold said. "I see."

Abraham Shakespeare was a young Black guy, probably around Maile's age, although Leipfold found it increasingly difficult to tell how old people were. Shakespeare was dressed in a sharp suit with fashionable brogues and a checked blue shirt beneath his blazer. He was also in a wheelchair.

"Perhaps we'd better go to the coffee shop," he said.

"What's wrong with your place?" Bram asked. "I've never been inside a PI's office before."

"Stairs," Maile said. "Didn't I mention?"

"You knew I was in a wheelchair when you offered me the interview."

"Yeah," Maile replied. "But you were the best person for the job.

I'm pretty sure it's illegal to discriminate against you just because you're in a wheelchair."

"That doesn't usually stop people," Bram said. "So you're Maile and this is Leipfold?"

"Yup."

"And I'm Jack Cholmondeley," the ex-copper added, leaning over to shake hands with Bram, who was looking back at him like a museum curator examining a potential new exhibit. "It's a pleasure to meet you, young man."

"The pleasure's all mine," Bram said. "So are we going to the coffee shop or not?"

"One of us should man the office," Leipfold said. "Sorry Jack, looks like you've drawn the short straw."

"All the world's an office," Cholmondeley said. "And every man must play his part. Give me the keys, then. And could you bring me back one of those hazelnut lattes?"

Leipfold chuckled and tossed his keys to Jack Cholmondeley, then turned around and strode off down the street with Shakespeare hot on his heels, easily keeping pace with him. Maile had to run to keep up.

Bram's wheelchair was a high-tech gizmo with all the bells and whistles a tech nerd could ask for. It had an electric motor, though he mostly wheeled himself, as well as a built-in laptop and a small LCD monitor that swung out on an arm so that he could use it as a second screen. It had Google Assistant hooked up to it and as they made their way towards the coffee shop, Bram asked it for the menu.

"I have a router," Bram said, noting Maile raising her eyebrows at him, her cheeks flushed with colour as she alternated between jogging and power walking. "It's only 3G, but it's better than nothing."

"Nice," Maile replied. "What's the battery life?"

"It's enough to get the job done."

The unusual trio held their meeting in the La Coco coffee shop, a trendy little place that was always full of hipsters. They were everywhere, drinking fancy lattes out of reusable cups and tapping away at their MacBook Pros, staring out at the world through pairs of horn-rimmed glasses.

"Ugh, *writers*," Leipfold murmured. "Everyone thinks they're a novelist these days."

"I write a little bit myself, Mr. Leipfold," Bram said. "Amongst other things."

"Of course," Leipfold said. "Shakespeare by name, Shakespeare by nature, eh?"

"Something like that."

The three of them sat at a table in one of the corners, Bram lifting himself out of his chair and on to the seat with his powerful arms. His suit bulged at the seams.

"So," Leipfold said. "To business. I understand that you've already talked to Maile and that she thinks you can cut the mustard. I'm not going to test you on your knowledge or interrogate you about your credentials. Honestly, even if I did, I wouldn't know what I was looking at."

"He's *good*, boss," Maile said. "Real good."

"We'll see," Leipfold replied. "Well, Bram, I'm sure Maile's told you what we're looking for. Our case load is picking up, and one Maile isn't enough to stay on top of it all. We need another one."

"Well, I don't have any tattoos and I like to think I've got better taste in clothing," Bram said. "But yeah, I can be a Maile."

"Even *I* don't know how to be a Maile," Maile said.

"Can you teach Bram on the job and show him the ropes?" Leipfold asked. "You're pretty busy at the moment. He's not going to slow you down?"

"I'm a fast learner," Bram said.

"And I'm a pretty good teacher," Maile added. "Honestly, boss, with Bram on board, we can grow Leipfold Investigations exponentially."

"I see," Leipfold said.

He got up, walked over to a nearby table and picked up an abandoned copy of *The Tribune.* Then he sat back down and threw the paper on to the table. "Got a pen, Bram?"

"Of course, Mr. Leipfold," he said. "I never go anywhere without one."

"Good," Leipfold replied. "I want you to do the crossword."

"The crossword?"

"The crossword, kid," Leipfold repeated. "Are you deaf as well as crippled?"

"*James!*"

"I've heard worse," Bram said, as he picked up the pen and paper. "It's okay, Maile."

"No," she said. "It really isn't."

While Bram tackled the crossword, Leipfold ordered a round of coffees before dropping his hands into his lap and staring off into the distance. Bram was too focused on the paper to notice his surroundings, and Leipfold was quite happy to look at the cream-coloured walls while he thought about his cases.

Maile was fidgeting on her seat, and Leipfold could tell what she was thinking. She hated inactivity, just like he did. But he could keep himself busy with his own thoughts, while Maile needed external stimuli.

Approximately nine and a half minutes later, Bram Shakespeare filled out the last few boxes, tossed the paper on the table and said, "Finished."

"Already?" Leipfold replied, a hint of amusement working its way into his voice. "That's not a bad time, kid. Not as good as mine, but not bad."

"Show-off," Maile murmured.

"How are you in the real world?" Leipfold asked. "What I mean is, have you ever worked on an active investigation?"

"Not really," Bram said. "I've never tracked down a long-lost kid or returned the family jewels to some ditzy heiress, but I can help in other ways."

"Bram's a white hat hacker," Maile said.

Leipfold looked at her.

"All right, it's like this," she explained. "When a boomer hears about a hacker, they—"

"A boomer?" Leipfold asked. Bram stifled a laugh and was saved from further embarrassment by the arrival of their coffees.

"Never mind," Maile said, as the waitress busied herself around the table. "The point is, when people hear about hackers, they think about some shady dude in a basement trying to hack the Pentagon or steal money from banks. Those guys are the bad guys, the black hats. The white hats are the good guys, the people who find bugs and security loopholes so they can report them and get them fixed."

"Some companies offer rewards for it," Bram added. "It's not much, but it's a living."

"Why the multi-coloured hats?"

"Ever watch a western?" Bram asked. "Back in the day, when they were in black and white, it was an easy way to tell the viewer who was who. Black is whack. White is right."

This time, it was Leipfold's turn to laugh. The nerdy kid in the wheelchair looked like a beefed-up Eddie Murphy and sounded like a white supremacist.

"I like you," Leipfold said. "You've got spunk."

"Gross."

"I'm talking about vim!" Leipfold said, flashing a stern but semi-amused look across at Maile. "Vigour! Get up and go!"

"*James!*"

"That one wasn't even—" Leipfold began, and then he thought about it. "Oh. Sorry, kid. It's nothing personal, but when you work in our line of work, people go for your weaknesses. Me? I don't think you have any."

"Am I supposed to say that my biggest flaw is that I'm hard-working and that I care too much?" Bram asked.

It was Maile's turn to laugh.

"All right," Leipfold said. "We'll give you a trial. But we might have a problem."

"What's that?" Bram asked.

"Wheelchair access," Leipfold replied. "I'm going to have to have a word with the landlord."

*　*　*

Jack Cholmondeley was back at the office. The phones had barely stopped ringing and he'd made no progress on the case he'd been assigned to, but he'd taken a bunch of names and numbers, and he thought Leipfold would be pleased when he got back from the interview.

He'd just put the phone back in its cradle for the seventh time when the buzzer went off. He hoped he remembered how to use the thing.

"Hello?" he said. "Who is it?"

"It's me, sir," the caller replied. "Constable Cohen."

"Are you alone?" Cholmondeley asked. "Were you followed?"

"Yes, sir," Cohen said. "And no, sir, I wasn't followed. I learned from the best."

"Of course," Cholmondeley replied. "You learned from me. Come on up."

He buzzed the intercom and let Cohen into the building, then waited for him to climb the stairs and to come in through the office's front door.

"It's good to see you, Mr. Cholmondeley," Cohen said.

"Ah," the old man replied, taking Cohen's coat and hanging it on a hook on the back of the door. "I see you've got used to my new position."

"Don't have much choice, sir," Cohen replied. "You know what the superintendent is like. Some of us still talk about you, of course, but the walls have ears. You've got powerful enemies, sir. Someone wants to make sure that you're forgotten."

"A word of advice, Constable," Cholmondeley said. "If you're going to call me Mr. Cholmondeley, you should probably drop the sir."

"Yes, sir."

Cholmondeley sighed and led Cohen towards the sofa, where he directed him to take a seat. Then he put the kettle on and started to root around for clean mugs and teaspoons. He found those without a problem, but his search for the sugar turned up nothing. He supposed it didn't matter. He didn't use the stuff, and Cohen had cut it out when he'd first joined the force, citing the need to maintain his physique.

Ah, to be young again.

"So what's new?" Cholmondeley asked, as he waited for the kettle to boil. Constable Cohen was already leaning back on the sofa and looking eagerly around the office as though he might spot the answer to some unsolved case on one of Leipfold's corkboards.

"Not much," Cohen said. "But I have a name for you. Richards is working for a guy called Terence Rowbotham. I'm not sure what his rank is, but he's pretty high up. I think he's the one behind this witch hunt to take you and those who are loyal to you down a peg. And that includes me, by the way. What's going on, sir?"

"Call me Jack," Cholmondeley said. "And I'm not quite sure, but I'm working on it. Have you ever heard of the Boys in Blue?"

"Aren't they just a legend?" Cohen asked.

"Well, precisely," Cholmondeley said. "They're supposed to be, but I'm starting to wonder if there's something to it. Don't they say that there's a grain of truth at the heart of every legend?"

"They do?"

"I'm not sure," Cholmondeley admitted. "Leipfold says so, but Leipfold says a lot of things."

"So you think there's something to it?"

"Perhaps," Cholmondeley said. "If they do exist, they'd make a powerful enemy."

"Let's hope it's just a story," Cohen said. "But just in case it's not, you should look after yourself."

"Likewise," Cholmondeley replied. He sighed. The kettle had finished boiling, and so he poured it out into their mugs and then left the teabags to stew. "I hope I'm wrong, because if I'm wrong then there isn't any danger. But if I'm right, we've stumbled onto something big."

"So what do you want me to do?"

"I want you to listen," Cholmondeley said. "Don't take any action, just report back to me. If you need me, you'll find me here, and if I'm not around then you can talk to James Leipfold or Maile O'Hara. You can trust them."

Cohen nodded and then stood up abruptly. Cholmondeley frowned at him.

"What's wrong?" Cholmondeley asked. "Not leaving already? What about your tea?"

"Don't worry about it."

"You think I'm crazy, don't you?" Cholmondeley said. "Bloody youngsters. You'll believe that the earth is flat or that UFOs exist, but you won't believe this?"

"Uh…"

"Mark my words, Constable Cohen," Cholmondeley said. "Something strange is going on, and I intend to find out what it is. You'll believe me one day."

"It's not that, sir," Cohen said, taking his coat back off the door and folding it over his arm. "It's just that I've got somewhere to be. I thought I'd stop by on my way over."

"Where are you going?"

"I'm going to see Constable Groves, sir," Cohen said. "Didn't you hear? She woke up. She's out of the coma."

*   *   *

Maile O'Hara was at a kick boxing class in a community centre with her housemate, Kat Cotteril. Kat was a couple of years older, but it often seemed like Maile was the wiser. She was certainly the more cynical and pessimistic. Kat thought the glass was half-full; Maile thought it was half-full of poison.

They took it in turns to wield the pads and kick the shit out of each other. There were a dozen people in their class and two instructors. After splitting them up and assigning everyone a partner, the instructors had started going from couple to couple and giving them pointers or demonstrating techniques.

"Hey, Kat," Maile said, as her housemate laid into the pads. "Go easy, there. You've got a lot of frustration."

"I need a man," she replied, aiming a well-placed kick at Maile's left hand.

"Why, so you can kick them?" Maile joked. "You don't need a man. No one *needs* a man. Although if you're desperate, I might be able to help."

"I'm not going on a date with James Leipfold," Kat growled, letting another kick fly, which failed to connect.

"Ew, no," Maile replied. "Not James. I was thinking of someone else."

"Who?"

"Ever heard of Shakespeare?" Maile asked. She laughed. "I don't mean—"

"Okay, ladies and gentlemen," one of the instructors shouted, cupping his hands over his mouth in a makeshift megaphone. "Change partners, please!"

Kat shot Maile a look that said "we'll talk about this later," and then they switched over to new partners. Kat paired off with a middle-aged man in a vest with a stray forest of chest hair poking out. Maile ended up with a lanky hipster with a beard, a dude-bro who looked like he drank soy lattes. He was at least eighteen inches taller than her.

"Let's go!" the instructor shouted, and Maile leapt into action. She acted on instinct, like a runner coming out of the blocks at the sound of a gunshot. She unleashed a flurry of kicks at the pads and hit with such ferocity that the hipster stepped backwards and tripped over his own feet, hitting the mats hard.

"Hey!" the hipster exclaimed, climbing back to his feet and reaffixing his glasses. "What the hell do you think you're doing?"

"Smashing the patriarchy," Maile said.

*　　*　　*

The following day was a slow one, and Leipfold and the gang spent most of it grafting. They resolved two different investigations, both low-to-mid-level jobs with decent paydays, but the wrap-ups were almost as complicated as the onboarding. There was a hell of a lot of paperwork.

Cholmondeley allowed himself the luxury of a chuckle. It was a hell of a lot of paperwork that he didn't have to worry about.

He treated himself to a new television on the way home and spent the early evening unpacking the thing and getting it up and running. The building had crappy reception, but he'd had a heads-up from Maile and so he'd also bought a digital box with a decent aerial so he could watch more channels. It had seemed like a good idea at the time.

Half an hour after he turned it on, he turned it back off again. He was already bored of the thing. Perhaps he'd ask Maile to give him some lessons on streaming sites, whatever they were. Not that he could use them. He didn't have an internet connection.

So he went to the communal kitchen to make himself a cup of tea instead, resigning himself to decaf due to the lateness of the hour. But there was a problem. He was out of milk.

For a brief, crazy moment, he thought about pinching some from one of his cohabiters, but he was a former copper and his code of ethics was hardwired into him. He left the kitchen and went to knock at the door of number four, but there was no answer. So he went back into his room to grab his coat and then headed out into the night.

The corner shop was closed, but the little Tesco along the way was open until ten. The problem was that it was also on the other side of the dual carriageway, and the only way to get there was through the underpass. He hated being underground at the best of times, a relic of an incident in his youth when he'd been trapped on a tube train that was stranded between stations. But he also had the Boys in Blue on his mind, and it was making him paranoid.

There was a young couple halfway along the tunnel who were clearly no threat to him, but there was also a middle-aged man strolling along the streets behind them, swinging an umbrella to and fro like a metronome. He reminded Jack Cholmondeley of the little clockwork toys that he'd played with as a kid, back when the closest thing to a computer game had been when they counted the numbers playing hopscotch.

Is he one of them? Cholmondeley wondered. But then he shook his head. *They don't exist.*

Still, he kept his wits about him as he continued through the underpass, even hastening his steps to catch up with the couple so that at least if he was attacked, there'd be a witness. It wasn't much comfort, but it staved off the anxiety and by the time that he was safe and dry on the other side, he was kicking himself for his foolishness.

There were only two other customers in the supermarket, and one of them was already settling up at the till. Normally, Cholmondeley was the type of shopper who liked to browse around and to check out what was new since his last visit, but that evening he knew exactly what he was looking for. He picked up a carton of semi-skimmed and made his way over to the till.

"No whiskey today, sir?" the shopkeeper asked by way of greeting. Cholmondeley frowned at him.

"Cheeky swine!" Cholmondeley replied. "Just this, please."

He settled up with the shopkeeper and declined the offer of a plastic bag, holding the milk carton by its handle as though it was a grenade and he was worried it might explode.

On his way back through the tunnel, he heard those echoing footsteps again, and he turned around and saw the same middle-aged man, who was still swinging his umbrella.

Jack Cholmondeley held his ground. He stopped halfway through the tunnel and put his milk on the floor to free his hands up. Then he turned to face the man with the umbrella and shouted, "What do you want from me?"

It had an immediate, visceral effect. The man almost leapt out of his skin, and he let go of the umbrella in his surprise and it swung through the air before skittering to a stop on the concrete. The man looked at it for a second, and then he looked at Jack Cholmondeley. Then he turned around and made a run for it, leaving his umbrella on the floor.

Cholmondeley walked over to the umbrella and picked it up, then swung it against his shoulder. He walked back to the milk carton and picked it up before returning to his apartment.

When he got back to the building, a nondescript-looking man was leaving number four. Cholmondeley walked past him in the corridor, but he barely even noticed. His mind was somewhere else.

He didn't even end up making his cup of tea.

*   *   *

Leipfold's landlord was a cantankerous old man who was utterly useless. The problem was that he owned three properties, and one of them was in the south of France. He spent half his time there and half his time in Manchester, which meant that getting him out to the office wasn't easy. It was his lowest priority, and the only time he visited was when Leipfold missed a payment and he wanted to collect his rent.

But Leipfold knew how to manipulate him, too. Normally, he would have preferred to have played it by the book, but his landlord was a dick and Leipfold wanted results.

"Hey, Mr. Taplow," Leipfold said, when he got hold of the guy on his mobile phone. "I need you to send someone over."

"What's the problem this time, Leipfold?" the old man whined, his voice sounding particularly harsh through the phone line. "Not the pipes again, I hope? I told you, I can't—"

"No, Mr. Taplow," Leipfold said hastily, trying to cut him off before he started ranting. "It's not the pipes. They're working just fine. But listen, have you heard of the Disability Discrimination Act of 1995?"

"The what now?"

"What about the Equality Act of 2010?" Leipfold continued. "I'm sure that as a responsible landlord of a public-facing business premises, you're well aware of the legal requirements."

"Well, I don't know if—"

"Here's how it works," Leipfold said. "I think you'll find they're mostly self-explanatory. The Disability Discrimination Act means that wheelchair users must be able to access all public buildings. The Equality Act means that it's your duty as a building owner to make reasonable adjustments for disabled people."

"Now, hang on, I—"

"We're taking on a new employee," Leipfold continued. "A chap called Shakespeare. But he's in a wheelchair."

"So?"

"So what are you going to do about it?" Leipfold asked.

"Are you threatening me, Mr. Leipfold?" his landlord asked. "Again?"

"No, not at all," Leipfold replied. "I'm just reminding you of your legal and moral obligations. I've asked around for a few quotes and I've found a chap who can start work on Monday. Shall I send the invoice over?"

The old man murmured something that Leipfold didn't catch, though it sounded remarkably like "I hate you." Then he came back on the line to say, "Fine. Send it over."

Leipfold smiled.

Chapter Eight:
Citizen's Arrest

IT WAS THE FOLLOWING night, a Friday, and Jack Cholmondeley was walking to the shop again. This time, he wanted a pack of ginger biscuits.

His senses were heightened, as they always were when it was dark out, and he had his eyes peeled for the middle-aged man he'd seen the night before. He was swinging the man's umbrella backwards and forwards, whistling softly to himself as he walked. He was about two thirds of the way through the tunnel when the attack began.

The first he knew of it was the echoing sound of running feet, and he whirled around just in time to see a shadow launching itself towards him with a flash of metal in its hand. Cholmondeley reacted on instinct, ducking the arm and then driving his head into the man's stomach, using his own momentum to push him back into the wall. He grabbed the man's arm and smacked it against the brickwork, then did it again and again until his knuckles cracked and the knife dropped to the floor.

But his adversary found a second wind and drove his elbow into Cholmondeley's stomach, sending the old man to the floor. He pounced at Cholmondeley and the former cop rolled over, then arced his umbrella through the air to smash its handle against the man's face. It caught him a good one just under the eye and he fell back. The two men hauled themselves unsteadily to their feet and then started to circle each other warily, like boxers in the ring who were waiting for the sound of the bell.

"Who are you?" Cholmondeley asked, panting noticeably but as stern-faced as ever. The drink had left him out of shape, but he was pleased to find that his survival instinct and his reflexes were still sharp. "And what do you want from me?"

"The Boys in Blue send their regards, Jack," the man replied, sneering at him. Cholmondeley could see that it wasn't the same guy who'd been following him the night before. He was younger for a start, and that also meant he was more dangerous.

"I should have known," Cholmondeley said. "I'm guessing you're not just here to say hello."

"You wish, old man," his adversary replied. "I'm here with a warning. Stay away from the Boys in Blue. You've already lost your job. It would be a shame if you lost your life. Or your wife."

Without warning, the man lunged at him with his arms, and Cholmondeley only just managed to duck, though he still caught a glancing blow to the collarbone. He heard more footsteps, the man's backup perhaps, but he didn't have a chance to look into them. His opponent had bent down to retrieve his blade, and that put Cholmondeley on the defensive again.

The blade swung towards him, and Cholmondeley could swear that he heard it piercing the air. He threw himself to his right and the blade passed just above his head, but it left him in a weakened position and the man was looming above him again with a ferocious leer on his face, like a butcher looking at piece of meat. Cholmondeley was reminded of some of the gangs that the major crimes unit was investigating. Several of them had their members carve gang signs and symbols into their enemies' flesh as initiations.

The man bent down towards him and then there was a sound like an aerosol and he was falling backwards, down to the floor and away from Cholmondeley.

The old cop backed away on his hands and knees, walking along the asphalt like an urban crab, and then he watched as his rescuer wound back her leg and then kicked the man in the crotch. She turned her head slightly and her features were illuminated by the strip lights.

"Citizen's arrest, dickhead," Maile O'Hara said.

*   *   *

Jack Cholmondeley had been forced to hand in his handcuffs along with his badge when he'd been placed on gardening leave, but that didn't matter much. He'd been a cop for a long time, and he knew how to restrain someone by bending their arms up behind their backs and frogmarching them along so that they didn't get a chance to fight their way out of it.

Cholmondeley marched the man along through the tunnel with Maile O'Hara beside him, her hands still wrapped around her pepper spray. She covered the man with the nozzle and went on ahead to make sure that there was no backup out there, lying in wait to ambush them. Once they made it out of the tunnel and emerged on the other side of the dual carriageway, they trekked the last hundred metres back to Cholmondeley's place. It wasn't perfect, but it would have to do.

Their prisoner was remarkably docile. He groaned in pain every now and then, but he'd taken a couple million Scovilles worth of chilli to the face and so that was unsurprising. His testicles had taken a beating, too. Thankfully, he didn't cry out or scream for help, which could have caused a few problems, and the streets were mostly empty. They passed a couple of people walking on the other side of the road, but they had their heads bowed to the wind and were paying little attention to anyone else. With the three of them pressed so closely together, they could have passed for a group of friends on their way home from the pub.

When they got back to Cholmondeley's place, they bundled their prisoner into the room and then used a couple of ties to bind the man's arms to the bedframe. He looked like a shackled prisoner in some medieval dungeon. By that time, he'd started to moan and whimper. They gagged him with a couple more ties, Cholmondeley grumbling about them being expensive.

"You got a better plan?" Maile asked.

"We could call James Leipfold," Cholmondeley said.

"I already sent him a text," Maile said. "He's on his way over. He said he'll bring some cable ties and tape."

"He doesn't mess around, does he?" Cholmondeley replied. "I hope we're doing the right thing. This is unlawful imprisonment."

"He attacked you," Maile reminded him. "If we're at fault, so is he. Besides, we have a couple of questions."

"What if he screams?"

Maile shrugged. "This is Brixton," she said. "No one will care."

"Still," Cholmondeley said. "I'd better give the neighbours a heads up."

Maile raised her eyebrow but said nothing.

"Can you keep an eye on him while I'm gone?" Cholmondeley asked.

"Sure," Maile replied. "And besides, Leipfold will get here soon."

"Excellent," Cholmondeley said, rubbing his hands together. "Perhaps we'll finally get some information."

Cholmondeley left his room and went to knock on a couple of doors. He didn't knock on all of them, just the ones that were directly adjacent to and above him. No one was home at number six, but a young man came to the door of number four and opened it up a crack, then poked his head out.

Cholmondeley guessed that he'd kept it on the chain, and he couldn't blame him. He would have done the same.

"What do you want?" he asked.

"Good evening," Cholmondeley said. "I'm sorry to disturb you."

"Yeah," the man said. "Whatever. What do you want?"

"I just wanted to apologise for any noise you might hear," Cholmondeley said. "Please don't call the police."

"Sounds legit," the man replied. "But okay, buddy, whatever you say."

"We're making a movie, you see," Cholmondeley added. "We've got some fantastic talent, but I'm afraid it can sound rather realistic. You might hear some shouting and some screaming. I just wanted you to know that it's all fine and above board. As I say, no need to call the police."

"Well, wouldn't you just know it?" the man replied, breaking into a smile. "We're shooting a little movie of our own."

* * *

James Leipfold headed over to Cholmondeley's place as quickly as he could, though he was delayed leaving the office when the phone rang. It was a potential new client asking for a quote, so Leipfold asked them to send over a written brief so he could get back to them in the morning. Time didn't exist for Leipfold Investigations, and half of their business came in out of hours.

When he got to Cholmondeley's place, he parked Camilla and chained her firmly to the railings, then buzzed the intercom and walked through to number five. When he entered Jack's little bedsit, he burst out laughing.

Their prisoner was still bound and gagged, stretched out on the bed in a grim parody of the Vitruvian Man. Jack Cholmondeley was standing over him, presumably keeping watch in case he tried to escape. Maile O'Hara was sitting on the floor with her back to the wall, tapping something out on her smartphone. Leipfold suspected she was checking her emails or seizing the opportunity to finish some report.

"Ah, James," Cholmondeley said. "I'm so glad you could join us.

We weren't quite sure what to do next."

"Have you thought about lighting a couple of candles and putting them beneath his toes?" Leipfold asked. He kept his tone steady and neutral and left it to Jack and Maile to decide whether he was joking.

"I've got a better plan," Maile said, without looking up from her smartphone.

"What is it?" Leipfold asked, quite literally giving her the floor. He closed the door behind him and went to sit down at the foot of the bed.

"Jack and I have already had a little chat with him," Maile said. "But I don't think he's going to talk, at least not easily. Now, unless you want to break a few laws and torture the guy, that leaves us with a quandary. What do we do with him?"

"And you have some ideas?" Leipfold asked.

"Exactly," Maile said. "Well, just one, but I think it's a good one. We use him to send a message."

"It's not going to involve a finger in a box, is it?" Cholmondeley asked, gloomily. The man on the bed squirmed, his eyes shooting open.

"No, not that," Maile said. "Jesus, what is it with you two today? No, no, we're not going to hurt this guy. We're going to free him so he can deliver a message."

"And what's the message?" Leipfold asked.

"You'll see," Maile said. "Pass me my lipstick."

*　　*　　*

The following day was a Saturday, and while there wasn't a new issue of *The Tribune* on the shelves, they had at least updated their website. Their escapades of the previous night were front page news.

Naked Man Found in Brixton, the headline read, and it was

accompanied by a pixelated photo of the man where only the message across his chest was visible. It was written in black lipstick and read, "We're coming for you."

Maile had loaded the story up on the screen, and she and Leipfold were having a good chuckle about it. Cholmondeley was out of the office, following up with a few leads and tailing a couple of the names on Mike Croft's list, augmenting his thoughts and notes with some data of his own about where the cops were going and what they were doing. So far, his surveillance had turned up nothing more than some minor corruption from an officer who was meeting up with a local drug dealer, and they had nothing concrete on the Boys in Blue.

"I've got something else for you," Maile said. "Bram's been in touch."

"Ah, yes," Leipfold said. "Mr. Shakespeare. How is he?"

"He's doing just fine," Maile said. "I've given him a few briefs to get started with, and he's sent over his first report. I took a look at it already. It's top rate stuff, boss."

"Yeah?"

"Yeah," Maile replied. "Remember those bots that Mr. Croft had us look into?"

"The test he set?"

"Yeah," Maile said. "Bram's done some more digging and found a couple of rogue IP addresses. They're still based in London, but he's seen them before. They're shell IPs belonging to an American firm. Some private security company with links to the Pentagon."

"Where did he find all this?"

"On the dark web on a site for conspiracy theorists," Maile admitted. "But get this. People are talking about the Boys in Blue."

"Anything good?" Leipfold asked.

"Maybe," Maile said. "I'll send it over. Most of it is rubbish, of course. It always is. But there are a few posts you'll want to take a look at. Especially this one, look. Some dude called Sniper79 says he used to be one of them, and now he's looking for allies to help take them down. A couple of people have already replied."

"Can you find out who they are?"

"I'll get Bram on it," she said. "This is more his area. In the meantime, I'll send his report over so you can check it out. I'm telling you, boss, it's really top-notch stuff. Did you speak to the landlord?"

"That useless old bastard?" Leipfold replied. He grinned. "Yeah, I did. We're going to get someone on it."

"So what's next?" Maile asked.

"We wait," Leipfold said. "And we work on our other cases. There's no mention of the Boys in Blue in *The Tribune*, but you can bet that they know what's happened. They won't thank us for putting one of their men on the front page."

Maile laughed. "They shouldn't have sent him after Jack Cholmondeley then," she said.

* * *

The rest of the weekend passed mostly without incident, though Maile kept her eye on the social networks because the article about the naked man in Brixton had got people talking. The web was rife with speculation, and it seemed like everyone and their dog had an opinion on the case, with most of them claiming it was some sort of message from the mafia. But it was just Maile O'Hara's lipstick.

Bram Shakespeare officially started at Leipfold Investigations on the Monday, although he'd only been promised ad-hoc work as and when clients came through the door. That suited Bram just fine, and it also bought them some time to get the new lift installed.

On Monday morning, a builder came over to poke around the place. Leipfold had been suspicious when the guy turned up, but only until he got the landlord on the phone and asked him to confirm the man's identity. Taplow said that the man was legit, but

Leipfold wasn't so sure. There was something familiar about him, but he couldn't tell what it was. That was unusual in itself. Leipfold had a good memory for names and faces, but if he'd ever met the builder before, he couldn't remember where or when.

It was a challenge, a puzzle that he couldn't solve. And he hated not being able to solve puzzles.

He told Cholmondeley not to let him out of his sight, and so the ex-cop spent half the day walking up and down the stairs as he showed the builder around the building. Eventually, he'd asked to speak to Leipfold so he could deliver his verdict.

"It won't come cheap, mind," the man said, presumably unaware that Leipfold wouldn't be the one paying his invoice. "But it's doable."

"How long will it take?" Leipfold asked.

The builder sighed theatrically and kissed his teeth. "That depends," he said. "It's a three-week job, but there's the waiting list to think about, too. I'll struggle to get you in before the summer."

"Well, that won't do," Leipfold said. "Is there any way you could give us priority?"

"If you're willing to pay for it," the builder said. "Time and a half."

"Excellent," Leipfold said. "My landlord will handle the paperwork. Can you start this week?"

"I mean, I'll have to—"

"Just get it done," Leipfold said. "My assistant will see you out."

Maile started to climb out of her seat, assuming that he was talking about her, but then he gestured for her to sit back down again.

"Jack," Leipfold said. "Please escort this man out of the building while I call Mr. Taplow. I want to make sure that there are no delays. The amount the old man's been charging me for rent should more than pay for the upgrades."

"Yes, boss," Cholmondeley said. "And then what?"

"Then come back here," Leipfold said. "I've got an unofficial assignment for you this evening. We're off to the Rose and Crown."

*   *   *

Leipfold wasn't drinking, and neither was Jack Cholmondeley. James had gone with his traditional lemonade, while Jack had opted for a can of ginger beer. Cedric, the moustachioed landlord, was watching inscrutably from behind the bar, where he was polishing the glasses with a rag that was only making them dirtier, leaving smears of oil across the inside of the glasses.

It was that kind of place.

"So, why did you bring me here, James?" Cholmondeley asked. "Is this some sort of test?"

"If it was, you would've passed it," Leipfold said, gesturing towards Cholmondeley's ginger beer. "But no, that's not why I brought you here."

"Then why *are* we here, James?"

"I want to talk to you about Mary," Leipfold replied. "I know you're suffering, Jack. I want to help you."

"How?"

"I don't know," Leipfold said. "I was never much good at doing people things. I'm glad you've stopped drinking, though. It's a solid start."

"It was getting me nowhere, James," Cholmondeley replied. "We both know that. I'll never get Mary back if I'm just a drunken bum. Besides, it was just an escape. Now, I think I know where we stand. I don't think we'll get back together."

"Ah," Leipfold said. An uncomfortable silence descended in which the sounds of the other punters seemed to wash over them. Leipfold took a swig of his lemonade and then smirked when Cholmondeley mimicked him and took a swig of his ginger beer. "The question is, Jack, do you want to get back together?"

"Of course," Cholmondeley replied. "But I'm trying to be realistic, James. I had my chance and I blew it, she as good as told me so herself."

"Was that before or after you forced your way into her house?"

"Please, James," Cholmondeley said. "My conscience is weighing heavily enough on me as it is. I'm going to try to make amends. Hell, it's all I *can* do."

"How?"

"I need to spend some time rediscovering myself," Cholmondeley said. "The truth is, old sport, I've been married to Mary for so long that I've forgotten who I am. Perhaps it's all for the best. Perhaps now that she's left me, I can get on with my life. I can find who I am and be the person I've always wanted to be."

"What's wrong with being Jack Cholmondeley?"

"To be honest, James, only one thing is keeping me going at the moment," he replied. "I want to chase the case and find out the truth about the Boys in Blue."

"Attaboy, Jack," Leipfold said. "I'll drink to that."

The two of them picked up their glasses and clinked them together, sending ice clattering around the rims. Then they downed their drinks, said goodbye to Cedric and took their leave.

Neither of them noticed that they were followed outside.

Chapter Nine:
The Mole

LEIPFOLD AND CHOLMONDELEY WERE back outside the older man's house when the person following them stepped out of the shadows and walked over to them. Cholmondeley tensed up immediately, but then he relaxed when he saw it was only Constable Cohen.

James Leipfold, Jack Cholmondeley and Constable Steve Cohen squeezed their way into Cholmondeley's tiny room and turned the television on so that if the walls were bugged, it'd run some interference. None of them knew if it would do anything, but it didn't really matter. If someone *had* bugged Jack Cholmondeley's place, he would have noticed. It's hard to hide a microphone in the walls when the walls themselves are falling down.

Besides, if anyone wanted to listen in, all they'd have to do would be to sit outside in the hall. The walls were so thin that when someone farted in the kitchen, the smell was as pervasive as the sound. If there was a fly in the communal bathroom, the sound of its wings against the tiles kept Cholmondeley up all night.

Or maybe that was just the weird buzzing he got in his head sometimes. It was hard to tell.

The three men scooched up together and sat in a row on Cholmondeley's bed like the world's worst Matryoshka dolls. If the scene hadn't been so sombre and serious, it might have been amusing.

"So," Cholmondeley said, clapping his hands together. He was sitting in the middle with Cohen to his left and Leipfold to the right. "What brings you here, Steve? I'm assuming that you're not just here for a social visit."

"Yes and no, sir," Cohen replied. "Call it a courtesy call. I just thought you'd like to know that there's going to be a raid tomorrow."

"A raid?" Cholmondeley exclaimed. "But what for? I've barely got a pot to piss in, lad. What do they think they'll find?"

But Cohen was shaking his head.

"You don't understand, sir," Cohen said. "This has nothing to do with the Boys in Blue, assuming they even exist. This is something else. It's the vice squad. They've had a tip-off that something strange is going on at number four."

*   *   *

Even though he'd been tipped off about the raid, Jack Cholmondeley still thought he was going to have a heart attack when he heard the battering rams. They were using standard shock and awe tactics, a heavy-handed move that seemed almost unnecessary. Cholmondeley had rarely had to authorise such force while in the line of duty, saving it for only the most extreme of situations when he'd known that his targets were armed and dangerous.

Cholmondeley wrapped himself up in his tartan dressing gown and eased himself into his slippers, grumbling as he bent down and pain flared up his back and into his aching muscles. He took another minute or so to brush his teeth before he went out into the hallway.

It was like a scene from *Apocalypse Now*, if *Apocalypse Now* had been a buddy cop movie. The hallway, which was never that big to begin with, looked even smaller now that it was packed full of burly coppers with their black body armour. They were armed cops too, a rarity even in London. When people said they were bringing out the big guns, this was who they were bringing.

And at the back of the big guns was a familiar face. It belonged to Sergeant Gary Mogford.

"Evening, Sarge," Cholmondeley said, slipping over towards the stairs to give the other men easier access to his neighbour's apartment. He was trying not to smile, but he couldn't help himself. "How are things?"

"Oh, you know," Mogford replied. "Keeping busy."

"So I see."

"What do you know about your neighbour?" Mogford asked, smiling unsettlingly at his former superior. Cholmondeley knew exactly what he was doing. He'd taught the man the same trick. He was trying to make questioning sound like casual conversation.

"Well, I suppose that depends," Cholmondeley replied. "Which one?"

"Sadie Jones," Mogford said. "Or Danielle Blasse. Or Gerald McDaniel, for that matter."

"Never heard of them," Cholmondeley said, truthfully. He wondered whether to tell Mogford about the other people he'd met from number four. "Why, what have they done?"

"Never you mind," Mogford said.

Cholmondeley decided not to tell him.

"What are you doing here, anyway?" Mogford asked. "I thought we'd seen the last of you when they put you on gardening leave."

"I live here," Cholmondeley said. "Or at least, I live here *now*."

"Oh yeah," Mogford replied. An ugly little smile passed across his face. "How's retirement treating you?"

"Can't complain," Cholmondeley said, although he could. "I'm just off to make a cuppa. Do you want one?"

"No thanks," Mogford replied.

"What about the rest of the boys?"

"Jack, I'm trying to do my job here," Mogford said. As though summoned by demonic decree, several armed cops emerged from number four with two young women in handcuffs. Shortly afterwards, a man came out with his hands behind his back and three rifles trained on him.

"Isn't this overkill?" Cholmondeley asked.

"Could be," Mogford grunted.

"Well, I think you're barking up the wrong tree," Cholmondeley said. "Now, if you'll excuse me—"

"Not so fast, old man," Mogford said. "You're going to come with me to the station."

"In my pyjamas?"

"Yes."

"On what grounds?"

"Oh, you're not under arrest," Mogford said. "But I know one or two people who'd like to have a word with you."

"Tell them to come and see me here," Cholmondeley said.

Mogford's cheeks turned into beetroot and he took a couple of steps towards Cholmondeley, getting right in the older man's face. Up this close and personal, Cholmondeley could smell the sour tang of pickled onion on his breath, probably from a chip shop or a bag of Monster Munch.

"Listen, *Jack*," Mogford said. "You're not the top dog anymore. In fact, I'm not sure you ever were. Now, you listen to me. You can come in by choice or I can find some reason to arrest you. It's up to you."

"Then I'll come with you," Cholmondeley said. "But we're going to make a compromise. You're going to let me change into my suit, brush my teeth and make a cuppa."

Mogford grunted.

*   *   *

Back at the Old Vic, Cholmondeley was ushered into one of the little interrogation rooms, although Constable Cohen was kind enough to top up his coffee. He'd already finished the one he'd taken with him in the back of the police car. It was inside a battered and chipped old mug that said "World's Greatest Copper."

After Mogford led Cholmondeley into the interview room, he winked at him and left the room, saying, "Good luck. You're going to need it."

They left him to sit it out in there for an hour or so, but Jack Cholmondeley didn't mind too much. In some ways, it was nice to be in a familiar location, even if the circumstances were somewhat unusual. His main problem was that after two cups of coffee, he was starting to need the toilet, and he supposed that his age was a factor. It seemed to Jack Cholmondeley that the older he got, the more time he spent standing in front of a toilet with his wrinkled dick in his hand.

Twenty minutes later, the door opened and a middle-aged man walked in. He looked vaguely familiar, and Cholmondeley tried to give the face a name. He wasn't in uniform, so he wasn't a beat cop, and he didn't think the guy was one of the higher-ups, either. He could be a new recruit or someone who'd been transferred in from another station, but his bearing and the way he held himself put Cholmondeley more in mind of the barristers and legal briefs who came in to try to get criminal scum out of trouble and, occasionally, to defend the innocent.

The man sat down on the other side of the table and looked at him dispassionately. Cholmondeley stared straight back, and then he started laughing when he finally figured out who the man was.

"You were following me the other day," Cholmondeley said. "You were the man with the umbrella."

"Indeed," the man said.

"Who are you?"

"That doesn't matter."

"I know my rights," Cholmondeley said. "You're required by law to identify yourself."

"Only if I arrest you," the man replied. "But you're here of your own volition."

"I'm not so sure about that," Cholmondeley murmured. He shifted uncomfortably on the chair and asked, "Is there any chance I can use the lavatory?"

"You can take a leak when I'm through with you," he said. "Don't worry, it won't take long. I have a simple message for you, a warning. Stay away from the Boys in Blue."

Cholmondeley whistled and looked theatrically around him at the interview room.

"I'm impressed," Cholmondeley said. "You have some nerve. What if someone's listening?"

"They're not," the man replied. "I made sure of that. But even if they were, we're just two new friends having a chat. Right?"

"Hmm."

"Let's face it," he continued, "you're old news, a has-been. But you still have a long retirement stretching out ahead of you. We took your job, Jack. Don't make us take your retirement, too. Think about it."

"Oh, I will," Cholmondeley said. "Is that everything?"

"For now."

"You still haven't told me your name."

"And I'm still not going to."

"I'll find out, you know," Cholmondeley said.

At that, the man chuckled, and Jack Cholmondeley took a deep breath and counted to ten to make sure that he didn't lose his temper.

"You won't, Jack," the man said. "Officially, I don't exist. But in case you're still not getting the message, let me spell it out for you. If you look into me, or if you interfere with the Boys in Blue in any way, I'll kill you. You have a nice day, now."

He let himself out of the room, and Cholmondeley was left behind for another fifteen or twenty minutes or so. He was just about to give up and take a leak in his coffee cup when Constable Cohen came to collect him and to escort him out.

"Who was that guy?" Cholmondeley asked.

But Cohen just shot him a panicked look and said nothing.

*   *   *

"Bram's come up trumps again," Maile said.

"He has?"

Leipfold, Maile and Cholmondeley were sitting together in the office. It was Tuesday morning, the day after Cholmondeley had been taken to the Old Vic, and they'd already covered the conversation he'd had there. He'd brought the man's discarded umbrella with him, and the three of them had investigated it for clues, but there was nothing. Leipfold felt secretly disappointed. He'd been hoping to find some sort of Russian spy umbrella with a built-in pellet gun, but no dice. It looked like it was just a plain black umbrella, albeit one that was well-made and of a superior quality to the crap they sold in the tourist shops.

"You remember the work he was doing on the dark web?" Maile asked. "The forum he joined?"

"I'm not sure that I fully understand it," Leipfold said. "But yeah, I remember."

"Well, he dug a little deeper," Maile replied. "He's found a portal linked to the Boys in Blue on an encrypted URL."

"Can you send it to me?"

"Do you have Tor?" Maile asked.

"I'm not bloody Glastonbury, Maile," Leipfold said. "You're not going to start talking about ley lines, are you?"

"Tor is a browser, you dinosaur," she said. "If you want to visit an onion link, you're going to need Tor."

"Stop talking about hills and root vegetables and get to the point, please."

Maile sighed.

"Fine," she said. "Basically, this portal is linked to the Boys in Blue and has a login screen, but we don't have a username or a password. Bram's making contact with some of the forum users to see what he can find, and I've got Krypt0 and Mayhem working on a brute force attack."

"Ah yes," Leipfold said. "Your internet friends. Any luck?"

"Not yet," Maile replied. "Give it time. Bram's also found a few sub-Reddits where people are sharing theories, though that's all they are. Nothing too interesting, just the usual accusations of corruption and the odd claim that they're behind bombings or lab-grown pandemics. I think we can probably discount that, but it's interesting nonetheless."

"Ah," Cholmondeley said, glancing across at her from his desk. "I'm not going to pretend that I understand everything you've been talking about, young lady, but I don't think the Boys in Blue are capable of something like that. Coercion? Yes. Murder? Perhaps. Mass murder? Absolutely not."

"I suppose we'll see," Leipfold said. "That's the purpose of an investigation, is it not?"

"There's something else," Maile continued. "A rumour, but one that's believable. People say that the Boys in Blue have infiltrated the press, including our friends at *The Tribune*."

"Hmm." Leipfold picked up a biro and chewed at the end of it as he stared thoughtfully into space. "Well then, I suppose we should pay them a visit."

*　*　*

Leipfold had a couple of contacts at *The Tribune*, including cruciverbalist Alan Phelps and the paper's editor, Siobhan Dent. He was hoping to speak to the latter, but he also knew she was a busy woman. And if the anonymous people on the internet were right, there was a good chance that she'd also been bought off. Phelps was more likely to talk to him, but he was less likely to have any useful information.

He'd left Jack and Maile at the office because there was a ton of work for the two of them, and so he'd wound his way through the streets alone, apart from Camilla. He was wearing a wire.

The Tribune's office was in one of the nicer parts of town, and Leipfold had no fears for Camilla when he parked her up round the back of the building. He hadn't made an appointment, but he never did. He took his helmet off and chained it, along with the bike, to the metal railings. Then he walked round to the front and pressed the buzzer.

As usual, the receptionist just buzzed him in without checking who he was.

"Oh," she said. "Mr. Leipfold, it's you. What is it this time? Did Mr. Phelps make a mistake in the crossword again?"

"Not this time," Leipfold replied, flashing her a smile. "Although I will say he's running out of ideas. I've spotted him reusing a couple of the same clues. Is the boss in?"

"Siobhan?" the receptionist replied. "Not for most people, no. But for you, Mr. Leipfold? Maybe. Can I ask what it's about?"

"You can ask," Leipfold said. "But that doesn't mean you'll get an answer. Just tell her it's important."

"If you say so, Mr. Leipfold," she replied. She placed a quick call to Siobhan's office, but there was no reply, and so she asked Leipfold to excuse her and wandered off to see if she could find her. Leipfold waited impatiently, ignoring the plush leather sofas that had been laid out for visitors, and several minutes later she returned and led him through to a private meeting room, where Siobhan Dent was sitting and waiting for him.

"It's good to see you again," Leipfold said, extending his hand for her to shake. She took it, but she didn't look too pleased. "How are things?"

"Busy," Dent replied. "What do you want, James? I hope you've got something good for me."

"I want to talk about the Boys in Blue," Leipfold said, watching her face closely and scrutinising her response.

Either she was an underrated actress, the kind of up-and-coming starlet in the making that could have been cast in a Tom Townsend play, or she knew nothing about it. Her brow furrowed, and a look of perplexity passed across her face.

"Is this some sort of riddle, James?" she asked. "If so, I don't get it. What, are they the British Men in Black?"

"Something like that," Leipfold said.

"I won't run a conspiracy theory," Dent said, eyeing him cautiously. "You know the deal we have."

"Yeah, yeah," Leipfold replied. "You have to have a story, and you have to have some proof. And I'm working on it. But that's not what I came to ask you."

Siobhan Dent laughed and then covered her mouth as though she hoped to somehow swallow her amusement.

"Always a favour, eh, James?"

"Always a favour," he agreed. "You really haven't heard of the Boys in Blue?"

"Really."

"I've been doing some research," Leipfold said. "They're a fraternity of sorts, a bit like the Masons except for coppers and old army types. We've been trying to dig up what information we can so we can expose their shady dealings to the public. We've even hired a new lad who can work miracles. He's found some sort of portal on the dark web, whatever the hell that is."

"You really are old school, aren't you, James?" Dent replied. "We've used it ourselves to provide a submissions portal for confidential informants."

"Yes, well," Leipfold said, taken aback. "We're still trying to work on a login. Perhaps more worrying is that we've come across some accusations about *The Tribune*. I think you have a mole."

"Cheeky swine," Dent replied. "I'll have you know I use concealer—"

But Leipfold was no longer listening. He was up on his feet and moving for the door, which he swung open before sticking his head outside. He'd spotted something that bothered him, one of those little details that insisted on making themselves known.

When they'd started talking, he'd noticed the sunlight shining through the keyhole from the big bay windows on the other side of *The Tribune*'s office. But at some point during their conversation, the sunlight had disappeared. Perhaps it had merely passed behind a cloud, but Leipfold wasn't so sure.

Either way, when he looked back out into the office, everything just looked…well, normal. Most of the journalists were at their desks, though a couple of the designers were working on a cutting board and Alan Phelps was running something through the photocopier. Leipfold took one last, suspicious look around the office and then closed the door.

"Something strange is going on," Leipfold said. "And I'm going to need your help to solve it. But we can't talk here. People are listening."

"Who?" Dent asked, her face contorted with confusion.

"That's what I plan to find out," Leipfold replied.

Chapter Ten:
Username and Password

ON WEDNESDAY MORNING, LEIPFOLD was focusing on the crossword while Jack and Maile sat in reception, drinking cups of tea and gossiping idly about their active cases. They had a Skype call lined up with Bram Shakespeare, and they were deciding what to brief him on before they dialed in.

"Has he found anything new on the Boys in Blue?" Cholmondeley asked.

"Give him a chance, Jack," Maile replied. "Have you?"

"Fair point," Cholmondeley said. "Okay, well let's play to our strengths. Ironically, you're a better writer than Shakespeare. Not related to Frank, are you?"

"Didn't he get hit by a golf buggy?" Leipfold asked.

"Oh yeah, Uncle Frank," Maile said, a deadpan expression on her face. She held it for a couple of seconds and then burst out laughing. "You two gentlemen are a hive of useless information. You're like every social network."

"Back in my day—"

"Get back to work, Jack," Leipfold said, without taking his eyes away from the crossword grid.

"I think I've got something that Bram can handle," Maile said, sweeping an unruly curl of hair out of her eyes. "We've got a client who's asked us to look into a suspected cryptocurrency scam. The theory is that someone's set up this currency so that once enough people have invested in it, they can dump their assets and cash in."

"And you think that Abraham can help?"

"He's just a Bram, Jack," Maile said. "And yes, he can help us. I've got another list of IP addresses for you to work through. Once you've filtered out the crap, I'll send them over to Bram."

"Ahem."

Leipfold had half-coughed, half-spoken, and Maile and Jack both turned around at the same time to look at him.

"Have you two finished?" Leipfold asked.

"Not really," Maile said. "We still need to talk to Bram."

"That can wait," Leipfold said. "I've found something you should take a look at."

Jack Cholmondeley remained on the sofa, sipping tea from his World's Best Copper mug, which he'd brought into the office. Maile raced over to Leipfold's side and took up a position a step and a half behind him so she could look over his shoulder. He had the puzzle pages of *The Tribune* spread out in front of him, and he'd already finished solving the day's crossword.

"Do you see it?" Leipfold asked.

"See what?" Maile replied. "That you finished the crossword? Well done, James. I'm very proud of you."

"Sarcasm doesn't suit you," Leipfold said, scowling at her. "No, I'm talking about *this*."

He took his pencil and used the tip of it to point to what appeared to be random sections of the crossword. After Maile stared at it and was clearly just as mystified as before, he elaborated.

"There's a message here," Leipfold said. "It's in a cipher, but it's there. If you take the first letter of every clue and pull them all together, it's an anagram."

"And you spotted that?"

"I like anagrams," Leipfold said, defensively. "I see them everywhere."

"Are you sure you're not dyslexic?"

"Har-bloody-har," Leipfold said. "And you told me off for making wheelchair jokes."

"That's different," Maile said.

"No, it's not," Leipfold replied. "Anyway, the point is, I think Mr. Phelps is trying to tell me something. But there's a problem. I've only got two of the words, and there's no way in hell I can figure out the rest without your help."

"Maile O'Hara to the rescue yet again," she said. "What do you need?"

"Well, that's just the thing," Leipfold said. "You'll probably figure it out when I tell you the two words that I figured out."

"Which are?"

"The first one was 'username'," Leipfold replied. "And the second one was 'password'."

*   *   *

Maile took the list of letters from the crossword clues and forwarded them to Bram, who was even better suited than she was to crack the code and unscramble the anagrams.

As for what they were the logins for, it was anyone's guess. Maile suspected it would let them into the site on the dark web, but why did Phelps have a login? And why had he hidden it in the crossword?

"I have a theory," Leipfold said, leaning lazily back on his chair with his feet up on his desk. "It's just a theory, mind."

"Your theories are usually better than most," Maile replied. "What's your theory?"

"When I was at their office, I thought someone was listening in at the keyhole while I was talking to Dent," Leipfold explained. "I saw Phelps lurking around nearby, but I thought he was just using the photocopier. Maybe he was listening in."

"Did you talk to Dent about the dark net site?"

Leipfold rubbed his chin thoughtfully, and Maile assumed he was walking through the weird mental mansion that was his mind, replaying the conversation with his near-eidetic memory.

"Yeah," Leipfold said. "I did."

"Phelps could have heard you talking about it," Maile reasoned. "He couldn't approach you directly because, well, someone might have seen him. He probably thought his phone and emails were being tracked. For all we know, they were. But he knows you're a crossword fan, he knows you're into cryptography, and he also knows you love an anagram."

"Sounds like a stretch to me," Cholmondeley murmured. Leipfold had got him working on some documentation, something that the ex-cop was surprisingly good at, and so he'd spent most of the last two days working on health and safety policies and an updated set of standard terms and conditions.

"You're used to playing by the rules," Leipfold reminded him. "A copper needs evidence. A private detective just follows his nose."

"Just as long as you don't get it chopped off, James," Cholmondeley said. "Good lord, this is all a bit too MI5 for my liking."

"It's too late for us to change our minds now, Jack," Leipfold said. "We're already in over our heads. We have to see this through to the end."

"Aye," Cholmondeley said. "As long as they don't kill us all before we figure out the answer to this bloody anagram."

* * *

None of them were murdered in their beds, not that night at least, and the following day saw them meeting up with Bram Shakespeare in the corner of the coffee shop. The place had good wheelchair access and brewed a decent bean juice, and it also afforded them a good view of the streets outside so that they could people-watch and comment on the passers-by. Sure, it wasn't the most private of places, but it did the job. And it wasn't as though Bram could get into the office.

Leipfold, Maile and Bram sat around a table and ordered drinks from the waitress before Bram pulled a laptop out and booted it up. He loaded up Tor and navigated through to the login portal.

"Check this out," Bram said, keying in a sequence of seemingly random letters into the username and password fields. "As far as I can tell, there's no rhyme or reason. It's the most secure way to create a username and password, although it's hard to remember the damn things."

"How did you find the right combination?" Leipfold asked.

"Trust me," Bram said. "You don't want to know. It took a lot of energy drinks. Can I put them on expenses?"

"I do," Maile murmured. "He doesn't check."

Leipfold glanced at her but said nothing. Meanwhile, Bram had finished keying in the digits and hit the login button, and though it took a while for the page to load, it made it in the end.

"Why's it so slow?" Leipfold asked.

"We're running through a VPN on coffee shop Wi-Fi," Bram replied. "What did you expect? We're in, though."

"What are we looking at?"

"Only the biggest story of the decade," Bram replied.

Now that they'd made it through the login screen, they could see the site for what it was—a discussion forum, much like the one where Shakespeare had found the link to the portal in the first place.

But this was no ordinary forum, even Leipfold could see that. Heavily encrypted and hidden away from private eyes on an anonymous server, they'd been lucky to stumble across it at all. It reminded Leipfold of a speakeasy during prohibition, where people could only get in if they knew the code word or the special knock. Someone had gone to great lengths to hide it.

Bram started browsing through the forums, scanning through

topics so quickly that Leipfold struggled to keep up with him, despite being a rapid reader. Bram seemed to be functioning more like a search engine or a human algorithm, speed-reading the screen and picking up on keywords, then moving the mouse or tapping away at the keyboard to load the next page while Leipfold was still on the second paragraph.

Still, it was enough for him to get a good idea of what was going on, and he could see from the stunned expression on his assistant's face that Maile was just as surprised as he was.

Right at the top of the page, a piece of digital graffiti art spelled out the words "BIB Chat," and it didn't take a genius to figure out what the acronym meant. The forums were divided into sub-forums, each of them themed based upon which branch of the forces it dealt with. All of the usernames consisted of a further string of random letters, providing the site's users with an extra layer of anonymity.

As for the discussions, they ranged from simple requests for promotion to more complicated plots where people were calling in mutual favours or offering bribes through untraceable cryptocurrencies. It was a veritable stock exchange of crime, the worst kind of black market. With just a username and password, which was only available via referral, anyone could pay anyone any amount to do anything. One guy was offering US passports for $9,000. Someone else was selling three tabs of Biggie Kat acid for £11.99 plus postage and packing. There were also a hell of a lot of people selling illegal email lists and porn site logins.

"The Blue Road," Maile murmured.

"What?"

"Oh, nothing."

"So what do we do?" Leipfold asked.

"I've got this," Bram said. In the same way that Leipfold was a natural frowner, Bram was a natural smiler. He looked like he'd smile if someone told him his mum was dead. It was the kind of

smile that filled people with confidence, which was why Maile—
and then Leipfold—had trusted him in the first place.

"So what's the plan?" Maile asked.

"Everyone's identified by a pseudonym," Bram said. "The letters
and numbers that make up their usernames. We need to figure out
who's behind the usernames."

"Jack Cholmondeley gave me a list of cops he thinks are bent,"
Leipfold said.

"James!" Maile scolded. "Steve Cohen is—"

"One of the good guys," Leipfold said. "Or at least, I think he is.
Hey, *Much Ado About Nothing*, if I give you the list of names, can
you work some magic?"

"I can try," Bram said. "If we have a list of usernames and a list
of suspects, I can carry out some analysis. Shouldn't be a problem.
We'll get an algorithm going and feed it as much data as we can.
If we can get some written samples from each of the suspects, we
can compare them to the samples from the dark web and see if we
can find some commonalities."

"I'm not going to pretend to understand all of that," Leipfold
said. "But if you can make it happen, do so. Let me know if you
need any budget."

"We have budget?" Maile asked, looking astonished at the mere
idea. "For *this*?"

"My personal savings," Leipfold replied. "They're not endless,
but they should be enough."

"No need," Bram said, looking excitedly across at them. The
grin was still plastered across his face, but it had been joined by
a twinkle behind the eyes that was reminiscent of the look that
possessed James Leipfold when he was gripped by the thrill of the
chase. "I can do all this from home."

"How much are we paying you again?"

"£10.50 an hour," he said.

"We'll make it £11," Leipfold said.

"Ooh," Maile murmured. "Big spender."

"Thanks, Mr. Leipfold," Bram said. "But I have a question. Something isn't right here. You say you got this login from Mr. Phelps and the crossword in *The Tribune*?"

"Yeah."

"I don't get it," Bram said. "Why is he helping you?"

Leipfold shrugged and said, "I have no idea, kid. That's something else for us to figure out."

*   *   *

Jack Cholmondeley was at the hospital, wearing his best tweed suit again and stinking of cologne. He'd driven the Beemer there and then struggled to find somewhere to park it. Most of the spaces were full, and those that weren't were either too small or had neighbouring cars encroaching into them. He'd finally found a space in a far corner of the car park, but then he'd realised that there were no machines nearby and so by the time he'd finished paying and displaying, he'd already killed ten minutes.

He didn't bother stopping at reception because he knew exactly where he was going. He'd spent a lot of time at the hospital over the years, mostly because of his job, and he could have found his way around in the darkness if he'd had to. Ward 9 was two floors below the operating theatre and housed patients who were recovering from major trauma.

The nurses were expecting him because he'd called ahead. Even though he was no longer a copper, he still had a lot of contacts, including many of the matrons and even one or two members of the hospital's board. It hadn't been difficult to pull a few strings.

He was greeted at the entrance to the ward by a dour-faced young nurse who shook him by the hand and then led him through to bed nineteen, where the patient was. She was sitting up in bed with an oxygen mask on her face and a canula in her arm. She'd lost a little weight, and it gave her an unusually gaunt appearance.

"It's good to see you, boss," Constable Groves said, her voice a little weak but otherwise not too far from normal. "I got shot."

"I know," Cholmondeley said. "I'm sorry about that. I feel responsible."

"You're not."

"The guy said it was a message for me," Cholmondeley reminded her.

"I wouldn't know about that," Groves said. "I don't remember it. I'm guessing that's why you're here? For information?"

"Not at all," Cholmondeley replied. "Believe it or not, I care. I wanted to see for my own eyes that you're healing up okay."

"I'm not quite as good as new," Groves said, "but I think I'll be just fine."

"I'm glad to hear that," Cholmondeley said awkwardly, sitting down in the visitor's chair at the side of her hospital bed. "Did you hear the news?"

"Yeah," she replied. "Cohen told me. He's been to visit me a couple of times."

She gestured to the bedside table, which was festooned with get well soon cards and the stalks of grapes that the constable had presumably brought for her to nibble on.

"I can't believe they put you on gardening leave," Groves said. "It's ridiculous. You're the best boss I've ever had."

"Easy, now," Cholmondeley said. "Exertion isn't good for you. You've been through a lot of trauma."

"Yeah," Groves said. "And it's not just physical. But the doctors say I'm on the mend, slowly but surely, and the operation to remove the bullet was successful. I'm looking at a couple months of rehabilitation and I won't be back at work until at least the summer, but I should count myself lucky. Another couple of inches to the right and that bullet would have hit me in the spine, and then where would we be?"

Cholmondeley shuddered at the thought. Groves flashed him a weak smile and looked around the room, then beckoned for him to come closer. He leaned in towards her and she whispered into his ear.

"Watch out for the Boys in Blue, sir," she said. "Constable Cohen told me all about it. I'm not going to lie, sir, I've had my suspicions."

Cholmondeley thought for a moment and then sighed.

"What would you have me do?" he asked. "I've put your life at risk, and to have done so inadvertently is even worse. Do you want revenge, is that it?"

"No, sir," Groves said weakly, leaning back against her pillow. "Nothing like that."

"Then what do you want?"

"Justice," Groves replied, weakly. "Now if you don't mind, sir, I'd like you to sod off. I need to take a nap."

*　*　*

The builder was round at Leipfold's place, making some final measurements before he started knocking down walls and bringing metal in. He'd managed to dig up the building's blueprints from somewhere and had spent most of the morning tapping at different walls and jotting down measurements.

Leipfold wasn't a builder, and he wasn't even a hobbyist when it came to DIY, and so he didn't know what the man was doing. He also didn't care. He wasn't the one who was footing the bill.

Still, it was difficult to concentrate with the man causing a ruckus every time he took a new tool out, and having an unfamiliar face around the place made him anxious and on edge. Every time Leipfold found himself sitting down to make some progress on one of his cases, he ended up getting distracted and going to check on the builder to make sure that he wasn't poking his nose in where it wasn't wanted or pinching all of the biscuits.

It was a lot of work for a new elevator.

Theoretically, Bram could have worked from home, but Leipfold preferred to have his employees where he could keep an eye on them. And besides, he had to admit that it couldn't do any harm. If nothing else, it meant that his office would be more accessible for his clients, though he couldn't remember the last time he'd been hired by someone with mobility issues.

The lift in question came as part of a kit, and it was being built to run between the corner of Leipfold's office and the downstairs lobby. Whenever the builder was in his office, Leipfold watched him with the intensity of a bird of prey staring at its next meal. When the man was downstairs in the lobby, the hammering, sawing and drilling was almost as much of a distraction.

They'd had to talk about their cases disjointedly, waiting for the man to leave the room before they covered anything sensitive or secret. That had affected Leipfold and Cholmondeley a lot more than Maile and Bram, who were already using ciphers to converse via secure instant messaging.

Finally, after what seemed like forever, the builder whistled a couple of times, wrote a few final notes in his notebook and then returned the pencil to its place above his ear and nodded at Leipfold before letting himself out of the building.

"About time," Cholmondeley said. "I've been dying to ask you, James. What are we going to do?"

"About what?"

"About the Boys in Blue," Cholmondeley said. "We have to report it."

"To who?" Leipfold scoffed. "The cops?"

"There's always the media," Cholmondeley said. "You told me yourself that they can be a powerful ally."

"Yeah," Leipfold said, "but there's a time and a place for it. Bram's still working his way through the data, although we've got a couple of likely matches. But I don't know, Jack. It's not enough."

"It would hold up in court," Cholmondeley said.

"No chance," Leipfold replied. "You're too much of an optimist. And besides, who can say if it would even *get* to court. The system is broken, Jack. Or at the very least, it's breaking."

"So what do we do?"

"We keep building the case," Leipfold said. "What choice do we have? We'll have to build a dossier and keep gathering evidence until there's enough to dispel reasonable doubt. I want you, Bram and Maile to work on that while I work on something else."

"What's that?" Cholmondeley asked.

"I need you to find us someone we can trust," Leipfold said. "Who are we going to tell about this, Jack? The cops? The press? They're both as corrupt as each other."

"I know what I'd do," Maile said. She'd been half-listening to them just like usual, her headphones stretched across her skull so they covered one ear but not the other. "I'd go straight to the masses. I'd use Reddit, or maybe Wikileaks."

"We'll see," Leipfold said. "It sounds like we might not have any choice, but I want to get a second opinion."

"I think we should—"

"Sorry, Jack," Leipfold said, cutting in before the ex-cop had time to derail his thought process. "I wasn't talking about you. I think we need to talk to the client. I think we need to talk to Croft."

*   *   *

Leipfold and the gang had a problem. Mike Croft had dropped off the face of the earth.

The phone number that he'd listed was going straight to voicemail, and he wasn't responding to emails either. Perhaps he was taking a long weekend, but it seemed unlikely. When Monday rolled around and there was still no response, Leipfold started to worry.

Then Bram Shakespeare made a breakthrough.

The three of them talked to him via a video chat. Maile had set it up on her machine and the three of them had scooched up around her monitor. It made for a surreal sight, in part because there wasn't room for them to bring their chairs over. Instead, all three of them were standing up, and Leipfold and Cholmondeley were crouching slightly to ensure that they stayed in frame.

"What's the 4-11?" Maile asked, once the connection had been established and they'd worked through the usual pleasantries, including a comment from Jack Cholmondeley about how lovely the weather was for the time of year.

"I've tied a few more suspects back to their usernames," Bram explained, his voice cutting out on the choppy connection. Maile had been asking Leipfold to upgrade to fiber optic ever since she'd started, but it was one of those nagging little jobs that he hadn't got round to. "I, uh…"

"Go on," Leipfold said.

"I parsed through the data we have on our servers," Bram said. "We have a few samples of Croft's writing style in his emails, and that was enough to make a comparison. There are no guarantees, you understand. Linguistic analysis is as much of an art as a science. Still, I make it a 99.7% chance that Mike Croft is af9r8ms9x0."

"You're going to have to write that down for me," Maile said.

"Af9r8ms9x0," Leipfold repeated, offhandedly. "Your memory sucks."

"Sorry, Rain Man."

"If I'm right," Bram continued, "then your client is as corrupt as the cops he's got you investigating. You should do a little digging on him."

"Who will watch the watchers?" Leipfold murmured.

"What was that?"

"Nothing," Leipfold said. "I think—"

But what he thought would have to wait, because there was a

buzz at the door and Leipfold asked Bram to wait while he went to answer it. He rushed across to the intercom and took the phone off its cradle.

"Yes?" he said.

The voice at the other end was instantly recognisable. Leipfold placed his hand over the receiver and turned around to look at his two co-workers.

"Holy shit," Leipfold said. "Croft is outside the office. He says he wants to come in."

Chapter Eleven:
Blue Movies at the Coffee Shop

THEY HAD TO THINK fast. Fortunately, they were good at it.

Leipfold stalled Croft for a couple of moments, making up an excuse by blaming the builder, and then he left the office and went down to greet their visitor. While he was doing that, Maile rushed round and fiddled with their computers and Jack Cholmondeley popped the kettle on and stashed some of their paperwork in the whiskey drawer in Leipfold's desk.

When Leipfold came back into the office, Croft was hot on his heels. He had a swagger to his walk that suggested he thought he owned the place, and Leipfold's distaste for the man's quiet confidence seemed to hang in the air like a malevolent cloud at a picnic. He kept it out of his voice, though.

"Good morning, Mr. Croft," Leipfold said. "Tea?"

"Not for me, thank you," Croft said. He looked imperiously around the room as though daring it to make some personal affront. When he seemed satisfied with whatever bizarre criteria he was grading them on, he helped himself to a seat. "I'll take some water, if you're offering."

"Of course," Leipfold said. He nodded at Cholmondeley as the kettle reached its crescendo and then sat down opposite his client. "So…"

"So?"

"So," Leipfold repeated. "You're one of them. You're one of the

Boys in Blue."

He hadn't been sure what reaction he'd receive, but it certainly wasn't the one that he got. Croft smiled, revealing a row of pristine teeth, and then he chuckled to himself.

"Yes," he said. "I wondered how long it would take you to figure that out. How did you do it?"

"Linguistic analysis," Leipfold said. He didn't elaborate.

"Well, that's one way to do it," Croft conceded. "There were other clues for those who looked for them."

"So you don't deny it?"

"I don't deny that I was an active member of the Boys in Blue, if that's your question," Croft said. "As it happens, my father was a former member, and so I was made an automatic member as soon as I joined the force. These guys don't mess around, Mr. Leipfold. I was given no choice in the matter. I became a member without even being consulted. Before I knew what was happening, I was in too deep."

"It's a touching story," Leipfold replied. "But is it true, I wonder?"

"Think about it," Croft insisted. "Why else would I have hired you?"

"To double cross us," Maile suggested, glaring at him from across the room with such ferocity that Leipfold wondered if she was trying to make his head explode with the power of her mind.

"Possible, I suppose," Croft said. He paused for a moment and looked around the room, first at James Leipfold and then at Maile O'Hara and Jack Cholmondeley. "Listen, I'm telling you the truth. I want to get out of the game. Sure, the old boys' club used to work back in the day, but that was when we were fighting fascists or trying not to get nuked by the Russkis."

Leipfold turned to look at Maile, but she didn't say anything.

"You gonna let him get away with 'Russkis'?" he asked.

She shrugged and said, "I tell you off because I think you're better than that. With him, I'm not so sure."

"Times have changed," Croft said, though his own existence suggested that they hadn't. "And the Boys in Blue haven't changed with them. When they were first founded, they were the strength at the heart of democracy, the very thing that made our country great. Now, they're a threat to democracy itself."

"I still don't believe you," Leipfold said. "We've got your account on the portal tied back to you and we've seen some of the stuff your name is attached to. You've been bribing journalists and setting convicts free."

"I have," Croft admitted. "But you have to believe me, I had orders of my own. You'll notice that I didn't touch the drugs and I stayed away from human trafficking."

"What do you want?" Cholmondeley growled. "A medal?"

"Easy, Jack," Leipfold said.

"Sorry, James," Cholmondeley replied. "It's just that I *hate* bent cops."

"But I was bent for a reason," Croft insisted. "I've been gathering as much intelligence as I could while minimising the harm I did. I'm no angel, I know that, but I did what I could to not be a devil. And perhaps I can help you out with something as an act of good faith."

"What's that, then?"

"I can give you the password to go along with my username," Croft says. "You can log in as me and continue your investigation from there. Just don't mess this up, okay? If they find out what we're doing, they'll kill me."

"If they find out what we're doing," Leipfold murmured, "they'll kill us, too. Go on, get out of here."

Croft opened his mouth to protest, but then he must have seen the look in Leipfold's eye because he closed it again and then leapt up from the chair as though the metal had burned a hole through the seat of his trousers. He shot Leipfold a look as though accusing him of putting tacks on the seat and then marched out of the office door, slamming the thing behind him. He didn't look back.

"Interesting," Leipfold said. "Did you get that?"

"Oh yes, boss," Maile replied. "I'm just saving and exporting it now. The audio quality's not great and it won't hold up in court, but it'll do."

"Good stuff," Leipfold said, rubbing his hands together. "Come, Watson, come! The game is afoot."

"What?"

"Nothing," Leipfold replied. "Email me that recording, will you? I'm going out for a walk."

*   *   *

The builder was back again the next day, and Leipfold spent it in his office, watching the guy's every move while getting occasional bits of research done and working on the company's finances. He'd delegated the investigation to Maile, with Jack Cholmondeley acting as her second-in-command.

The two of them met Bram Shakespeare at the same cafeteria and found themselves sitting in the same spot. Leipfold had given Maile the company credit card, and she used it to order a round of coffees and a half dozen croissants. She took the drinks back to the table on a tray and handed them out, then sat down with her back to the entrance.

Jack Cholmondeley had taken the corner seat, the one that Leipfold had sat in on their last visit, and Maile smirked to herself. It was the policeman's seat, the one with the best view of the rest of the room, and both men had gravitated towards it out of habit.

She smiled at Bram, who was sitting opposite her with Cholmondeley on his right, and said, "So what have we got?"

"Information," he replied. "At least, I think so. I was up until dawn with the login you gave me, parsing through all the data I could find."

"Croft's login opened up a whole bunch of new sub-forums," Maile said. "What did you find in them?"

"A lot more of the same," Bram replied. "More old boys calling in favours so they can shape the direction of society. But get this. It looks like Croft has been working on a pornography ring."

"Why?" Maile asked.

"Money, I guess," Bram said. "Apparently people still pay for it, especially the niche stuff. They've been getting up to some pretty kinky shit."

"Kids?" Cholmondeley asked. There was a harshness to his voice that Maile had never heard before.

"No," Bram said.

"Good," Cholmondeley replied, cracking his knuckles and leaning back in his chair. Maile had always thought of Jack Cholmondeley as a mild-tempered old man, but for a split second he'd shown a glimpse of a darker side. He looked like an avenging angel from the Old Testament.

"It's hard to tell from this exactly what's going on," Bram said. "The porn itself is pretty brutal, that violent stuff with names like 'Choke-Fucking My Bitch Ex-Girlfriend'. You know what I'm talking about."

"I do?" Cholmondeley asked.

"I do," Maile said. Bram and Cholmondeley turned to look at her. "What? I go on 4Chan."

"Ah," Bram said, as though that explained everything, which it did. "Anyway, my point is, there's some pretty depraved shit going on. Fake snuff films, furry porn, borderline incest, all that kind of stuff. But it's not the porn that I'm worried about."

"You're worried about the girls," Maile said.

"Yeah," Bram replied. "I mean, even if it's totally legit, it's morally reprehensible. The cops might be bankrolling it, but they'd have to hire film crews and producers. A lot of those guys are as sketchy as they come. Some of the girls might have been tricked into shooting these films after being told it was just a regular porno."

"Or worse," Cholmondeley said, leaning forwards again. That

look had reappeared. Maile could see it in his eyes, and it scared her. "I've come across cases like these before. A lot of the girls are trafficking victims who barely speak any English."

"We have to find them," Maile said. "If we can track them down, we can ask them and get them the hell out of there if they're in danger or being held against their will."

Bram and Cholmondeley both nodded, and a tense silence descended upon the three of them as they figured out what to do next. Maile took a swig of her coffee and sighed.

"We're going to have to watch the movies they've been making," she said. "See if we can't get some screenshots of the girls so we can track them down."

"If you insist," Bram said, his fingers flashing deftly across the keyboard.

"What are you doing?"

"You said—"

"I didn't mean *here*," Maile said, looking uneasily around. "We're in a freakin' hipster coffee shop."

"Relax," Bram said. "We're in the corner, and I've muted it. See, if we're careful, we don't even have to—"

"Hey!" Cholmondeley exclaimed, shooting up to his feet and catching his knee on the bottom of the table. "I know that girl!"

"Watch a lot of porn, do you?" Bram asked.

"Less of that, young man," Cholmondeley said. "I'm a married man."

Then his face dropped, and Maile guessed that he'd just thought about Mary and his shitty little bedsit.

"What I mean to say is," Cholmondeley began, "I recognise her. Come to think of it, I think I know where they've been filming."

"Where?" Maile asked, leaning forward. "Tell me!"

"When I met her, she told me her name was Natasha Raynor," Cholmondeley said. "She was living in my building. At least, I thought she was. Some strange things have been going on in the flat next door to me. Perhaps it's time I found out exactly what."

* * *

The four employees of Leipfold Investigations spent the rest of that day and most of the next working on a plan of attack. The hands on the clock moved imperceptibly slowly, and by the time that they shut up shop at 6 PM, tensions were running high.

"Does Bram *have* to come?" Maile asked, checking her Fitbit for the thirtieth time that afternoon.

"He says he wants to," Leipfold said, shrugging. "He's paying the taxi fare himself. Who am I to say no?"

"But what if he gets hurt?"

"He won't," Cholmondeley said, grimly. Maile had seen more and more of his dark side over the last twenty-four hours, and she was starting to wish that the old Jack would come back. It was almost as bad as when he'd been moping around and talking non-stop about Mary.

"Anyway," Leipfold added, clearly trying to dispel the tension and doing a terrible job of it. "You've got your pepper spray."

"Fresh canister, baby," Maile said.

They killed a little more time at the office as they waited for the clock to do its thing, until it finally ticked around to 6:30 PM, which they'd agreed would be the signal. Somewhere on the other side of the city, Bram was hopping into the back of a taxi.

"Let's do this," Leipfold said.

Maile rode with Jack Cholmondeley, stretching herself out in the luxurious leather seats of his pristine Beemer, and Leipfold followed behind them on Camilla. Maile knew how fast she could go when he opened her up, and so she assumed that he was deliberately taking it easy so that he didn't overtake them.

When they got to Jack Cholmondeley's place, Bram was being helped out of a cab by a nondescript taxi driver, the kind of guy who looked like he might be a Dave and who probably spent his downtime playing cards and ranting about immigrants.

The four of them split up, with Bram and Maile taking Cholmondeley's bedsit and the ex-cop buddying up with Leipfold in the kitchen. They said they planned to maintain their cover by making spag bol, and Maile wished she could be a fly on the wall to watch them at it. She couldn't imagine either of them in such a domestic setting.

The noises started up at about 8:30, and the two of them had long since finished cooking. They'd even served up a couple of bowls to Maile and Bram and used it as a pretext to knock on a few doors, though they didn't find anything. Only one of the neighbours answered, and he didn't speak a word of English.

He didn't want any spaghetti.

The noises sounded like deer rutting in the mating season. It wasn't a pleasant sound, and it didn't sound all that sexual. It did, however, sound a hell of a lot like the audio they'd heard on the clips they'd watched during their research.

Maile watched from the door of Cholmondeley's flat as he carried out the next part of the plan with Leipfold. It was a pretty standard tactic. Leipfold stood to one side, out of sight of the peephole, while Cholmondeley knocked at the door with a parcel in his hand. They'd rehearsed this in advance, and Maile herself had wrapped the parcel, which just contained Leipfold's copy of *The Brothers Karamazov.*

The door opened a crack and a suspicious eye peered through it, but that was all the two men needed. Cholmondeley wedged his foot in the crack and then Leipfold hit the door at a run, barging it open and sending it smashing into the inside wall, narrowly missing the face that the eye belonged to. The chain snapped away from both the door and the wall and went catapulting away into the hallway, clattering off the door of number seven.

There was a scream, and then Leipfold and Cholmondeley

stood aside as a Muslim woman ran past them and out into the hallway. Maile backed out of the way too, and Bram rolled past her and along the hallway. Maile glanced in his direction and saw that he'd caught up with the woman at the door and started talking to her, and then she turned her attention back to Leipfold and Cholmondeley, who'd entered the neighbour's place and were out of sight.

She stepped out of Cholmondeley's bedsit, leaving the door on the latch so she could duck back in if she needed to. Then she stepped cautiously across the hallway and peeped her head into the neighbours' flat.

The place reeked of sex and marijuana, as well as a hint of some chemical that set her teeth on edge. The inside of the apartment still showed signs of the police raid from a couple of days earlier, and while there was little light filtering in through the windows, it was brightly lit by artificial lighting. It wasn't from hydroponics, though. Maile recognised the quality of the light. It was studio lighting for photographers and film-makers.

Still standing in the doorway, she listened as Leipfold and Cholmondeley asked a couple of questions, and then a deep voice replied to them. Maile couldn't make out what was being said, but it didn't matter. The boys would update her when they got back to the office.

She turned around and made eye contact with Bram, who was still trying to talk to the Muslim woman.

"She doesn't speak any English," Bram said. "We'll have to find a translator."

"Google it," Maile said. "The company will cover it."

"How am I supposed to tell what language she's speaking?" he replied.

While he was talking, the woman continued to babble away. Maile put her finger to her lips for a moment and listened.

"It's Arabic," she said. "She's—"

"Look out!"

Maile whirled around, just in time to see a man rushing past her. She had an impression of plain black clothing and a wisp of grey hair and then he was gone. She turned around again and saw the man racing towards the front door. The Muslim woman cowered back against the wall as though seeking comfort in the arms of the building itself, but he showed no signs of attacking or interfering with her. Bram was moving too, edging his wheelchair to one side and rummaging for something.

Maile started running after him, but the man was already at the door and he'd swung it open. He was two steps away from freedom. And then Bram unfolded his collapsible baton and swung it at the back of his legs. He went down hard and hit his head off the door.

Chapter Twelve:
Feminine Intuition

THE MAN THAT BRAM had captured had been in the bathroom when Leipfold and Cholmondeley had forced through the door, and they'd had their hands full with two other guys. There were also three women in there.

Number four wasn't as small as Cholmondeley's place, but it wasn't exactly big, either. The building was a former Victorian alms house and had been designed with larger apartments in mind. As the price of land in the capital had continued to rise, however, the building's owners had decided to add a few extra walls and doors to squeeze more money out of it. Number four had survived the worst of the changes and so instead of being a single room, it had a living room/kitchen and a bedroom, as well as its own bathroom. It wasn't exactly spacious, but it was better than Cholmondeley's place.

After Bram incapacitated the third man, Cholmondeley came out to see what the commotion was and secured the man's wrists behind his back with cable ties before frogmarching him back inside. Maile followed them, while Bram took the Muslim woman into Cholmondeley's room.

The inside of the apartment was squalid and dingy, making it more like a squat or a hovel than a home. In one of the corners, a dozen or so cardboard boxes were stacked on top of each other. She couldn't see what was inside them, but she was willing to bet they were Blu-Rays with names like *Ahmina Tequila Loses Her BDSM Virginity.*

Leipfold and Cholmondeley had already deployed the cable ties on the other two men, and the three of them were sitting slumped on a tattered old sofa. They weren't gagged, but that wasn't a problem. They either assumed that no one would come to their aid if they cried out or they didn't want to draw more attention to themselves. As though word of the raid a couple days earlier hadn't already spread throughout the complex like an Australian forest fire.

"Who are you guys?" one of the men asked. "And what do you want from us? Money?"

"We want information," Leipfold said. "More specifically, we want to know who you're working for."

"Don't say anything, Trev," another man added, looking pointedly at the first. "They'll nick us."

"We're not the cops," Leipfold said. Then he paused before pointing at Jack Cholmondeley. "Well, he is, or was, or whatever. My name's James Leipfold, and I'm a private detective. We're working a case."

"And it brought you here?"

"Exactly," Leipfold said. "I have no desire to cause you any more inconvenience than we already have. If you provide us with the information we need, we'll be on our way."

"You'll dob us in the moment you leave."

"Only if you don't give us any info," Leipfold said. "But you'll find that if you scratch our backs, we'll scratch yours."

"What about the cripple?" the third man said, scowling up at the two men while massaging the backs of his knees. "He assaulted me."

"You brought it on yourself," Cholmondeley growled, playing the part of the bad cop to perfection. He had that look about him. "And if you call him a cripple again, I'll dislocate your shoulder."

"Jack!" Maile exclaimed. "You can't do that!"

"I'll put it back afterwards."

"Still, I—"

"Enough," Leipfold said, holding his hand up for silence. He glanced over towards the bedroom door, which was open and afforded a view of the scantily clad women inside it. "Who's behind your operation?"

"We don't know," Trev said. "It's all anonymous. We're paid in bitcoin and sent encrypted instructions."

Leipfold looked at Maile, who nodded.

"Could be legit," she said. "We know these guys are tech savvy. If they're using the dark web to communicate, I can believe they know their stuff when it comes to encryption. And if they paid through bitcoin, we won't be able to track it."

"Hmm," Leipfold said, turning back to look at the men on the couch. "Ever heard of the Boys in Blue?"

"Sorry," the second man replied. "I don't listen to pop music."

"Well, I'm convinced," Cholmondeley murmured.

"Where do the girls come from?" Leipfold asked. "We're concerned about their welfare."

"Search me, pal. We just show up when we're told to and start shooting."

"There is *something*," Trev said. "Not a name, really. Mr. M. Is he your man?"

"Could be," Leipfold said, evenly. "I'm going to need to take your names and numbers. Your *real* names and numbers. I'll want to speak to you again."

"You're going to let us go?"

"For now," Leipfold said. "But we'll be keeping an eye on you. And you're going to do something for us."

"We are?"

"Yes," Leipfold said. "You're going to down tools and stop shooting. And as soon as you get your next batch of instructions, you're going to tell us."

"And if we don't?"

"If you don't, we'll find you," Leipfold replied. He nodded at Cholmondeley, who was vibrating with a nervous energy. "Jack Cholmondeley here will track you down in a dark alley with a sock full of marbles."

*   *   *

The following day, at Leipfold's office, all three of them were finding it difficult to concentrate. The builder was back, and this time he'd brought a couple of friends, as well as an HGV full of equipment that he'd parked two hundred yards down the street because there wasn't enough space to manoeuvre it to the double yellows outside Leipfold's office.

Leipfold had a niggling feeling that he recognised one of them, but he wasn't sure. His memory was sharp enough for him to know what he'd had for breakfast two months ago and the phone number of the first girl he'd ever asked out, but something was different about this guy. He'd changed somehow—aged, perhaps—and Leipfold couldn't put his finger on where he'd seen him before. But he guessed that it didn't matter. It had probably just been in some pub somewhere.

The builders were working on the elevator, and they were due to stay on site for the next three weeks or so. Leipfold had given Maile and Jack permission to work from home if they wanted to, but they'd both still showed up. As a counteroffer, Leipfold had also given them free reign to dip into the petty cash if they wanted to go and sit in the cafeteria to get away from the banging and the drilling.

Leipfold's office was in an old Victorian building with wide eaves and a high ceiling. This worked in their favour, because it also meant that the stairwell was light and airy, with plenty of room to put in a basic elevator. It wasn't anything fancy, and it was barely big enough for four people. A wheelchair user would have to make the ride alone. But the size of the thing was also an advantage because it kept costs down and reduced the installation time from months to weeks. They were hoping to have it done by the end of April.

Leipfold had been suspicious of the builders to begin with, but keeping an eye on them had quickly proved to be too boring. Instead, he'd had Maile set up some security cameras throughout the building that she could access from her smartphone. She'd had no interest in watching the men as they went about their business, though, so she'd also installed the app on Leipfold's phone and laboriously taught him how to use it.

He'd quickly become hooked to it and had spent half the day with his phone propped up on his desk, slowly scrolling through the bank of cameras and watching what the builders were up to.

At around three in the afternoon, the buzzer went off and Maile answered the door because her desk was the closest and she was already standing up. When she heard who it was, her eyebrows raised so quickly it felt like they were trying to take off from her head.

"Holy shit, boss," she said, calling across the office to Leipfold, who was staring at his phone again when he was supposed to be working. "You'll never guess who's here."

"Who?"

"Alan Phelps," Maile said. "From *The Tribune*. He says he wants to talk to you about the Boys in Blue."

"Then I guess you'd better buzz him in."

When Phelps entered the office, the first thing that Maile noticed was how exhausted he looked. The bags under his eyes could have carried his shopping. He looked like he needed two cans of Monster and a shot of adrenaline. He reminded Maile of a zombie in a low-budget horror flick.

"Afternoon, James," Phelps said. "I thought I'd stop by. I'd better not stay for long, though. You never know who's watching us."

"Indeed," Leipfold said. "You said you wanted to talk about the Boys in Blue."

"Is it safe here?"

"It's as safe as you're going to get," Jack Cholmondeley said. He'd been listening in on the conversation and had walked over to offer Phelps a cuppa. The newspaperman refused the offer, but Cholmondeley popped the kettle on anyway.

"We don't have much time," Phelps said. "I'm being followed."

"So that's why you used the cypher?"

"Oh, that," Phelps said. "No, that was just me having a little fun with you. Damned fool that I am. It didn't occur to me until afterwards that you're not the only one who does the crossword."

"But surely a hidden message in a crossword is obscure enough to escape their notice."

"You'd be surprised," Phelps replied. "They have eyes everywhere."

"Are you a member?" Leipfold asked.

"Of course," Phelps said. "They don't give you much of a choice, you understand. But their power and their reach are waning."

"Let me guess," Maile said. "You want out."

"Got it in one, young lady," Phelps replied. "How did you know?"

"Call it my feminine intuition," Maile said sweetly, staring daggers at the man from behind a frozen smile. Phelps took her at her word, not catching the bitter sarcasm, and grinned back across at her like a dog looking out of the window at a passing butterfly.

"Let's face it," Phelps said. "Being a middle-class white guy is no longer in fashion."

"That's easy to say with the benefit of privilege," Maile murmured.

The kettle finished boiling and clicked off as steam billowed forth from the spout. Cholmondeley gripped the kettle and poured water into a couple of mugs, then took them around the office to drop them off to Maile and Leipfold.

"Okay," Phelps said. "Here's the deal. There's a growing number of us who want out of the Boys in Blue. The problem is that once you're in, you're in. They don't let you leave."

"Have you tried?"

"Hell no," Phelps replied. "I'm not a hero, and I won't become a martyr. That's for better, braver men than me. But people *have* tried to leave, or at least they've talked about it. They've been getting braver, too. You've probably seen some rumours on the discussion forum."

"I've seen a couple," Maile said. "But I figured they were baiting the hook to see who bit."

"You could be right," Phelps said. "It's hard to tell. They use their own secrecy as a way to keep members on edge. No one knows whom to trust, so we don't trust anyone. Why do you think I contacted you?"

"I figured Mike Croft told you to," Leipfold replied.

"Who?"

Maile was still learning the art of spotting a lie from someone's body language, but Leipfold and Cholmondeley were good teachers and she was a diligent student. She wasn't sure, but if she'd had to put money on it, she would have said that Phelps' confusion was genuine.

"It was just a test," Leipfold said. "I guess you passed it."

"Listen, James," Phelps said, looking nervously around the office again. Nothing had changed, and even the bothersome builders were nowhere to be seen, though the sound of an electric drill could be heard from somewhere in the stairwell. "I don't have much time, so let me get to the point. I want you to do something for me."

Phelps reached into his pocket and pulled out a sleek black flash drive. It was designed to be as small as possible and looked more like a wireless dongle than a traditional USB stick. Maile had used them before, of course, but she'd always been disappointed. The manufacturers usually made concessions when it came to storage space so they could keep the physical dimensions as small as possible. That was fine when they were being used to store and share documents, but it made them a pain in the backside when they were being used to share larger files, like video footage.

"What's on it?" Maile asked, noting that Phelps was handing it to Leipfold and not her, even though Leipfold still struggled to set his alarm clock.

"Names and contact details," Phelps said, not missing a beat. "All encoded and encrypted, of course. You'll have no problem getting into them, I'm sure. You can decipher it using the code from the crossword."

"And what do you expect in return?" Leipfold asked.

"Oh, not much," Phelps replied. "Like I said, I want out. So do the guys on this list, at least as far as I can tell. I can't take it to the cops and if I print this stuff, I'm a dead man. The only thing I could think of was to give it to you."

Leipfold took the flash stick and Phelps looked nervously around again, then took a couple of steps towards the door.

"Leaving so soon?" Leipfold asked.

"I've stayed too long as it is," Phelps replied. "You have no idea what you're dealing with, Mr. Leipfold. They have eyes everywhere. Did you know that London is the most watched city in the world? I wouldn't be surprised if they're behind it. No, I have to go."

He paused for a moment, then turned around and walked over to Leipfold. He shook his hand.

"What was that for?" Leipfold asked.

"In case I never see you again," Phelps replied.

*　*　*

For the rest of that week and all throughout the weekend, the gang focused their efforts on the investigation into the mysterious Mr.

M, the purported leader of the pornography ring. There were a couple of mentions of him on the dark web forum, but they'd mostly overlooked them during the investigation because there were hundreds of references to urban legends, from Slenderman to the Babadook. Mr. M had seemed like another one of those, an alias for some sort of Voldemort-like figure at the top of the totem pole.

Now he seemed disturbingly real.

Leipfold had grown frustrated with the problem and given up on it, focusing instead on a couple of new cases that had come through the doors. Cholmondeley had been interviewing the girls they'd found in the makeshift porn studio, using translators when he needed to. Most of them had been recruited abroad from underprivileged families and promised a better life in the United Kingdom. One or two of them had even paid for the trip themselves, only to end up living at a Croydon hostel. They weren't technically hostages, but they also weren't really free, either. Either way, they were in the country illegally, brought in across the channel by the organised gangs that the home secretary kept going on about in the House of Commons. Roger Gough had little sympathy for both the gang and its victims, but his policies were popular with the growing anti-immigration movement.

Their hosts usually let them stay pro bono for a couple of weeks, but then they started charging them for room and board. As inexperienced young women in a foreign city, it had been easy to coerce them into pornography and prostitution, especially after they'd been introduced to the hazy wonders of black tar heroin.

That just left Maile and Bram, who'd dedicated themselves to tracking down more information on Mr. M and carrying out some background research on the names that Phelps had provided them. Leipfold had wanted to pay each of them a visit, but Cholmondeley had cautioned him against making a rash move and told him to approach it like a copper instead.

So they'd asked Bram and Maile to do a little extra research on each of the names on their list to build a dossier on the suspects before they went to speak to them. With the names that Phelps had supplied, along with the list of cops that Cholmondeley had created and the names they'd tied back to usernames on the dark web forum, there were over one hundred fact sheets for them to work on, each of them requiring constant updates thanks to the flow of new information from social networking sites and search engines.

The two of them had their work cut out for them, and they spent most of the weekend augmenting the work they'd already done with further notes on the Boys in Blue. By Monday morning, they'd finally caved and switched to a piece of software that was normally used by writers to plot the complex worlds of their fantasy novels. They used the character sheet tool to create a searchable log for each of the suspects, and they modified the magic system tool to catalogue potential cross-references and relationships, such as those between bent cops and corrupt journalists or those who'd been identified as having links to the porn ring.

But their real success had been with the family tree tool, which had allowed them to build a hierarchy with the elusive Mr. M right at the top of it. They'd chatted via encrypted instant messaging until the early hours of Monday morning until they were finally ready to present their findings to the rest of the team.

They caught up in the hipster coffee shop again, and this time all four of them were there. Now that Leipfold could keep an eye on the builders from his smartphone, he was much less reticent to leave the office.

"So here's how it is," Bram said, by way of introduction. "You know how you like crosswords, Mr. Leipfold?"

"I don't just *like* them," Leipfold replied. "They're the reason why I get out of bed in the morning."

"Weird flex, but okay," Bram said. "My point is that just like you love crosswords, I love logic problems. We approached the challenge of researching the Boys in Blue in the same way. A regular logic problem is two dimensional, and all of the information that's provided is assumed to be true. In this case, we had all of these statements and these lines of enquiry, but we didn't know what was true and what was false."

"Ah yes," Cholmondeley said. "The perpetual problem. Unfortunately, it's harder to tell the truth from a lie when there's no body language behind it."

"I just assume that everything I read online is a lie," Maile murmured. "It makes things easier."

"Will you guys pipe down?" Bram said. "I'm trying to explain something here."

His three co-workers looked sheepishly at each other and then hung their heads, giving off the appearance of people who were unnaturally interested in the contents of their coffee cups.

"Now," Bram said. "Where was I?"

"Logic problems," Maile said.

"That's right," he continued. "Logic problems. So we took our records on Mr. M from the forums and correlated them with what our suspects have been doing out there in the real world. It's not exactly a science, more of an art form, but it should be enough to give us a good guess at what's actually going on."

"And what *is* going on?" Cholmondeley asked.

"See, that's where it gets interesting," Maile said, unable to help herself from jumping in and taking the reins. "It's a bit like chaos theory and the butterfly effect. You know, how the ripple of a butterfly's wings can cause a tsunami on the other side of the world?"

"I saw the movie," Leipfold said.

"Good," Maile replied. "Then you know how it ties in with parallel universes."

"It was a long time ago," Leipfold admitted.

"What movie?" Cholmondeley asked.

"Whatever," Maile said. "The point is, we have all of these theories lined up, and each of them works based on the data that we have so far. The problem is that we don't know which one is correct. It's like running a scientific experiment with a bunch of potential outcomes."

"Or like opening Schrödinger's box," Bram supplied.

"Exactly," Maile said. "The only way to figure out if the Boys in Blue are dead or alive is to open the box and see if the isotope has decayed. And that's why we need you two. It's time for you to carry out a little recon so we can get to the bottom of this thing."

Chapter Thirteen:
The Downstairs Office

IT WAS TUESDAY MORNING, and James Leipfold was in a sour mood. He'd been up late the night before, trying to help Jack Cholmondeley to get his life back on track by working through his finances and looking at rentals on Rightmove. Leipfold felt for the guy, but he also knew that he needed some closure. His instincts told him that the marriage was over, if it had ever been under to begin with, and Jack Cholmondeley was doing himself no favours by continuing to live in a shithole that no woman would ever want to go back to.

Not that he was one to talk.

Cholmondeley had kept Leipfold talking until closing time, and it had been past midnight by the time that he'd made it home on the back of Camilla. He hadn't eaten, so he took twenty minutes to whip up a stir fry and wolfed it down as quickly as he could before retiring to his bed with a hefty non-fiction book about Alan Turing. It was a good read, but it didn't help him sleep. It was light outside by the time he drifted off, and it was barely two hours later when his alarm went off.

All the coffee in the world wasn't enough to make him feel human, but that didn't stop him from giving it a good go. He was on his fourth cup by 10 AM, when the landlord popped round to check on the progress. Ironically, Leipfold had finally started trusting the builders and was checking the cameras for what he told himself would be the last time that day when he saw that they'd already let the old codger inside and were chatting animatedly to him on the stairs. The one that Leipfold half-recognised was there again, and he still couldn't put his finger on where he knew him from. But to his credit, whoever he was, the guy seemed to be a hard worker—at least, he was whenever he wasn't shooting the breeze with one of Leipfold's visitors.

He cursed to himself and walked over to the door, opening it before his landlord, Mr. Taplow, had a chance to knock at it.

"Nice chaps downstairs," he said by way of greeting.

"They certainly make the place look untidy," Leipfold replied. "What can I do for you?"

"I've been thinking, Mr. Leipfold," his landlord said. "You know, ever since that unpleasant business with the graphic designers downstairs, the bottom floor of this building has been empty."

"That's how I like it," Leipfold replied. "It keeps things nice and quiet and avoids any mix-ups with the postman."

"You know, you have quite the reputation," Mr. Taplow said, inviting himself into the office and sitting down in the reception area. He looked like a man in need of a cup of tea, but Leipfold was in no mood to offer him one. He shot Cholmondeley and Maile a look that he hoped they'd be able to interpret.

"I live on my reputation," Leipfold replied.

"Yes," Mr. Taplow said, removing his glasses and polishing them on the fabric of his shirt. "But I have to make a living too. The problem is that I can't find a tenant to take the place on. There's not much demand for it, what with one thing and another, and as soon as anyone expresses interest, they Google the place and pull up results about your agency."

"I'm not doing anything that goes against the contract," Leipfold said.

"I know," his landlord replied. "I checked it several times, once with my lawyer. And seeing as you've just signed on the dotted line for another five years, I thought I'd make you an offer."

"I'm listening."

"Well, this elevator business has got me thinking," Taplow said. "We'll still install the thing, of course. We've come too far now to turn back. But I thought if you were to cover the cost of the install—"

"We've been through this," Leipfold began. "I—"

"You're not listening to me," Taplow pressed. "I could give you a one-year lease on the offices downstairs. It'd work out as an extra twenty-five percent on your rent and you'd get double the space."

"So I get my upstairs office to myself and can move my employees downstairs," Leipfold said. "But why not just offer me the ground floor office? Then you wouldn't have to install the elevator."

"You'd say no," Taplow replied. "I know how attached you are to this place. And besides, I'd still have the same problem. No one wants to share a building with you. At least this way, I cut my losses and make enough from you to cover the mortgage."

"And the elevator?"

"We've already signed the contract," Taplow said. He chuckled. "I noticed that you've put some cameras up, by the way. I didn't give you permission to do that."

"I'm protecting your investment," Leipfold said.

"Quite," Mr. Taplow replied. "And now you mention it, that's precisely what's in it for me. It's better to have the place occupied and in good working order. You think about it, okay? I'll let myself out."

*   *   *

Jack Cholmondeley spent most of the day tailing suspects and cross-referencing their movements with the different theories that Maile and Bram's three-dimensional logic problem had spewed out.

It turned out that a lot of the cops at the Old Vic were either corrupt or inept. If they'd been working on Cholmondeley's team, he would have had them out patrolling the streets or knocking doors and interviewing suspects. Instead, they were acting as though they were professional socialites whose job it was to be seen about town.

He was exhausted when he got home from work, but at least the noise from his neighbours had quietened down. All that was left was the strange old man upstairs who sometimes screamed because of night terrors. He was too tired to think about his personal life. That would have to wait.

The following day was a Wednesday, and he was the first to arrive at the office. Even the builders weren't there, although they were supposed to be. He ended up sauntering down the street for a coffee at the hipster joint, but he got it in a biodegradable cup to go and by the time he was back at the office, Leipfold was just parking up and preparing to set up shop for the day.

"Ah," he said, spotting Cholmondeley striding along the street towards him. "Jack, just the man. I've been meaning to talk to you."

"I've been meaning to talk to you too, James," Cholmondeley replied. "I was hoping we could—"

"Later," Leipfold said. "Jack, I'm going to take the landlord up on his offer. We're going to take over the ground floor."

"Excellent," Cholmondeley said. "Well then—"

"If I take the deal, I'm going to have to make a few choices," Leipfold continued, raising his voice slightly so that it rose over his friend and colleague. "I can't afford to pay you, Bram, Maile and myself if I'm going to spunk my savings up the wall to expand the office."

"You're letting me go," Cholmondeley said, drily. "I understand. Jesus, James. You've got the bedside manner of Harold Shipman."

"Sorry, Jack," Leipfold said. "You know how it is. I've got to make a living."

"So do I," Cholmondeley replied. "But don't worry. Mary wants to buy me out of my half of the house. If I take her up on it, I'll have enough to see me through until my retirement. And in the meantime, James, I don't think you'll be getting rid of me anytime soon."

Leipfold sighed, though it was over-theatrical to his own ears. He hoped that the others hadn't noticed. Like Emperor Palpatine, everything was proceeding as he'd foreseen.

"He just wants you to work for free," Maile said, somewhat scuppering his plans by stating the obvious. "It worked on me for a while, too."

"Oh, I know," Cholmondeley replied. He smiled at them. "Listen, James, you've been doing me a favour as it is, so now it's time for me to return it. I'll keep working here until we crack the Boys in Blue case, and then I'll leave you to it. In the meantime, you make sure that you pay young Shakespeare what he's worth. I have a feeling that you're going to need him."

*   *   *

Mr. Taplow sent over the paperwork later that afternoon, and Leipfold signed it in the evening and returned it. The following morning, he showed up at the office with a new set of keys in his hands, and just like that, Leipfold Investigations found itself with double the amount of office space.

Cholmondeley was out tailing suspects and Maile had popped out to interview a new client at the hipster coffee shop, and so other than the builders, Leipfold was on his own. He did the most logical thing and called Bram Shakespeare, then made himself a cup of coffee and sat down to do the crossword. Maile got back to the office just as Bram was arriving in the back of a black cab, and so only Cholmondeley was missing when Leipfold opened the downstairs door for the first time.

The graphic designers had left the place in a hurry after a scandal had hit the company and its owners had cut and run with all of the assets they could get their hands on. As far as they could tell, no one had been inside the place for a couple of years, but it didn't look too bad.

The room was similar to the main office, although it looked sparser because anything of any value had been plundered when its previous owners had gone bust. Still, there were a couple of desks and a few chairs, as well as a riot of potted plants and a couple of flimsy-looking filing cabinets. In one corner of the room, a smaller office had been sectioned off behind glass partitioning.

"I call dibs," Maile said.

It was the first thing that any of them had said since they'd opened the door. Bram had wheeled himself in at the head of the party with Maile a step behind him. Leipfold had taken the rear and had immediately started searching the room for anything of note, though it was the filing cabinets that held the most interest for him and they'd have to wait for another day.

"It's perfect," Leipfold said. "I mean sure, we'll need to clean the place up a bit, but we'll get there."

"As long as I get the corner office," Maile replied.

"Take it," Leipfold said. "We'll move the reception down here and I'll have the upstairs as a private office and storage room."

"What about me?" Bram asked.

"You're working reception," Leipfold said. "Maile, you've been promoted. What time is it?"

"Eleven thirty," Bram said.

"Good," Leipfold replied. "We'll take until two to move a few things around and get you set up down here, and then we're back to work on the Boys in Blue."

*   *   *

Bram and Maile were getting to know each other a little more, and they'd already developed a solid set of in-jokes as well as nicknames for the majority of the company's clients. While Leipfold spearheaded the investigation into the Boys in Blue, Bram and Maile shot the shit and worked on the routine stuff, the investigations into cheating spouses and the cases of industrial espionage that paid the bills and kept the lights on.

Maile had learned that Bram was single, and that had given her an idea.

"What kind of girls do you like, Bram?" she asked. "You do like girls, right?"

"That's like asking a man dying of thirst whether he'd prefer still or sparkling water," Bram replied. "Since you ask, I'm bisexual. Why?"

"I think I know someone you might be interested in."

"Is it you?" he asked.

"Hell no."

"Good," Bram said.

"Hey! What's wrong with me?"

"Nothing," Bram replied. "But you're already my work wife."

"Your work wife?"

"Yeah," Bram said. "You know, the person I work the most closely with. No offence, but if we were spending every night together as well as every day, I don't think it would end well."

"Well, I haven't used my pepper spray on you yet," Maile replied. "But I had someone else in mind. My housemate, Kat."

"What's she like?"

"She's uh…cool."

"Good enough for me," Bram said. "Does she mind the wheelchair?"

"I haven't asked," Maile admitted. "But if you're up for it, I'll see what she says."

"Is she cute?"

"Here," Maile said, reaching into her pocket and pulling out her phone. "I'll show you a photo."

*   *   *

The employees of Leipfold Investigations spent the rest of the working week focusing on the Boys in Blue, though with the priority still on monitoring the suspects and cross-referencing their movements, Maile and Bram were freed up to focus on some of the new clients.

In some ways, the company was starting to become a victim of its own success. Now that they had more resources, they could take on more cases, but the gigs coming in were mostly humdrum professional stalking jobs where some jealous client asked them to follow a spouse. When it wasn't that, it was some little old lady asking them to track down a missing cat or budgerigar.

And it looked as though they were at the bottom of a ladder with their feet on the first rung. The foot traffic had increased notably thanks to the simple expedient of putting a big sign up in the downstairs window and turning the lights on. Balcombe Street wasn't exactly busy, but it still witnessed its fair share of passers-by. Being on the first floor, Leipfold's windows were unremarkable from street level, but the ground floor office was so close to the street that if they lifted the blinds, they could make eye contact with people as they wandered past.

Bram had started running the reception with a newfound level of precision, and he had Leipfold and Cholmondeley on the streets like a taxi operator taking calls and routing drivers to their next pickup. It was an unorthodox system, but it worked, up to a point. Because Bram was working reception, it also fell to him to greet the walk-ins, and there were half a dozen of them on the Friday, mostly in the mid-afternoon. They fell into a new routine in which Bram screened them as they came in and then handed them over to Maile for further interviews if they cut the mustard. Maile took notes and prepared a briefing for Leipfold, and he ultimately decided whether to take the case on. Only then did they write up a contract and agree upon the terms.

By Saturday morning, they'd already onboarded three new clients, and Leipfold had made the decision to route all of the website and telephone enquiries through Bram and Maile too. As with most business processes, it took a greater amount of time to do the same job, but it also meant they could focus on only the quirkiest of cases.

It was an arse-about-face way of doing business, but it ensured that they only took on cases that Leipfold was interested in. The main drawback was that if a client couldn't afford his fees, Leipfold would rather give them a discount than drop the case and take on a different client who could afford to pay him. The agency had more work than ever, though with Bram and Cholmondeley they had plenty of room to grow and to work on their side projects, like the investigation into the Boys in Blue.

Everything seemed to be going swimmingly.

Then someone threw a brick through the window.

Chapter Fourteen:
Nightingale

THEY DREW STRAWS TO decide who'd clean the glass up, and it was Bram who pulled the shortest. Maile had offered to take his place, but Bram had insisted and Leipfold had burst out laughing.

"I think he proved back at Cholmondeley's place that he's more than capable," Leipfold said. "If he can damn near break someone's leg with a nightstick, he can sweep up broken glass."

"I am *here*, you know," Bram said, not bothering to look up from the dustpan and brush. "Just because my legs are fucked, it doesn't mean my ears are. Why don't you two make yourselves useful?"

"Already on it," Leipfold said. He was on his hands and knees, examining the brick as though he expected it to yield up the secrets of the pharaohs or some ancient, arcane knowledge.

"Did you find anything?" Maile asked.

"Yeah," Leipfold said, thoughtfully. It hadn't exactly been subtle. "There's a message on it, but it just says, 'Fuck off'."

"The question is, who threw it?" Bram said. "The Boys in Blue?"

"If it is, that settles it," Leipfold said. "We've got to take those bastards down and bring them to justice. I need to know where to send the invoice. Find a glazier, will you, Maile?"

The atmosphere in the office was subdued that day. Leipfold spent most of the day upstairs, calmly and methodically bringing all of Maile's possessions downstairs into the new room. It wasn't anything personal. It was just that the upstairs office was *his* space. It always had been, since long before Maile had joined the company. Now that she had an office of her own, he could arrange things just so. Better still, because they'd moved the sofa downstairs and built a new reception area, he had more space than ever before.

Maile and Bram were happy, too. For Bram, it meant that he was finally an official part of the team and not just some freelance resource who worked from home. For Maile, it meant that she had her own space in which to express herself, and if she was working inside her office, there was no reason why she couldn't listen to whatever music she wanted to.

All three of them had brought in a few knick-knacks from home—framed photos of family members, motivational posters and electronic gadgetry. Bram had convinced Leipfold to part with a couple hundred quid to buy him a dock for his laptop, and Maile had brought in a decent sound system as well as a second monitor that she could watch YouTube on while she worked.

Even Jack Cholmondeley had brought in a few personal possessions, though he was spending less and less time in the office. When he was there, he had a desk of his own in the no-man's land between Maile's office and the reception desk. He'd brought in a couple of books and a framed photograph of him and his wife from when they'd taken a cruise around the Seychelles.

The future was looking bright. But there was a blue cloud on the horizon.

*   *   *

When Monday morning rolled around, all four of them showed up to the office early. There was a spirit of excitement in the air, a shared vibe about the week ahead. Jack Cholmondeley had signed up to a dating site, the very same site that his soon-to-be ex-wife had been using. Bram Shakespeare was looking forward to the release of a new MMORPG, which was due to come out at midnight. Maile was stoked because she was an empath, and she was feeding off everyone else's emotions.

Leipfold was just excited because he'd treated himself to a new pen. He was that kind of guy.

Their excitement reached fever pitch just as they were tucking into elevenses. Cholmondeley had brought in a couple of packs of ginger biscuits, and Leipfold had broken with tradition by making the whole team a cup of tea. Then he'd settled in to get the crossword done. When he turned the page and read the article there, he went off like a rocket. His surprised ejaculation was so loud that the others could hear it from the floor below him, and so Maile and Cholmondeley rushed up and burst through the door as though expecting him to be in hand-to-hand combat with a burglar.

"What is it, James?" Cholmondeley asked, breathlessly. He wasn't as young as he used to be and the rush up the stairs had taken his breath away.

"The Boys in Blue," Leipfold replied, calmly.

He was sitting back in his office chair with his feet up on the desk. Now that much of the furniture had been moved downstairs, his office seemed airy and spacious, and yet he was still maintaining the same spot in the corner of the room. He'd bought an easel, a canvas and some paints from an arts shop, but he hadn't had time to start painting. Even with the addition of the canvas, the room still felt bare. In some places, the carpet was discoloured from where the furniture had squashed it down and blocked off the sunlight.

Leipfold beckoned the others over and they came to stand behind him and to look over his shoulders. It was immediately obvious what had caught his attention. There was a two-page spread on the Boys in Blue on page seventeen of *The Tribune*.

"What's it about?" Maile asked.

"It's an exposé about their involvement in the human trafficking ring," Leipfold replied.

"Anything about the corruption?" Cholmondeley asked. "Don't get me wrong, I want to nail them for the human trafficking, but I'm more concerned about them perverting the course of justice. Who knows how many times we've been forced to turn a blind eye to this kind of stuff?"

"Nothing," Leipfold said. "Not yet, at least."

"I don't get it," Maile said. "What's going on?"

"There's no by-line," Leipfold murmured. "I wonder who wrote it."

"Call them and find out," Cholmondeley suggested.

"I will," Leipfold said. "I'll call Phelps and meet you downstairs so we can chat it through with Bram. Make sure you put the kettle on."

By the time that his call with the journalist was over, Leipfold's coffee was ready and the other two had brought Bram up to speed with what had happened.

"Look at this, boss," Maile said, when he entered the downstairs office. "They've published it online as well, only it's a couple thousand words longer with a few extra details. What did Phelps say?"

"He's just as confused as we are," Leipfold replied. "Either that or he's one hell of an actor. The good news is that I know exactly who to turn to. Siobhan Dent."

"The editor?"

"Exactly," Leipfold said. "If nothing else, she'll know who filed the story. Hell, maybe she wrote it herself. But there's something bothering me."

"You're not the only one," Cholmondeley murmured.

"When I spoke to her, she said she'd never heard of the Boys in Blue," Leipfold said. "Maybe she hadn't and something came in after I spoke to her, but I don't buy it. I know those journos and I know how long their lead times are. This is a feature, not a news story. If *The Tribune* was covering it, she should have known about it."

*   *   *

Leipfold went to see Dent by himself, grateful for the chance to be alone with his thoughts again as he wound through the city's streets on the back of Camilla. He knew the route to *The Tribune*'s offices by memory, and that meant he could cruise along on autopilot, letting his reflexes do the work as he lost himself in the world inside his head.

It was a mess up there, like two dozen spider webs inside a rusted old shed that hadn't seen the sunlight for too many moons. Everything was connected, and it reminded James Leipfold of filling out a crossword puzzle. Every time he hit a dead end, he could just switch to a different clue and solve that one, giving himself another one of the letters. Eventually, all of the pieces fell into place.

The problem was that with a crossword, there was a specific end-goal in mind, as well as neat and tidy little answers. When it came to the Boys in Blue, the clues were cryptic, encoded and damned near impossible to solve, and they didn't tell you how many letters the right answer contained, either.

It was just how he liked it, a challenge so big that it was difficult to comprehend it or to look at it head on. It didn't matter that he had no real evidence of anything, other than a bunch of accusations and some computer wizardry that he didn't understand. He'd get the bastards—if they existed and the whole mess wasn't just an elaborate hoax.

But then someone had shot Constable Groves, and while she was out of the hospital and back at home, she still faced an uphill battle with her rehabilitation.

"Hoaxes don't shoot people," he murmured and promptly

swerved to avoid steering Camilla straight into the back of a milk float that had slammed on the brakes when the traffic lights changed.

The car park at *The Tribune*'s office was empty, almost suspiciously so, but that was okay with Leipfold. It meant less chance of someone bashing his bike when they opened their car door. The last time someone had done that, Leipfold had broken a finger punching the wall of his office after they'd exchanged insurance details and he'd excused himself.

When he buzzed at the door, he had to wait a while for a response. And when that response came, it was from the very person he was hoping for.

"Who is it?" Dent asked.

"Delivery," Leipfold replied, throwing his voice in a passable impression of Maile O'Hara, who was the first person he thought of.

"Come in."

It was as easy as that.

Leipfold pushed the door and walked into the office, then meandered his way onto the main floor, where the banks of desks housed the old school Windows Vista machines that the journalists used to write their stories. Siobhan Dent was in her partitioned office beside the boardroom, and she was talking on her mobile phone when Leipfold entered.

She stuck her head through the door and shouted, "Just leave it on the front desk." Then she saw who it was and spoke into her phone to say, "Jason, I'm going to have to call you back."

She cut the call and then turned to look at Leipfold.

"All right," she said. "Better make this quick."

"Where is everyone?" Leipfold asked.

"It's Saturday," Dent replied. "Next question."

"Why did you lie to me about the Boys in Blue?"

Dent's face went pale. She looked desperately around the room and then beckoned Leipfold wordlessly into her office, closing the door behind her. As soon as the door was closed, she locked it from the inside. Then she pulled the blinds down and put some music on, going old school with a CD player.

"Jazz," she explained. "It plays havoc with microphones. I sweep this place every day just on principle, but you never know."

"Are they likely to be listening?"

"They have ears everywhere," Dent replied. "They have friends everywhere, too. You're here to ask about the piece we ran, aren't you?"

"Ten points," Leipfold said. "But how do I know I can trust you? You've lied to me once. What's to stop you from doing it again?"

"You of all people should know better than to trust the press, James," Dent said, reprovingly.

"Okay," Leipfold said. "Let me rephrase my question. How do I know you're not one of the Boys in Blue?"

"Do I look like I have a penis?"

"No," Leipfold admitted. "But you never know, and I wouldn't like to make assumptions."

"About my gender?"

"About the Boys in Blue," Leipfold said. "Maybe they decided to move with the times and to take on women."

"Yeah," Dent replied. "And maybe the pope took a shit in his cap and stuck his dick in it."

"You have a way with words," Leipfold said. "I suppose it goes with the territory."

"James, the Boys in Blue represent the establishment," Dent said. "They're the epitome of the privately educated white male. They have fingers in every pie. They make the damn pies and they tell us when to eat them. I want them brought down as much as anyone."

"Then talk to me," Leipfold said. "Tell me everything you can, starting with that story you ran in the newspaper."

"I was given the story and told to run it," Dent said. "It happens more often than you might think."

"How often are we talking?"

"Three or four times an issue," Dent replied. "Plus the occasional online release. We have an anonymous submission form on the dark web, the same sort of stuff you see from Wikileaks. Occasionally, maybe three or four times a year, we get something worth publishing from a genuine source. The rest of the time, it's from the Boys in Blue."

"How do you know it's from them?" Leipfold asked.

Dent paused. Her eyes swept nervously around the room again and she scooched over to the door to peer through the keyhole and out into the office beyond. Then she turned the volume up a little more.

"There's a code," she said. "Each message is encrypted with the passphrase 'nightingale' and signed by Mr. M."

"I notice there was no mention of him in your article."

"What can I say?" she replied. "For as long as I've been here, it's been an open secret. It's practically built into the company. In the early days, we were funded by the Boys in Blue. The current owner is a member. If I speak out, I'll lose my job, or worse. So tell me, what would you do?"

"I'd hire a private investigator," Leipfold said. "But why? I don't understand. Why did they draw attention to themselves?"

Dent smiled, but it wasn't a happy smile. It was the smile of a crocodile with an empty stomach and a toothache.

"That's their little masterstroke," Dent said. "It's a pre-emptive strike. They know you're working their case, James. You might want to watch your back."

Realisation dawned and Leipfold's jaw dropped.

"They knew if they ran the story now, it would sound like some mad conspiracy," Leipfold said. "So now any future reveal will lose its impact."

"That's their plan, at least," Dent replied. "Whether it will work or not is anyone's guess. But I can tell you one thing, Mr. Leipfold."

"What's that?"

"If you pushed them to take action, you must be doing something right," she said. "Look at them, James. You've got them on the back foot. Get some use out of nightingale. Press home your advantage before it's too late."

* * *

"It just goes deeper and deeper," Bram said.

Cholmondeley grunted and Maile smirked. She was listening to the two of them from her office, her door perpetually open as though she was a Fortune 500 executive on a mission to prove herself as one of the shit-lickers.

It was Monday morning, and Leipfold had finished his daily debrief a half hour earlier and then retreated into the safety of his office. Jack Cholmondeley had stopped by the office for a cup of tea between tailing suspects, and he had a lead on a potential meeting place.

"If money's involved, so are the Boys in Blue," Cholmondeley said.

"But a titty bar?"

"They're called gentlemen's clubs, Abraham," Cholmondeley replied, reprovingly.

"Abraham is my dad," Bram said. "And he'd call them titty bars."

"Your dad is probably younger than me, kid," Cholmondeley said. "We'll call them gentlemen's clubs. The point is, it looks like we know where they meet. Maybe we can get in there somehow."

"Well, I guess I'm ruled out," Maile murmured to herself. She picked up her laptop and scooched over to the doorway in her chair to better watch the conversation.

"I'm a little conspicuous," Bram said. "I'm guessing they don't have many young Black guys in wheelchairs."

"James could pull it off, maybe," Cholmondeley said. "And I could give it a go."

"You just want to go to a titty bar," Bram murmured.

"Enough," Maile said, wheeling herself through the doorway and into the main office. "Tell James. He'll decide what to do. In the meantime, we've got another problem. Now that the Boys in Blue have beaten us to the punch, how are we going to release our dossier?"

"Ha!" Bram exclaimed. "That one's easy. We cut out the middleman and go directly to the public."

"How?"

"I've got some ideas," Bram said. "The real problem is making people aware that this thing exists in the first place. We could reach out to some of the conspiracy sites, perhaps."

"Hell no," Maile replied. "We need to establish credibility, not destroy it."

"So let's do it," Bram said thoughtfully. He rolled backwards on his chair and stared thoughtfully at an indeterminate spot on the other side of the downstairs office. "Let's turn their own weapon against them. We could use the dark web to find forums and chatrooms where we can anonymously dump the data."

Maile paused, then she too started staring at the wall. "It could work," she said. "We could go a step further and whip up a website. Something untraceable. If we host it on the dark web and cover our tracks, they won't be able to take it down."

"We could set up a torrent, too."

"Good call," Maile said. "We can do both, then dump the lot when we go public. We can set up a bunch of drone accounts on social networks and spam the link until people take notice. After that, it'll spread by itself."

"And if they try to take it down, it'll spread even farther," Bram added.

"The Streisand Effect."

"Excuse me," Cholmondeley said, raising his hand sheepishly and backing up on his own chair. "But what on earth are you two talking about?"

Chapter Fifteen:
Purple Dinosaur

LEIPFOLD AND CHOLMONDELEY WERE dressed up for a night on the town, although that wasn't saying much. Jack Cholmondeley was wearing his old tweed suit, and James Leipfold was wearing his black funeral gear, the only smart clothing he owned.

They were off to Purple Dinosaur, a swanky gentleman's club in the East End where the drinks were expensive and the girls even more so. It had also been mentioned several times on the Boys in Blue discussion forum as a preferred hangout for the elite.

Cholmondeley had been there once before when it was trading under a different name, long before he'd first met Mary. Leipfold had never been. The closest thing he'd seen had been the strippers in the windows of Amsterdam's Red Light District, and he'd paid them no more than vague attention as he'd been passing through while hunting for *vlaamsefrites*.

They drove to the place in Cholmondeley's black Beemer, reasoning that they might as well arrive in style. Leipfold wasn't drinking, of course, and he'd cautioned Cholmondeley to do the same. They'd need their wits about them.

It was the kind of place where there was no need to park because they had a valet. Leipfold got out first, gesturing furiously at Cholmondeley to do the same. The old man did so, but he clearly wasn't happy about it. He was mumbling something about the paintwork, but he quickly brightened up when Leipfold tipped the valet thirty quid to give the thing a thorough waxing.

"Come on, old boy," Leipfold said. "Let's go inside."

The bouncers at the door looked like Vikings, six-foot tall Scandinavian types with long blond hair and fashionable beards. They were checking IDs at the door, but only to take note of who their visitors were. Leipfold and Cholmondeley were waved in with barely a second glance.

"Not much security," Cholmondeley murmured, as they walked through the entrance hall. It was a huge, expansive space that was full of marble, with a well-dressed young lady in a red uniform sitting behind a tidy little desk with a telephone.

"There's no need," Leipfold replied, keeping his voice low so that it didn't echo around the massive entryway. "Our adversary might meet here, but they don't own the place. It's open to the public, and we're just two gentlemen out for a nightcap."

"But we're not drinking," Cholmondeley said.

Leipfold didn't reply.

They walked to the left of the reception desk and through an expansive archway that led to the club proper. The inside was dark and gloomy, despite the opulent chandeliers and the reflected light from the metal poles, and that suited Leipfold just fine. They found an empty booth towards one of the corners and slipped into it, then ordered a couple of mocktails so they wouldn't look conspicuous, though there wasn't much cause for concern. Their suits made them look like a couple of businessmen, especially with the lights down. Leipfold just hoped the deception would hold.

"Now remember," Leipfold said. "We're just a couple of ordinary gentlemen going out for some leisurely drinks."

"There's nothing ordinary about us, James."

"Then we'll have to pretend," Leipfold said.

The music started up again, and the two men fell silent as several strippers took centre stage. The club was playing jazz—

sophisticated stuff—and it seemed at odds with the semi-naked women gyrating around poles with power tools in their hands. One of them was wielding a chainsaw and bringing it down towards her crotch, grinding it against a metal chastity belt and sending sparks flying into the air.

"That doesn't look safe," Cholmondeley murmured. "What if she slips?"

"I suspect that she tries not to," Leipfold replied. "Hey, who's that?"

One of the girls had climbed down from her platform and walked across to a booth on the other side of the room. In the darkness of the club, it was hard to make out the punter's face, but whoever it was, they were clearly a big shot. The table was littered with empty bottles of champagne and he was throwing bank notes at the girl as she gave him a private lap dance.

"I have no idea," Cholmondeley said. "But I need to take a leak, so I'll check him out."

Leipfold nodded and Cholmondeley stood up and strolled away in search of the little boys' room. Without Jack there to distract him, Leipfold's senses were sharpened and he found himself listening to random snatches of conversation that crept out above the music.

He was paying particular attention to the two conversations on either side of him. From the booth to his left, he could hear a couple of people talking about the Oyster Club, another members-only club that Leipfold had heard of from one of his other cases. To his right, four middle-aged men were having a spirited conversation about pornography.

"We need to find a new location," one of them was saying. "Somewhere else to film."

"We're going to need another director, too."

"Yes, well," the first replied. "I don't think Mr. M will want—"

The music kicked back in, and by the time that he heard them again, Jack Cholmondeley had returned. He'd bought another round of mocktails including one that came with a little umbrella and a sparkler.

"I think we might be on to something," Cholmondeley said as he sat down. "There's a chap over there who—"

"Shh," Leipfold growled, putting a finger to his lips and nodding to the table to his right. "Listen."

They only caught a couple of words, but it was enough. Leipfold took his phone out and hit the record button, hoping they'd be able to clean it up later on and that it'd be admissible in court. At the very least, it would be enough to light a fire beneath the conspiracy nuts and get them blogging about the Boys in Blue and the corruption that they were responsible for.

It didn't take a genius to understand what the men were talking about. The porno ring was looking for new blood, and by the sounds of it, they were also bribing several members of the Metropolitan Police to turn a blind eye. It was nothing new, but it tied in with what Cholmondeley and Leipfold already knew, and because this was a face-to-face and not some anonymous chatroom on the dark web, they were using names. Leipfold didn't need to check to know that many of the names tallied with their dossier, and while a good lawyer might be able to argue it was coincidental, it was a pretty colossal coincidence.

Every now and then, when they remembered, Leipfold and Cholmondeley chatted to each other about anything and everything, though it mostly revolved around Cholmondeley's plan to slowly but surely get back into dating.

"You should try the Oyster Club," Leipfold murmured.

"What was that?"

"Never mind," Leipfold said. "My round, is it?"

"It is indeed," Cholmondeley said. "You wait until you see the prices. It's a scandal."

"It's London," Leipfold said, excusing himself and heading

out of the booth and towards the bar. He was gone for six or seven minutes, and he was still laughing when he sat back down in the booth with Jack Cholmondeley. He had two more of the ridiculously-priced mocktails in his hands.

"What is it, James?" Cholmondeley asked.

Leipfold took a couple of deep breaths and then forced a neutral expression onto his face.

"It's nothing," he said. "Don't worry about it. It's just the guy you told me to look out for."

"What about him?"

"I know him," Leipfold said. "He's bloody Mike Croft."

"Who?"

"He's the client, you silly sod."

Chapter Sixteen:
138 Words Per Minute

IT WAS AN EVENTFUL night.

Leipfold and Cholmondeley waited until closing time, when most of the other punters were three sheets to the wind. A couple of them were four or five sheets to the wind, and one guy who was six sheets to the wind got thrown out on his arse by one of the bouncers, who carried him like a farmer picking up a piglet.

The two of them left separately, each of them tailing a different suspect. They picked two of the drunkest, likeliest-looking marks and split up on foot, then met up at the office the following morning to discuss their findings.

The two men had dark bags under their eyes and looked as though sleep was a distant memory to them. Bram and Maile, both of whom were night owls and who usually struggled to make it to the office before 9:30 AM, looked comparatively fresh.

"What's your secret?" Leipfold asked.

"Energy drinks," Maile replied, holding up a can of Monster and pointing to Bram's Red Bull.

"Are they any good?"

"Better than coffee," Bram said.

"Good," Leipfold replied. "Run to the shops and get me one."

"Piss off," Bram said. "You wouldn't tell a blind man to keep an eye out."

"I didn't mean you," Leipfold said. "I was talking to Jack."

"Me?"

"Yes, you," Leipfold said. "Get one for yourself while you're at it."

"An energy drink?" Cholmondeley repeated, pronouncing the words as though he was speaking a foreign language in a strange country and he was afraid of offending the locals. "Really, James? What if I have a heart attack?"

"You won't have a heart attack," Leipfold said.

"He *might* have a heart attack," Maile murmured.

"Besides, you should be used to it," Leipfold added. "Back in your day, there was cocaine in the Coca-Cola."

Cholmondeley grumbled about it, but he also acquiesced and went on the supply run. By the time he got back, Leipfold had finished the day's crossword. Cholmondeley handed over the drinks with a bashful look on his face and Leipfold popped them open. He handed one of them to Cholmondeley and took a long swig of the other.

"Ugh," he said. "It tastes like chemicals."

"Yeah," Maile replied. "Aspartame and caffeine. Everything a growing girl needs."

"Can we get on with things?" Cholmondeley asked gloomily, taking a sip from his own drink. "I'd like to get this over and done with before I keel over and get carried out of here in a body bag."

"That won't be because of the energy drink, Jack," Leipfold said. "But sure, let's do it."

Maile and Bram downed tools and scooted over while Leipfold and Cholmondeley sat down awkwardly on an uncomfortable sofa that the graphic designers had left behind.

Leipfold led the briefing, supported by occasional contributions from Cholmondeley, who seemed happy to play second fiddle. He brought them up to date on their adventures the night before and then the two of them took it in turns to report on what they'd learned.

"I followed my mark to Hammersmith, where I lost him," Cholmondeley said. "He got in the back of an Uber. By the time I got back to the Beemer, he could have been anywhere."

"Too bad, Jack," Leipfold said, flashing him a cheeky grin. "I had much more success. I tailed my guy to Stratford and watched him going into a warehouse. Then I followed him inside."

"And?" Maile asked impatiently, glaring at Leipfold as he paused to take a sip from his energy drink. The caffeine was hitting him like a steamroller, and he started to talk a little faster.

"I won't bore you with the details," Leipfold said. "At first, I thought it was a hideout, but he turned out to be scoring some coke, presumably to keep the party going. I watched them make the trade, waited for the dealer to skedaddle and then confronted our little friend with a few questions."

"I hope you didn't break the law, James," Cholmondeley said. "You know I hate it when you do that."

"It's the law of the jungle, Jack," Leipfold replied. "Sometimes you have to break the law to get results. You of all people should know that."

"What's that supposed to mean?"

"Nothing," Leipfold said. "It's not important. The point is, with a little coercion, I was able to get some more information. More names to add to our database, as well as some extra info on a few of the key players."

"Great," Maile said. "More work for us."

"I also got a description of Mr. M," Leipfold continued, slipping comfortably into his narrative. "And get this. I think we know him."

"He's on our database?"

"More than that," Leipfold said. "The description he gave me could only be one man. Mike Croft."

"Surprise, surprise," Maile murmured. She'd wheeled her chair out into the main office and was sitting beside Bram, who absorbed the information in stony-faced silence. Only Jack Cholmondeley seemed animated.

"I bloody well told you, James," the ex-cop said. "You should have let me follow him."

"To what end?" Leipfold asked. "So he could catch you in some dark alleyway? These men are dangerous, Jack."

"I didn't know you cared."

"I don't," Leipfold said, chuckling and rubbing the ginger stubble around his jaw. "But if Croft knows we're on to him, we're finished. He still thinks we're on his side."

"And are we?"

"I have no idea," Leipfold said. "We need to do some more digging and find out what his real name is."

"You mean it's not Mike Croft?"

"Jack, you're supposed to be a copper," Leipfold scolded. "Did you never read Sherlock Holmes?"

"Never had the time," Cholmondeley replied. "I've not had much chance to read anything other than case notes and reports."

"That settles it," Leipfold said. "Take a tenner out of the petty cash and go to Waterstones. I'm giving you the afternoon off."

"Give my love to the pygmy," Bram said.

"And give my love to the Mormons when you get to *The Valley of Fear*," Maile added.

Leipfold grinned in spite of himself and made a mental note to dig up his old Miss Marples. Cholmondeley's next mission would be to pay a visit to St. Mary Mead.

*　*　*

On Wednesday, the gang played host to an unexpected visitor. It was the woman from Jack Cholmondeley's apartment building, and she was accompanied by a young woman called Tabitha Swordrock from the translation agency.

Leipfold winced when Maile told him who was waiting for him in the downstairs reception area. He knew what her hourly rate was.

With six of them in the downstairs office, the place felt almost crowded, although Leipfold remembered its heyday when there were eighteen graphic designers and an admin team in the space.

"How can we help?" Leipfold asked, while Maile was busying herself with a round of drinks. Bram was sitting at his desk, but he had his laptop in front of him and Leipfold had asked him to record notes, something that wasn't a problem for Mr. Shakespeare. He typed at 138 words per minute.

"My client, Miss Acharya, wants to speak to you," Swordrock said. "She asked me to come with her so I could interpret for her and ask her any questions that you might have."

"Why now?" Leipfold asked. "I mean no offence, you understand, but when we talked before, she said she had nothing to tell us. What's changed?"

There was a pause for a few moments as Swordrock translated Leipfold's question into Arabic and processed the response. While that was happening, Maile came back in with six cups of coffee on a plastic tray. The mugs were a strange assortment of souvenirs that Leipfold had picked up throughout the years, and most of them were stained a shit-splattered brown from years of strong coffee.

"She says she fears for her life," Swordrock translated. "She always feared for her life, but she hoped that the worst was over. She says that after you guys shut down filming, she thought they'd let her go and that she could finally start her life here."

"And that didn't happen?"

There was another heated exchange of Arabic, and Leipfold took the opportunity to take a swig from his coffee. It was still red hot, but Leipfold had an asbestos throat and he swallowed it greedily as though it was a glass of cold water.

"She says they've been following her ever since," Swordrock explained. "She's been living in a halfway house. She says she came from Lebanon and was told she'd be moving to Paris to live with a distant relative. Instead, she ended up in a Spanish brothel."

"Where?" Leipfold asked.

"Does that matter?" Cholmondeley added.

"Barcelona," Swordrock said. "She says she stayed there for a couple of months, being rented out each night or being forced to sit at the roadside on a deck chair with her minder watching from a distance. She says those days were her favourite because at least she got to see the sunlight. After that, they loaded her and a bunch of other girls into a shipping container and she was brought here."

The woman carried on talking, her hand gestures getting more and more animated until it looked as though she was trying to summon some Cthulian hell-beast from the planet Zog. The translator struggled to keep up with her.

"She says that there were thirteen of them in the shipping container," Swordrock explained. "They were left in there for ten days. They had food and water, but it was cold in there and they had nowhere to go to the toilet. She says that even after all of the other horrors and indignities, that was the worst. Eventually, they were taken out of the shipping container and taken to another safe house. It took her a few weeks to realise she was in the UK, although she knew she was no longer in Spain."

"Human trafficking," Cholmondeley murmured. "The worst of the worst."

"Well, she can't stay where she's been staying," Leipfold said. "Ask her if she wants to stay here, at the office. We can set up a bed somewhere and—"

"That won't be necessary," Swordrock said, and Leipfold noticed that this time, she hadn't waited for her client to speak. "We work with a number of charities that specialise in human trafficking. We can give her some temporary housing."

"Can you protect her?"

"No," Swordrock admitted. "But we can go one better. We can give her anonymity. They'll never find her."

"You sure about that?"

"As sure as we can be."

"Then I suppose that will have to do," Leipfold said. "I wonder if your client would mind doing something for us. I'd like to show her some photos. Perhaps she'd be kind enough to let us know if she recognises any of the people in them."

The woman and her client conversed quietly in Arabic and then they both nodded their heads.

"That would be acceptable," Swordrock said.

"Good," Leipfold replied. "Then let's get started."

*　*　*

In the end, the woman gave them positive IDs on a half dozen of the people in their dossier, including the suspect that Leipfold had tailed after their trip to the gentlemen's club.

She also recognised Mike Croft and said she'd be prepared to stand up in court to point the finger at him as the head of the pornography ring, or at least the sector of it that she'd been exposed to. She'd only met him once, when he'd paid an off-the-record visit to the makeshift studio while they were in the middle of a shoot, but from the way that the others had deferred to him, it had seemed as though he was in charge.

Leipfold knew what she meant. Croft had an air of power to him that he recognised from the army. It was something in the body language or the way he talked. When Croft spoke, Leipfold could tell that he expected to be listened to and obeyed.

With Croft as the main focus of their investigation, Leipfold had handed him over to Jack Cholmondeley, who spent the rest of the working week tailing him, although he witnessed nothing that they could use to build their case. It seemed that Croft was meticulous about appearances, going out of his way to seem like a normal, upstanding member of society, a man to be admired.

But Leipfold and co. knew better, and Jack Cholmondeley in particular had a grudge against the man.

While Cholmondeley was out on the streets tailing Croft all over town as he went from meeting to uninspiring meeting, Bram and Maile were working on the dossier. By the time that five o'clock on Friday rolled around, they were as close to finished as they were likely to get. The whole damn thing had been digitised and added to a database on the dark web, and they'd created a torrent for the information, too. All of the infrastructure was in place, and while they could continue to update the dossier as more and more information came in from Jack Cholmondeley and their listening tools, they were also ready to release it at a moment's notice. They'd even set up a bot network to spam the link on discussion forums and social networking sites to make sure that they got some visibility. If nothing else, people would see the link. It would be up to them whether they clicked it and whether they acted upon the information that they discovered.

Bram had come up trumps with another idea, too. Maile had put him in touch with Mayhem, one of her online friends, and the two of them had been working on a machine, learning algorithm that used natural language processing to parse through their data and to pick up on any links that had previously gone unnoticed. The database was already a huge interlinking web, but the algorithm added new nodes and made it even more self-referential.

The digital visualisations of the network were a wonder to behold, huge three-dimensional things with almost as many layers of complexity as a human brain. Coupled with their strict logs of their suspects' movements and the data they'd parsed from social networks, they had a compelling case, not only against individual members but also against the organisation as a whole.

The investigation was proceeding well, and while it was taking up increasing amounts of the company's resources, they'd also closed a couple of active cases for their other clients. For once, both their workload and their financial situation seemed stable. New leads were still coming in, but not at the same rate as they had been, and that gave them a little breathing room to work on their own projects. Jack Cholmondeley had even started writing a novel, although Leipfold had forbidden him from working on it from his phone when he was supposed to be tailing people.

On Saturday, April 22, Maile and Bram were taking the weekend off while Leipfold and Cholmondeley followed up on a few loose ends.

Leipfold was following Terence Rowbotham, a senior cop who'd made it into their dossier for a number of different reasons, including manipulating the press and laundering money through a complex system of betting shops that the Boys in Blue were funding with their ill-gotten cryptocurrency.

Rowbotham was a normal-looking guy with the feel of an out of work actor. He had salt and pepper hair that fell across his forehead in a floppy fringe, and he was wearing the kind of anonymous blue shirt that was sold en masse in department stores around the country. The most unique thing about him was the way he walked, which reminded Leipfold of a Monty Python sketch.

It also made him difficult to follow, but Leipfold was a master of the art. Like an urban chameleon, he could melt into the background and become just another face in the crowd, and by varying his outfit and taking unorthodox routes around the city's alleyways, he was able to keep a visual on Rowbotham without putting himself at risk of discovery.

So far, it had all been in vain. Rowbotham had been on duty all day, meandering from place to place with the casualness of a copper who thought that his job was to be seen and not to actually accomplish anything. Jack Cholmondeley had warned Leipfold about Rowbotham before he'd left, although he only knew him by reputation. He was one of the lifers, the old coppers who were still on the force because of the people they knew, rather than because of their proficiency.

By the late afternoon, Leipfold was considering calling it a day. He decided to let fate dictate his next move for him and tossed a coin. It landed heads, which meant that he'd give it another half hour.

Rowbotham emerged again, leaving the Old Vic to walk to the nearby supermarket. Leipfold watched out of the corner of his eye while pretending to busy himself with the ingredients on a pack of dry-roasted peanuts. The copper bought himself a meal deal, a bottle of wine and a packet of extra strong mints.

"What a waste of time," Leipfold murmured, though secretly he appreciated the break. He came up with some of his best ideas when he was walking the streets and following a mark, and it reminded him of his younger days when he'd followed people because they interested him instead of because he was being paid.

On the way back out, Rowbotham took an unexpected right and struck off across the car park. Leipfold followed cautiously, increasing the distance between the two of them, and felt his confusion mounting as the man headed for the far corner of the lot. Rowbotham had arrived on foot, and the only things in that direction were the donation banks for used clothing and the steel fence that circled the car park. Leipfold wasn't sure whether they were there to keep people out or in.

"Hello," Leipfold murmured. "What's this?"

A car had pulled up, an anonymous-looking sedan. Its drab brown colour and uninspiring hubcaps were like a form of urban camouflage. It was the kind of car that would still be there in the morning even if the doors were left unlocked and the keys were in the ignition. It wasn't worth the effort of stealing.

He picked up his phone and dashed off a quick message to Jack Cholmondeley, who'd been running vehicular surveillance on a couple of the other top cops. He was just around the corner, and it was the work of a couple of seconds to send instructions.

Cholmondeley was just pulling up when the driver got out of the vehicle and Rowbotham climbed in. Leipfold dashed out another set of instructions and hoped that Cholmondeley got them, then ducked out of the way when the vehicle's former driver started to walk towards him. Even at a distance, Leipfold could see exactly who it was.

"Mike Croft," he murmured. "If you're not Mr. M, I'll eat my hat."

*   *   *

Jack Cholmondeley followed the ugly brown sedan as it wound its way through the streets towards the north of London. It had always been more difficult to tail people in vehicles than on foot, and London's roads exacerbated the problem thanks to one-way systems, multi-laned highways and the endless roadworks that plagued the city like teenage acne.

Fortunately, he'd taken a course on evasion and pursuit a couple of years ago, and while it had admittedly been a while since he'd brushed up on his skills, it was like learning to ride a bike. The old habits and routines didn't abandon him in his hour of need, and he'd carried out so much surveillance over the last couple of days that it was all old hat.

Rowbotham continued to drive the tan sedan north, and Cholmondeley followed lazily behind, occasionally dropping back in the traffic to give his quarry some lead time. Black Mercedes were popular in London because they acted like a badge of honour for the wealthy elite, but Cholmondeley didn't want to take his chances.

They were nearing the outskirts of the city when Rowbotham took a sudden and unexpected left into a cul-de-sac. Cholmondeley cursed and drove past it, craning his neck to the left and right in search of somewhere to turn around. He couldn't see anywhere likely, but there wasn't much traffic and so he pulled off a sneaky and illegal three-point turn and drove back towards the cul-de-sac.

When he got there, Terence Rowbotham was waiting. He'd parked his car and was sitting on the bonnet, staring straight at Jack Cholmondeley as he cruised down the street towards him. For a brief, crazy moment, Cholmondeley thought about putting his foot down and smashing his Beemer into the man. His foot was on the pedal before he knew it, but he took a deep breath and talked himself down. He moved his right foot off the accelerator and pushed his left foot down on the brakes. Then he slowed to a stop in front of Rowbotham, parked the car and climbed out of it.

"Fancy seeing you here, Jack."

"You know me?" Cholmondeley replied. "That's not good."

"Not from your career, you understand," Rowbotham said. "I hear that you served well but without distinction. No, no. I'd never heard of you until you started investigating the Boys in Blue."

"Ah," Cholmondeley said. "So you admit they exist?"

Rowbotham laughed and then jumped down from the hood of his vehicle. He walked up to Jack Cholmondeley and looked him dead in the eye.

"Come off it, Jack," Rowbotham said. "We both know that I know that you know."

"Ah," Cholmondeley said. "But do I know that you know that we both know that I know that you know?"

"I'm not sure," Rowbotham said. "Too many clauses."

"How did you know I was following you?"

"You know that course you went on?"

"Yeah."

"Who do you think created the damn thing?" Rowbotham asked.

"I see," Cholmondeley replied.

"Listen, Jack, I'd like to offer you a deal," Rowbotham said. "I know how important your job was to you. Perhaps we were a little too harsh when we dismissed you."

"You didn't dismiss me," Cholmondeley said. "I was placed on gardening leave."

"Either way," Rowbotham continued, "we could use more hardworking, enterprising cops like you. How about I get you your old job back?"

"You can do that?"

"If I want to," Rowbotham said. "The real question is whether you're going to make it worth my while."

Chapter Seventeen:
WWJCD?

WHILE JACK CHOLMONDELEY WAS tailing Terence Rowbotham, Leipfold was on foot, following Mike Croft as he made his way across the city. He'd ducked into a tube station and headed east, and so Leipfold had followed him, hanging from the straps of the next carriage along. Croft seemed oblivious to the fact he was being followed, and he barely looked up throughout his journey. Instead, he appeared to be unusually interested in the fishnetted legs of two teenage girls.

It gave Leipfold a hollow feeling in his stomach. They were young enough to have been Croft's grandchildren, and they were almost as old as the women that had found themselves in his porno ring, like flies at the mercy of some giant spider.

Croft got off the tube in the East End, and Leipfold pursued him at a distance, occasionally ducking behind vehicles or letting him gain some distance. They walked along one of the city's many nondescript high streets and then along the river.

Leipfold was just starting to wonder where they were wandering when Croft took an unexpected right and strolled down an alleyway. Leipfold poked his nose cautiously around the corner and, when he saw that Croft had his back to him, he leaned out a little farther.

Mike Croft was standing in front of a steel door at the end of the alley. He rapped assertively against it, hammering out what sounded to Leipfold's ears like a predetermined signal.

Croft looked around and Leipfold shrank back out of sight. When he looked around the corner again, the door had been opened and Croft was disappearing inside it. The door slammed closed and shut Leipfold out, but it almost didn't matter. Standing there at the end of the alleyway, Leipfold laughed softly to himself.

He'd seen the face of the man that Croft was meeting, and he'd recognised it. It was Roger Gough, the home secretary.

*   *   *

Leipfold and the gang reconvened on Monday morning to sort through the week's workload and to plan their next move against the Boys in Blue.

"Are we going to dump the data?" Maile asked.

"Not yet," Leipfold replied. "But we're close."

Then he told her about Mike Croft's disappearance through the door and his presumed meeting with the home secretary.

"I've never heard of him," Bram said.

"*Psht*," Cholmondeley murmured. "Kids these days."

"If Croft's with the Boys in Blue and he's meeting with the home secretary, their reach is deeper than we thought," Leipfold said. "The man's the second most important person in the country. The corruption must go right to the top."

"If that's true," Cholmondeley said, "we should double down on security."

"Yes," Leipfold said. "We're lucky that they've only made a move on Constable Groves, and even then only as a warning. How is she, by the way?"

"She'll live," Cholmondeley said, gloomily. "But it's going to be a while before she walks the beat again. James, there's something else."

"What is it?"

"Terence Rowbotham caught me when I was tailing him," Cholmondeley said. "At first, I thought there was going to be trouble, but then he made me an offer. He wants to give me my old job back."

"Are you going to take him up on it?"

"I have to, James," Cholmondeley said. "All I ever wanted was to be a copper."

"Your job doesn't define you, Jack."

"No, but it does play into your sense of self, James," Cholmondeley replied. "I start next Monday."

"So much for gardening leave, huh?" Leipfold said. He sighed. "Fine, I can't say I blame you, and it's not as though you can live on your savings forever."

"Exactly," Cholmondeley said. "I appreciate the opportunity you've given me, James. And I'm sure you're already aware that there's something in it for you."

"Yeah," Leipfold said. "You can feed me information. Just don't get caught."

"I'll try my best."

"Ahem," Maile said, theatrically. "If you two gentlemen have quite finished, Bram and I have got an update. We've had some results back from our algorithm over the weekend, and we now have a total of 684 members of the Boys in Blue, fully-profiled with the cases against them."

"Christ," Leipfold said. "That's a lot."

"We have fourteen thousand more names on the maybe list," Maile replied. "The damn organisation is huge. For all we know, this is just the tip of the iceberg."

"How are we doing with the usernames from the dark web?"

"We've got a couple hundred of those tied back to real people," Bram said. "They form the backbone of some of our cases. At the latest count, there are over thirty thousand members, though some of them could be duplicates."

"A single person having multiple logins and that sort of thing," Maile supplied.

"The point is, this is the real deal," Bram said. "That's 684 cases that should stand up in court, Mr. Leipfold. Even if half of them get off, that's still good enough to cause a stir. People won't stand for it. They'll demand a full investigation."

"They won't need one," Leipfold said. "We'll have done it for them. Okay, let's work to a deadline. Jack is going back to the Old Vic on Monday. We'll give him a week to settle in and to share any final information. Then we'll go live with what we have the Monday after."

* * *

But as often seemed to happen at Leipfold Investigations, things didn't quite go according to plan.

Maile and Bram were in the downstairs office, gossiping about one of their new clients, when the buzzer exploded into life and demanded their attention. At first, Maile thought it was the builders, because they kept locking themselves out and asking to be let back in. But when it kept buzzing even as she scooched across the room to answer it, she realised it was something more sinister.

"Let me in!"

"Who is it?" Maile asked, trying to inject some normality into her tone even though the desperate voice on the other end had tugged at her nerves and filled her with fear. She was already pressing the button to let them in when the reply came.

"It's Swordrock," they said. "Oh God, they took her. They took her."

Maile got up and went to meet the woman in the hallway, then led her straight upstairs into Leipfold's office. She had a feeling that he'd want to speak to her right away, and there was something else to consider. She sounded as though she feared for her life. If those fears were grounded and someone really *was* after her, she'd be safer in Leipfold's office than in their reception area.

Maile knocked on the door and then let herself into Leipfold's office without waiting for a response. With the top floor to himself, he'd rearranged the furniture like some feng shui master trying to harness the power of a ley line. Maile's desk was downstairs and he had no need for a reception, so Leipfold had expanded his collection of maps and filing cabinets to fill the space. Far from helping him to keep the space tidy, he seemed to have taken Maile's departure as permission to be as messy as he wanted.

"Hey!" Leipfold said, not looking up from his computer screen as Maile opened the door. "I thought I told you to knock and wait. I'm working on something very delicate here and—"

"James," Maile said patiently, "you're going to want to hear what Ms. Swordrock has to say."

"Ms. Who?"

"They took her," Swordrock said, the tension and the fear leaking out of her like sweat on a summer's day. It was contagious, and Maile wondered what her Fitbit would say if she checked her heart rate. She had a feeling she was in fat burn mode, and she'd only been standing for a couple of minutes.

"Who?" Leipfold asked.

"Who do you think?" she snapped. She looked unsteady on her feet and Maile went to fetch her a chair, though she didn't sit down on it. "I went to the safe house today, and she's gone. They took her."

"Were there signs of a struggle?"

"The whole damn place had been turned upside down," Swordrock said. "There was blood on the carpet, although not enough to convince me that they killed her. They must want her alive. They probably want to find out what she knows. And then there was this."

She reached into her handbag and pulled out a letter, which she handed to Leipfold. Maile came to stand behind him so she could see what he was seeing. The note was like something out of a bad spy movie, a sheet of A4 copier paper with letters cut from newspapers to spell out a simple, anonymous message.

TeLl jaMEs LeIpfoLD 2 Dr0P ThE CAsE OR sH3 DiES.

"Ah," Leipfold said. "My notoriety proceeds me."

"You have to do something," Swordrock said. Some of the colour had returned to her face, but she still looked like an albino cosplaying as Casper the Friendly Ghost. "Promise me, Mr. Leipfold. You have to find her."

"She's right, boss," Maile supplied. "If nothing else, if we catch them in the act, we'll have a case against them for false imprisonment."

"WWJCD," Leipfold said.

"Huh?"

"What would Jack Cholmondeley do?" he said. He smiled. "I'd better give the old man a call. We'll need his help with this."

"I'm sorry," Swordrock said, finally sitting down on the chair that Maile had brought for her. "You're going to have to start at the beginning, I'm afraid. I have absolutely no idea what you're talking about."

Leipfold looked pained for a moment, as though whatever he'd had for breakfast had suddenly disagreed with him. He grimaced, then nodded at Maile.

"Go on, then," he said. "Bring her up to speed with the investigation. I think we can trust her, and you never know. She might be useful."

*   *   *

"Thanks for agreeing to see us, ma'am."

"Not a problem, Constable Groves."

The three of them were sitting in Groves' mother's living room, drinking builder's tea from the best china cups and sitting on the chintz sofas. Constable Groves was sitting uncomfortably on one of the sofas while Constable Cohen and Superintendent Richards took the other one.

A half-empty teapot and a small jug of milk had been placed on a table between the two sofas. Cohen helped himself to a sugar cube and stirred it into his tea with a silver spoon.

"I expect you're wondering why I asked you to come here," Groves said.

"The thought had crossed my mind," Richards admitted. "Of course, I'm more than happy to make time for you. You've more than earned it. You have an exemplary record, and I'm grateful for everything you've done for us. I was sorry to learn that you'd been injured."

"I appreciate it, ma'am."

Cohen cleared his throat and glanced meaningfully across at Groves.

"The thing is," Groves continued, "I have a favour to ask of you."

"If it's about the shooting, you know I can't comment on an active investigation," Richards replied.

"No, it's not that," Groves said. "Constable Cohen and I have a request to make. We want you to bring Cholmondeley back."

"Jack?" Richards said. "Why?"

"Well, let's face it," Cohen replied. "We've got a problem with the Boys in Blue. Jack Cholmondeley might be the only person we can trust to take them down."

"Are you crazy?" Richards said. "You don't just *talk* about the Boys in Blue. How do you know I'm not a member?"

"You're a woman," Cohen said. "So is Groves, and I'm gay. They only take straight, white males. None of us are eligible."

"But what about Jack?"

"What about him?" Groves asked.

"He's a straight white male," Richards replied. "In other words, he's just the kind of man that the Boys in Blue might want on their books."

"Exactly," Cohen said. "So perhaps you should bring him back and see what he can ferret out."

*   *   *

Leipfold's team spent the rest of the morning planning their next move while Bram updated their dossier with some new evidence that Swordrock had provided. There was nothing concrete, but she'd noticed a couple of strange-looking men at her office and outside the safe house.

More damning still was the official visit that had happened while she'd been out of the office on a training course. She'd not seen him herself, but the visit had been a hot topic for weeks afterwards, and with good reason. It's not every day that the home secretary pays a visit to a private translation agency.

Leipfold had seized on that as further proof that the corruption went right to the top, but other than a glimpse of the man through a door and a little watercooler gossip, they didn't have much against him.

"Remember," Maile said, "he could still be innocent. In the eyes of the law, he is until he's proven guilty."

"He's a politician," Leipfold said. "He's definitely guilty of something."

Bram, meanwhile, had been following the investigation in a different direction, trying to map out a blueprint of the Boys in Blue and their influence amongst the press.

"If Rupert Murdoch isn't a member of the Boys in Blue, I'll eat my wheelchair," Bram said. "But it's not just the *Daily Fail* and *The Sun*. It's the whole of the right-wing press, including stuff in Australia and the States. If we publish what we know, they'll come after us. You know what the press is like."

"So much for free speech," Leipfold said. He pinched the bridge of his nose and sighed. Then he looked around the room at the three pairs of eyes that were all looking hopefully back at him. "All right, let them come. They say there's no such thing as bad publicity. If nothing else, we'll get more walk-ins."

"Ha-ha," Bram said. "Very funny."

"What are we going to do about the woman?" Cholmondeley asked. He was standing awkwardly beside a couple of Leipfold's filing cabinets, holding a hot cup of coffee in his hand and looking out of place like a gaudy coat stand.

"I'm glad you asked, Jack," Leipfold replied. "How do you feel about working outside of the law?"

"You know I hate it when you do that, James."

"Sometimes, there isn't any choice," Leipfold said. "If we want to find the missing woman and shut down the human trafficking ring, we're going to have to be a little…shall we say, flexible?"

Cholmondeley sighed and said, "So what's the plan?"

"We need to do some breaking and entering," Leipfold said. "Let's start with the apartment opposite your place. They'll have cleared out by now, but perhaps we can find some clue about where they were going."

*   *   *

In the end, Leipfold drew the short straw and was tasked with the job of breaking into the apartment. Bram couldn't do it, and Maile wasn't keen to risk a criminal record. They couldn't ask Swordrock to do it, and Cholmondeley was worried about "pissing on his own doorstep."

"Fine," Leipfold said. "I'll do it. But I'm going to have to get myself a new crowbar."

Cholmondeley still played a part, though. He lurked in the building's communal areas while Leipfold waited around the corner, dressed in his black motorcycle gear and with a bandana pulled low over his face. Cholmondeley waited for the evening rush to be over and for the building's other inhabitants to finish prepping their microwave meals. Then he sent him a message consisting of a single word of two characters: *Go.*

The porno apartment was on the ground floor, and so Leipfold didn't have to worry about scaling walls. He also knew the layout of the building, and so it was simple enough for him to follow the exterior around to the right place. The apartment was at the rear of the building, backing on to a low alleyway that encircled the house and which led to where the bins were stored.

He dragged a bin over so it was beneath one of the windows and then climbed on top of it and inserted his crowbar into a gap. It was a typical urban window of the kind that could be locked while open. Leipfold had the same design at his office, although he kept them closed at all times because he knew how easy they were to compromise.

That particular window was a perfect example. After Leipfold inserted the crowbar, all it took was a little love-tap and the bolts bent and the window came free of its casing. Then he lifted it open and climbed inside like a snake squeezing through a sewage pipe.

He went in head first and hit the floor in a roll, then came straight up against a wall and slowed to an undignified stop. It hurt like hell, and he reminded himself that he wasn't as young as he used to be. That old line from the movies was starting to seem like less of a cliché and more like observational comedy.

Leipfold pulled himself to his feet and looked around. He'd entered the apartment via the bedroom, but it looked very different. The furniture was still there, but everything else had been taken out. The wardrobe was empty, the bed was unmade and consisted solely of a bare mattress with no quilt or pillows, and when he let himself out through the door and into the rest of the apartment, the scene was much the same.

"They must have cleared out as soon as we busted them," Leipfold murmured, examining the light layer of dust that coated the apartment. The living room, the kitchen and the hallway were equally Spartan, and the flat had an air of neglect to it, a kind of silence that reminded Leipfold of a morgue.

He picked up his phone and called Cholmondeley.

"Yeah?"

"There's nothing here, Jack," Leipfold said.

"Keep looking."

"Any chance of you coming to give me a hand?"

"Can't," Cholmondeley said. "I'm busy keeping watch."

Leipfold sighed and cut the call before starting back on his search. It was relatively easy because there wasn't any clutter for clues to hide behind. All of the cupboards were empty.

"There has to be *something*," he murmured.

Then he hit the jackpot. When he moved the bed out of the way, he spotted a patch of discoloured wallpaper behind the headboard. He ran his hands over it and then tapped against the wall. It echoed, a good indication that there was a hollow space.

Leipfold took a step back to look at the wall from a different angle. Then he moved forward again and caressed the wall until he found what he was looking for: an indentation where it wasn't solid. He pushed against it and the wall shuddered. He pushed again, this time using the friction against his hand to shove the wall to the left.

It slid open like something out of *Star Trek* and revealed a cubbyhole within. Leipfold picked his phone up and called Cholmondeley, then started speaking as soon as the call connected.

"Jack, come here," he said. "You're going to want to see this."

"What is it?" Cholmondeley asked.

"It's like something out of Scooby Doo," he said. "Come and have a look."

Leipfold cut the call and strolled back into the hall to open the front door, then returned to the secret compartment in the bedroom. It was roughly the size of an airing cupboard, and Leipfold suspected that it had once been a walk-in wardrobe. With the modifications in place, however, it reminded him more of a jail cell. And there was a reason for that.

The secret room could have held four people if they didn't mind getting up close and personal, and it looked as though it had been used for exactly that purpose. There was a smell to it that took Leipfold back to his army days, the unpleasant acidic smell of unwashed bodies. But whoever had hidden there was long gone, and they hadn't left much behind.

Or had they?

Leipfold leaned a little closer. There were a couple of soiled pairs of underpants on the floor, but other than that, the space was remarkably bare. There was a shelf at head height, but when Leipfold climbed on the bed to look inside, he saw that it was empty except for a lonely packet of silicone gel. Sighing and cursing inwardly when his knee flared up in a painful protest, he climbed back down from the bed.

Cholmondeley had joined him, and he was leaning into the space and using a battery-powered flashlight to look into the corners.

"Where did you get that?" Leipfold asked.

Cholmondeley shrugged and said, "I keep it under my bed, just in case. We get a lot of power cuts here. We're not exactly on EDF's priority list. Hey, look at this."

"What?" Leipfold asked, edging over to stand beside him. He stuck his head inside and looked at where Cholmondeley was shining his flashlight. "Hmm, interesting."

Someone had scratched something into the wall, possibly with a fingernail. It was a sloppy job and some of the plaster had peeled away completely, but it looked like most of the message remained intact. It was difficult to tell.

It was written in Arabic.

Chapter Eighteen:
The Raid

IN THE MORNING, WHEN Leipfold arrived at the office, Swordrock was already waiting outside for him. She was lurking in the shadows outside and watching the door nervously as though she was expecting the Boys in Blue to burst out of it and to take her down with a nightstick or a rag of chloroform.

When Leipfold approached, she ran over and threw her arms around him, which was awkward because he was in the process of dismounting Camilla and he had his helmet in his hands. He stood there impatiently for a couple of seconds, then cleared his throat and said, "Yes, well."

He let them into the building and surveyed the ground floor of the precinct. The builders had finished putting in the new lift, and Bram had already tested it out a few times to do a tea run or to brief Leipfold in person when he couldn't be bothered to go downstairs. Today was the builders' last day in the office, and all they had to do was to clean up the last of the mess they'd made and to carry out a few tests.

Leipfold took Swordrock up to his office and sat her down, then disappeared downstairs to make them both a cup of coffee. Cholmondeley arrived while he was in the kitchen area, and the two of them went back upstairs to begin the interview.

"Tell me you've got good news, Mr. Leipfold," Swordrock said. Her face was pale and she looked as though she'd seen someone get hit by a Megabus.

"I'm not sure if it's good," Leipfold said, "but I've got something. We didn't find any sign of your client, but we *did* find a hidden room with a message scratched into the plaster. The problem is, we can't read it. Any idea what this means?"

Leipfold pulled up a photograph on his phone and pinched at the screen to zoom in. Then he held it out to her.

"Hmm," Swordrock said. "Yeah, that's Arabic, all right. It looks like…I mean, it's just a name."

"What's the name?"

"It's the name of a mosque," Swordrock replied. "The East London Mosque, to be more precise. It's on Whitechapel Road."

"Then we'd better pay them a little visit," Leipfold said.

"It's not as easy as that," Swordrock replied. "There are social mores here, codes of conduct. It's a close-knit community. You can't just barge in there."

"Why not?"

"How do you think a bunch of little old ladies at a church fete would react if some guy with a suntan, a beard and a rucksack showed up and started asking questions?" Swordrock said. "It's a different world."

"You can guide us."

"I can't," she said. "I'm a stranger there, just as much as you are."

"Listen," Leipfold said. "Do you want to find her or not?"

"Of course," Swordrock said. She sighed. "Okay, we'll check it out."

"I know that place," Cholmondeley said. "There's a little pub just outside it. The Swan."

"Then it's settled," Leipfold said. "Jack, get your keys. You're driving."

* * *

"Well," Leipfold said. "I knew you were old, Jack, but I didn't know you were that old."

The pub had seen better days. For a start, it wasn't open, and it looked like it hadn't been open for several years. The windows had been boarded up and the walls were covered with graffiti tags and gang symbols. A couple of CCTV cameras hung out from the eaves, but Leipfold guessed that they hadn't seen service for a while. The cameras looked so old that he doubted they were still being manufactured.

"Hmm," Cholmondeley said. "It was always a dodgy little boozer, but it never used to look quite like this."

"Oh well," Leipfold said. "I don't drink and you're driving, Jack."

They turned around and looked over to the other side of the road, where the mosque loomed up out of the darkness. It was a bland building, not owing too much to Middle Eastern design, but it was also massive, towering high above the rest of the street, though it was lost amongst the wider city.

It was the early afternoon and it looked relatively empty, though people came and went at regular intervals. Leipfold supposed that they were offering childcare or hosting community groups.

Leipfold and Jack Cholmondeley lurked there for twenty minutes or so, getting their bearings and establishing a feel for the area. It was an old trick that kicked in subconsciously, and one that had served them both well on the streets. Without even knowing they were doing it, they scanned familiar areas for something different and looked at new areas to mark out any points of reference. That allowed them to pick up on details that other people might not have noticed.

Right then, it had alerted Leipfold to an unusual noise coming from behind them. It was the distant echo of muted conversation, voices where there shouldn't be voices. He caught Cholmondeley's eye and held a hand up to his ear, then they looked around for the source of the sound.

"It's coming from inside the pub," Leipfold whispered.

"Could be builders?"

"Come off it, Jack," he said. "The only builders that place is going to see is the wrecking crew when they come to tear it down. We've got to investigate."

"I was afraid you were going to say that."

Leipfold led the way, with Cholmondeley following close behind them. Swordrock had come with them, but they'd long since left her sitting in the passenger seat of Jack Cholmondeley's Beemer so that she could move it if a traffic warden came along. Nobody had thought to ask whether she held a license.

Leipfold reached one of the windows and examined it, finding a small gap in the woodwork where it wasn't quite boarded up. There was a light in there, and Leipfold guessed from its flickering quality that it was a candle or a fire. He couldn't see much, but he *could* see a figure on a chair. Her hands were tied behind her back and a black hood was over her face, but he had a pretty good guess who she was.

"You fool," someone was saying. "Don't you see? This can only bring us more attention."

"But you said—"

"I know what I said," the first person continued. "But things have changed. Jack Cholmondeley's going back to the Old Vic, and we're going to ask him to join the Boys in Blue."

Leipfold and Cholmondeley exchanged glances. There was movement from inside and then the prisoner in the hood shifted. One of the men slapped her firmly across the back of the head and she cried out in pain, then rattled off a series of curses in Arabic.

"It's definitely her, James," Cholmondeley said. "What are we going to do?"

"We're going to do the right thing, Jack," Leipfold said. "We're going to call in your mates from the Old Vic."

"You mean you're going to call the police?" Cholmondeley

asked. "But, James, I thought the police were compromised."

"They are," Leipfold said. "But not all of them. If enough cops show up and they catch these guys in the act, it'll force it all out into the open. And besides, Jack. They could be armed."

"Let's hope they are," Cholmondeley said, grimly. "That way, the first responders will shoot to kill. I'll call in a few favours and see what I can do. There must be an armed response team somewhere with nothing better to do."

*　　*　　*

Leipfold and Cholmondeley worked late that night and caught a couple hours of sleep in the office. Leipfold had already stashed a sleeping bag in the building, and Cholmondeley stretched out downstairs on the sofa, though his lanky frame left his legs and feet dangling over the end.

Cholmondeley had put in a call to Constable Cohen, and Cohen had roped Sergeant Mogford in to act as senior officer. Cohen had been briefed to give Mogford the information, but to tell him that it came from an anonymous informant.

"Gary Mogford is a good cop," Cholmondeley said. "But he's also as stubborn as they come. If he thinks I'm trying to issue orders to him by proxy, he won't help us. If he thinks he's acting on his own initiative, he's ours."

Somehow, Cohen and Mogford were able to obtain a rapid response search warrant, and Cohen put in an extra shift to create and brief a SWAT team. Go time was 6 AM, so Leipfold and Cholmondeley set their alarms for five and made their way back to the pub and the mosque.

The sun was just rising when the SWAT team arrived, and Leipfold and Cholmondeley milled about in front of the mosque, watching the raid unfold while occasionally sidestepping the morning worshippers.

The black van rolled silently up to the pub, an old police trick that Leipfold had used from time to time, too. They must have cut the engine farther down the street and rolled on with its momentum, giving them the added advantage of stealth. There was no knock on the door, just the heavy thud of the bosher as it smashed into the wood and sent splinters flying through the air.

"Armed police! Nobody move!"

The rapid response team crashed against the building like a tidal wave, rushing inside in single file. Leipfold and Cholmondeley couldn't see what was happening, and so they listened instead for the sound of gunfire, though there wasn't any.

"Should we go over and take a closer look?" Cholmondeley asked.

"Better not," Leipfold replied. "We'd only get in the way. Plus, do you think it's a good idea to peer in through a window at a bunch of people with guns?"

"Point taken."

They waited out the rest of the raid in silence, though both men were clearly anxious. Leipfold couldn't stop pacing backwards and forwards, and he noticed that Jack Cholmondeley was biting his nails again, an old habit that he'd thought the man had kicked twenty years ago. It was the wait that was the hard part. The whole thing took less than ten minutes, but it felt like half a lifetime and Leipfold wouldn't have been surprised to find that his carrot-coloured hair had started to go grey.

The van pulled up outside the pub, and Leipfold surmised that it had been summoned in. The back door of the van swung open and a familiar face hopped out and onto the pavement. Gary Mogford looked up and down the street, forcing Leipfold and Cholmondeley to hide behind a post box, and then he strode into the pub as though he didn't have a care in the world.

"It's all over, then," Cholmondeley said. "Mogford might be a good cop, but he's no idiot. He wouldn't put himself in any unnecessary danger. He'd only risk going in there if he knew that any active shooters had been taken down."

"Better not let him see us," Leipfold added.

Gary Mogford came back out several minutes later, and this time he was accompanying the Arabic woman, who was no longer hooded and bound and who looked scared out of her wits, even from a distance. She had an angry welt on the side of her face and dried blood caked across her jawline. She was shouting something desperately in Arabic, and one of the coppers was trying to calm her down by speaking her language back to her. So far at least, it seemed that they'd been unsuccessful.

Leipfold wasn't surprised. With what the woman knew about the Boys in Blue, she probably thought she was heading out of the frying pan and into the fire.

"Maybe this wasn't such a good idea after all," Leipfold said.

"How so?"

"If they take her back to the Old Vic, we're sending her into the lion's den," Leipfold said. "If the Boys in Blue want to get to her, they'll find a way to reach her in the cells."

"They wouldn't dare," Cholmondeley replied. "If they did, they'd have to explain it. It would be a PR nightmare. And besides, Gary Mogford is a good lad. I don't think he'll take her back to the Old Vic. He'll take her to the hospital to get her checked over."

"Hello," Leipfold said. "Who's that?"

Cholmondeley followed Leipfold's outstretched finger, and his eyes alighted on a single, solitary man who was climbing out of a first-floor window. He'd slid the thing open, lowered himself out by his fingertips and was dangling ten feet from the ground. As they watched, the man let go of the windowsill and dropped to the ground. He hit it hard and his legs buckled, then he rolled on to his side and came to a stop on the pavement.

Leipfold was already moving, and so was Cholmondeley, although he was a couple of steps behind him. Leipfold put that down to his age. But they were both too far away, and the man had a head start, even if he was wounded. The two men were approaching from the southwest and he was running to the northeast, and they lost sight of him for a while as the abandoned pub rose up in front of them. The riot cops were spilling out of the door too, and then all of them were running down the street, like some perverse take on cheese rolling. Leipfold half expected a Morris dancer to saunter past.

Then there was a roar of rubber on asphalt, and Leipfold felt himself stumbling as Cholmondeley dragged him to the side. It was just in time to stop him from being clipped by the black BMW as it picked up speed and roared off down the road.

It was up to about forty-five when it hit the running man and sent him pirouetting through the air. He hit the asphalt with a sickening, disturbing crunch.

*   *   *

Jack Cholmondeley was in a bad mood, but that was no surprise. After the dust had settled, he'd been left with the sobering reality of a totalled BMW.

"I only have third-party insurance," he said, gloomily. He had dark black bags beneath his eyes and was cradling a coffee as though it was some sort of lifeline. "The car's a bloody write-off. Do you have any idea how much it's going to cost me?"

"I dread to think," Leipfold replied.

"I'll have to dip into my savings again."

"Yes," Leipfold said. "Well, at least we got our man."

"Indeed," Cholmondeley brooded. "He won't be running anywhere any time soon."

"You know who it was, right?"

"Yeah," Cholmondeley said. "I know."

"We're going to have to publish," Leipfold said. "We have no choice. That woman might have wrecked your car, Jack, but it doesn't have to ruin the case. We have to strike now, while the iron's hot."

"You can bet that the media is already eyeing up the story," Cholmondeley said. "I'm surprised it's not in the news already."

"The Boys in Blue are trying to suppress it," Leipfold said. He shrugged. "Hey, at least they didn't try to paint it as a terror attack."

"They could have done," Cholmondeley replied, gazing thoughtfully into space. "He's the home secretary."

"But don't you see, Jack?" Leipfold said. "They want to hush this up and move on. We have them on the back foot. We need to press our advantage. I'll get Maile and Bram on it."

* * *

While the two older men were having their meeting, Bram Shakespeare and Maile O'Hara were in the downstairs office, chatting idly about the shows they'd been streaming and a new ARG that was making the rounds online.

"I wonder who's running it," Bram said.

"Who cares?" Maile replied. "They say on the internet, no one knows if you're a dog. It's true, man. They could be sapient canines from outer space and we wouldn't find out if they covered their tracks well."

"Sapient canines?"

"You know what I mean," Maile said. "You have to take precautions, that's all I'm saying. That's why you carry your nightstick."

"And it's why you carry your pepper spray," Bram added.

"Exactly," she said, flashing him a winning smile. He was at his desk, and she was lying on the visitors' sofa with her feet on the upholstery and her machine on her lap. "Not much use against guns."

"I wouldn't know," Bram said. "I'd never had to use it until I started working with you guys. To tell you the truth, I've been looking for an excuse."

"Well, you found one," Maile said. "It happens a lot when you work for Leipfold. Did I ever tell you about Tom Townsend?"

"That asshole?" Bram replied. He smiled weakly at her. "Yeah, you told me about him."

"When you come up against creeps like that," Maile said, "you'll be glad you have your nightstick."

"What does the boss carry?"

Maile paused and thought about it for a moment. Then she shrugged. "Nothing, I guess," she said. "Just his wits and his fists."

"Maybe we should get him a taser," Bram said.

"Let's wait until Christmas," Maile replied. "The damn things are surprisingly expensive. Speaking of which, Kat tells me that you took her out for dinner in the West End."

"Oh, yeah?" Bram said, his expression neutral. "What did she say?"

"Not much," Maile admitted. "She said you went to see a play and then grabbed a bite to eat."

"Did she have fun?"

"She said the play was shit."

"Yeah, it was," Bram said. "Did you know that she used to do makeup and prosthetics for theatre companies back in the day?"

"Yeah, I did," Maile replied. "She also said that the food was good and that the company was even better. It sounds like you made a good impression. Are you going to take her out again?"

"A gentleman never tells."

Maile laughed, and then the two of them turned to look at the door, which was swinging open. Leipfold entered first, with Jack Cholmondeley hot on his heels. Maile sat up properly and scooched over so that Cholmondeley could sit down, and Leipfold perched on the end of Bram's desk with his legs crossed and his arms folded.

"Okay, listen up," Leipfold said. "The home secretary's been knocked down by Jack's black BMW. The Boys in Blue are keeping it quiet at the moment, but you can bet your boots that they're planning something. We've got to beat them to the punch."

"Are you saying what I think you're saying?" Maile asked.

Leipfold nodded. "Yeah," he replied. "It's time to dump the data."

Chapter Nineteen:
Back to Work

AT LUNCHTIME, WHILE BRAM and Maile were in the downstairs office working on the data dump, Jack Cholmondeley was in the boss' office. Leipfold himself wasn't in there, though. He'd begrudgingly agreed to pop out to read his book at the coffee shop so that Jack could use his office.

He'd arranged a meeting with Superintendent Richards.

When she entered the office, she hung her coat up on the back of the door and then went to sit down at Leipfold's desk. She leaned back in the chair and crossed her legs.

"So, Jack," she said, by way of greeting. "I hear you're all set to re-join us."

"Aye," Cholmondeley replied, warily. "No thanks to you."

"It was nothing personal, Jack," Richards said. "I was under orders, you understand."

"From the Boys in Blue."

"Yes, well," Richards said. "One doesn't fuck with the Boys in Blue."

"Indeed."

"Between you and me, Jack," she said, leaning forwards conspiratorially and dropping her voice to a whisper, "I'm rather happy you're coming back. You're not dropping your investigation, are you?"

"Well, I…"

"Good," Richards said. "I want you to do a little digging. Take the Boys in Blue up on their offer and join them, then bring them down from the inside."

"How did you know about their offer?"

"Please, Jack," Richards said, dismissively. "I have sources of my own. How else am I supposed to stay one step ahead of them? But that doesn't mean I'm happy with the status quo. We owe it to the world, Jack. We have to bring the Boys in Blue down a peg."

"Then it's a good job I have a plan," Cholmondeley replied. "But I might need your help."

"You've got it, Jack," Richards said. "But I need you to make me a promise. I can't afford to take direct action against them unless I know they're going to go down."

"I can't promise that," Cholmondeley said. "You know I can't. But I can promise that I'll at least do my best. Is that good enough?"

"It'll have to do."

*   *   *

Jack Cholmondeley returned to work the following day, and it didn't take him long to make first contact. He'd been given his office back, and he was spending his lunchtime having a tidy and taking down his photos of him and Mary when there was a knock at the door.

"Come in," he said.

The door swung open and Sergeant Joe Riggs from the forensics team entered the room, scanning the corridor behind him before he closed the door as though making sure that the two of them were alone. For a brief, hallucinatory moment, Cholmondeley pictured a weapon in the man's hand. It would be ironic if his life were to end with him being murdered inside the Old Vic.

"Welcome back, Jack," Riggs said. "How are things?"

"Can't complain," Cholmondeley replied, in a tone that sounded as though he wanted to do just that. "Some bugger's been in my office, moving my files around."

"Well, we didn't know if you were coming back," Riggs said. He sat down on a chair on the other side of Cholmondeley's desk and then looked around the room as though expecting something to climb out of the walls and attack him. "We had your office swept and we're pretty sure it's free of bugs and devices. We should be able to talk freely here."

"Yes?" Cholmondeley replied. "About what?"

"The Boys in Blue," Riggs said. "We want you to join us."

A tense silence descended and Cholmondeley took a moment to appraise Riggs and take stock of him. The two of them had worked together before, though it was infrequent. Riggs was of the newer breed of cops that understood technology and knew how to put it to work for them. They were a world away from the old school cops like Jack Cholmondeley, who'd earned their stripes from walking the beat and getting to know the community.

Riggs was a handsome man in his mid-thirties with designer stubble and short hair that was styled with some product or other so that he always looked windswept. Cholmondeley was aware of his reputation as a manly man, a tough guy who'd had a rough upbringing and come out the other side. In charge of coordinating crime scene investigations and cleanups, he'd seen things throughout his career that lesser men would have been unable to deal with. Cholmondeley couldn't help wondering how the guy slept at night.

Cholmondeley had once heard someone remark that it was a good job that Riggs was on their side of the law, because if he'd been a criminal, he would've been good at it. And now it seemed that the man was a recruiting officer for the Boys in Blue.

Cholmondeley chose his words carefully.

"You want me to join the Boys in Blue?"

"Not me personally," Riggs said. "I'm just the messenger. But yes, that's the gist of it."

"What's in it for me?" Cholmondeley asked.

"Power," Riggs replied. "Power and money."

"Ah," Cholmondeley said. "You should have said."

"We're offering you a flat million for your first assignment."

Cholmondeley whistled and said, "That's a lot of money."

"That's the carrot," Riggs said. "Then there's the stick."

"The stick?"

"You saw what we did to Constable Groves," Riggs replied. "That was just to send you a warning. Imagine what we could do if we had to make a serious statement."

"I'm listening."

"How's your wife, Jack?"

"She's soon to be my ex-wife," Cholmondeley replied.

"If you don't do what we say, you'll be a widower before she gets a chance to serve you with your papers."

"Are you threatening me?"

"Does the Pope shit in the woods?"

"That's a mixed metaphor," Cholmondeley said. "But I understand what you're trying to tell me. Let's say that hypothetically, I accept your offer. How do I sign up?""

"It's not as simple as that," Riggs explained. "You'll have to pass the initiation. If you do that, you'll get your money. We'll also give you a login to our discussion forum and a decryption list so you know who's behind the usernames."

"That all sounds too complicated for me, Riggs," Cholmondeley replied. "I might need a little help to wrap my head around the techie side."

"I'll see what I can do, Jack," Riggs said. "And in the meantime, there's your initiation. It's fairly simple. I want you to kill James Leipfold."

*   *   *

It was a couple of days later, and James Leipfold was lying in a pool of blood, sprawled out on his office floor. He looked peaceful, almost as though he was sleeping.

There was a baseball bat on the floor beside him, which had been wrapped in barbed wire and was covered with gore and viscera. There was a corresponding lump on the back of Leipfold's head, though it was mostly concealed because of the way that his body was laying on the floor. The blood had seeped into the carpet and stained it a deep crimson.

Detective Inspector Jack Cholmondeley was standing over the body, looking down at his old friend with an expression of sympathy and regret on his face. He reached into his pocket and withdrew his mobile phone, then took a few snaps of the corpse from different angles, along with another one of the murder weapon. Then he sent them to Riggs' burner phone and waited for a response.

His phone buzzed into life a minute or so later.

"Jack Cholmondeley," he said, by way of introduction.

"It's me," Riggs replied. "Nice work, Jack. Did anyone see you?"

"No," Cholmondeley said. "I kept my eye on the place and waited until he was alone. I told him it was a social visit and he let me in. Then I waited until his back was turned, took the bat out of my bag and started swinging."

"Is he dead?"

"What do you think?"

"Excellent," Riggs replied. "Okay, Jack, get the hell out of there. You'll find an envelope attached to the bottom of your car, and that will contain your login and your next instructions. We'll wait for someone to find him and to call it in. You'll get your pay once my team has processed the crime scene and trashed any evidence you left behind."

* * *

Sergeant Gary Mogford and Constable Steve Cohen were the first responders to the incident at Leipfold's office, and they quickly pronounced the scene secure and called in forensics. Then they stayed at the office until Riggs and his team arrived.

The forensics man paid no attention to Bram Shakespeare or Maile O'Hara, other than to briefly nod at them after they let him in. It wasn't his job to deal with the witnesses, the unfortunate friends and family members who found the victims. It was his job to process the crime scene, and that was exactly what he planned to do.

He led the way up the narrow staircase with two of his colleagues behind him. Mogford and Cohen were standing just outside the door to the office, and they stepped aside once Riggs flashed his police ID. Riggs went in first, and his two colleagues followed behind shortly afterwards. One of them was holding a camera, which he was using to snap photos of the scene. The other was carrying the forensics kit. All three of them were dressed from head-to-toe in PPE gear.

"Where first, boss?"

"Let's start with the body," Riggs said. "I want you to document where it's lying and to prep it for transit to the morgue."

"Don't do that," Leipfold said. "I hear it's cold there."

Riggs swore, and the man with the DSLR was so shocked that he took a couple of steps backwards and tripped over a chair, dropping the camera as he went. The other forensic investigator simply froze.

James Leipfold pulled himself to his feet.

"Not quite what you expected, Mr. Riggs?"

"I should've known we'd be double-crossed," he said. "But you won't take me down without a fight. I guess if you want a job done properly, you need to do it yourself."

Riggs' hand went to his sides, and he ripped open his PPE gear and pulled a hidden pistol from a holster. Then he levelled it out and pointed it at Leipfold's head.

But that was as far as he got, because that was the moment Jack Cholmondeley shouted Riggs' name, causing him to spin around towards the coat rack behind the door, where the old cop had been hiding. The barrel of the gun swung around again, but before he had a chance to squeeze the trigger, Constable Cohen had burst through the door and thrown himself at Riggs' legs.

Sergeant Mogford was hot on his heels, although he was pushed back when the gun went off and struck the plaster, a foot or so to the right of his head.

And then Leipfold was there, kicking Riggs in the hand and sending his gun scattering across the floor. Riggs fought back like a lion trying to avoid captivity, but without his weapon, he was quickly overpowered while the other two forensic officers watched on. They didn't lift a hand to help him.

"I'm not sure if your little friends are with the Boys in Blue or not," Mogford said, wheezing slightly from exertion even though he was the one who'd done the least. "We'll carry out a full investigation, of course. But I'll be sure to note that they didn't get in the way of an officer carrying out his duty."

"I'm a cop too, you asshole."

"I *hate* bent cops," Mogford grunted. He drew back a foot and kicked Riggs in the stomach, knocking the air out of him.

"Easy now, Gary," Cholmondeley said. "And now, if you'd be so good as to lend me your cuffs."

Mogford grunted again and took his handcuffs from his belt, then passed them across to Cholmondeley.

"Joseph Riggs," Cholmondeley said, slipping the cuffs around his wrists, which were being held behind his back by Constable Cohen and a gore-covered James Leipfold. "I'm arresting you on suspicion of solicitation to murder. You do not have to say anything, but it may harm your defence if you do not mention when questioned something which you later rely on in court. Anything you do say may be given in evidence."

He paused and then flashed a grin at Leipfold.

Then he added, "We've got you now, Sonny Jim."

* * *

After the cops left, Leipfold and the gang had a debriefing.

"That went well," Leipfold said.

"Yeah," Bram replied. "Better than expected."

"Kat did a great job with the makeup," Maile said. "I knew she was good, but I didn't know she was that good."

"It's remarkable what you can do with a half-gallon of pig blood, some papier mâché and a heck of a lot of makeup," Leipfold replied. "Although I must admit, I doubt I'll be eating a bacon sandwich anytime soon."

"It was good of Jack Cholmondeley to give us the heads up," Bram said. "Imagine what could have happened if he'd actually taken the Boys in Blue up on their offer."

"He never would have," Leipfold replied. "He'd rather die than disgrace his badge. They should have known that. Instead, they gave us the bait we needed to set a trap for them."

"And the trap worked," Maile said. "At least, to an extent. Did Jack get the information we needed?"

"Yeah," Leipfold replied. "A list of names and usernames that shows corruption amongst the ranks of the cops at the Old Vic. I've got a copy of it here."

He reached into his jacket and withdrew a nondescript manila envelope, then slid it across the table to Maile.

"When we're done here," Leipfold continued, "I want you to take this document and cross-reference it with the research we've already done. Then you can add it to our data dump and get ready to release it. And quickly, mind. We're going to release the dossier in time for tomorrow's news cycle. Any questions?"

"Yeah," Bram said. "I've got one. Did Jack Cholmondeley get his money?"

Leipfold laughed and shook his head.

Chapter Twenty:
The Calm Before the Storm

LEIPFOLD HELD HIS MEETING that night, under the cover of darkness. There was a reason for that. They were due to dump their data at midnight, and as soon as their evidence went live, there'd be hell to pay. Secrecy was paramount, especially on the run up to the release. But he also needed some help from the press.

"Thanks for coming," Leipfold said, ushering Alan Phelps and Siobhan Dent into the office. It looked as though Dent had recently had her hair done, while Phelps was wearing a garish pink tie which Leipfold surmised had probably been a Christmas gift from someone who didn't like him. "I'll keep this brief."

"Good," Dent said. "I was supposed to be going out for dinner tonight."

"I'll make it worth your while," Leipfold said. "If you want, I'll give you a fiver so you can get a kebab."

"I'd rather eat my own hand," Dent said.

Leipfold grinned and gestured for her and Phelps to make themselves more comfortable. As for himself, he sat down heavily in his chair and then leaned back on it, putting his feet up on the desk.

"Hurry up, James," Dent said. "I don't want to be stuck here all night."

"Indeed," Leipfold said. "Well, it's like this. I've brought you here to talk about the Boys in Blue."

He'd been working the case for long enough that he wasn't surprised when they automatically looked up and around, as though the Boys in Blue could be summoned by the mere mention of their name.

"It's like this," Leipfold said. "My team has been working on a comprehensive investigation and we're dumping the results at midnight. I wanted you and *The Tribune* to have first refusal on the story."

"What story?"

"We have dozens of coppers bang to rights," Leipfold said. "Most of them are guilty of corruption, taking bribes to turn a blind eye or dropping charges. We also have some confirmed cases of human trafficking for the purposes of prostitution and the production of pornography. Oh, and the home secretary is in a private hospital bed after being hit by Jack Cholmondeley's car."

"Who was behind the wheel?"

"One of the women that he's been routing through a human trafficking ring," Leipfold said. His voice was a low rumble, making him sound like an angry animal that was trapped inside a cage. "My team has provided a dossier with all of the highlights. This is big, Siobhan."

"Call me Ms. Dent, please."

"Fine," Leipfold said. "I'll call you Lonnie Donnegan if it'll make you happy. The point is, we've got the data, we've got the names, and we've got the evidence we need to nail these bastards. As I see it, you've got a choice to make."

"A choice?" Phelps asked.

"You can side with the Boys in Blue and suppress publication," Leipfold said. "You might buy them some time, but the truth will out eventually."

"Citizen journalism," Phelps murmured.

"Your other option is to run the story first," Leipfold continued. "You could publish an exposé. You could take our data and run with it. You could even publish a special issue."

"And paint a bullseye on our chests?"

"The Boys in Blue are only a threat if they maintain their hold on power," Leipfold said. "But the balance of power is shifting. It's time for you to pick a side."

Dent shook her head slowly, and Phelps stared gloomily at the floor, biting his fingernails. Leipfold watched them impassively, his inscrutable eyes boring holes into their defences. Then he loaded up a picture on his smartphone and showed it to them.

"Who's that?" Dent asked.

"It's Constable Jenny Groves," Leipfold replied. "She's a policewoman who was shot and nearly killed by the Boys in Blue. She'll be in recovery for months. If you won't do this for me, do it for her."

"If she was a warning, what will they do to us if we run the story?" Phelps asked.

"Sometimes, good people have to put themselves at risk if they want to do what's right," Dent replied. She paused. "You've given me a lot to think about, Mr. Leipfold."

"Better think fast," Leipfold said. "You've only got a few hours until we publish the data."

*   *   *

The data went live with little fanfare, and Leipfold spent the night pacing up and down in his office, expecting it to be raided by the Boys in Blue at a moment's notice.

By the time that the sun rose and his employees came into the office for the day, the news had started to spread. Maile checked the analytics as soon as she came into the office and found that it had been accessed 67,000 times.

"That's not bad," Leipfold said, "but it could be better. Has anyone seen *The Tribune* this morning?"

"I've seen their website," Maile said.

"And I've got the paper here," Cholmondeley added.

"And?" Leipfold asked. "Did they cover it?"

"You're damn right they did," Maile said. "It's all over the front page, and their breaking news section is still being updated."

"I've been checking out their feeds on social media," Bram added. "I sent Dent a direct message to get the lowdown. She ignored me at first, but then I told her who I work for and once she was satisfied that I was who I said I was, she was happy to give me some info. Dent and Phelps stayed up all night at the office. They've hired private security to keep the place safe. Maybe we should do the same."

"We don't need to," Leipfold said. "You've still got your nightstick. But security is, of course, a concern."

"So what are we going to do?" Cholmondeley asked. "Don't tell me you're planning on getting a gun. I know you can handle those things, James, but I—"

"Relax," Leipfold said, holding his hand up. He nodded at Bram and then looked towards the kettle, and that was as good as a verbal instruction. Bram sighed but rolled obediently over towards it.

"I'll relax once I know we're safe," Cholmondeley said. "A cup of tea isn't going to lull me into a false sense of security, if that's what you're hoping for."

"Of course not," Leipfold said. "Don't you worry about me, Jack. Maile bought me a taser."

"From the dark web," she murmured.

"Besides," Leipfold continued, "it's not us I'm worried about."

"Oh?"

"Constable Groves," Leipfold said. "Where is she?"

"She's at her mother's," Cholmondeley replied. "Somewhere in Croydon, I believe. Not much of a garden, but I hear the rehabilitation is going well. Why do you ask?"

"Isn't it obvious?" Leipfold asked. "If they want to threaten us, they'll go for her."

"Then we need to go and protect her."

* * *

In the end, they decided to split into teams. Maile and Bram were in charge of keeping tabs on the data and using anonymous email accounts to send further updates to key journalists, though they had better success with some than with others.

Cholmondeley was in charge of protecting Constable Groves, who'd been remarkably receptive to the idea. Her mother's house was an old Georgian affair with a couple of spare bedrooms, and she was more than happy to welcome the old cop into her house once she learned who he was and why he was there.

Leipfold, meanwhile, was running security at the office. The builders had finally finished, and so he spent most of Thursday morning pacing around the building and looking for weaknesses. Maile had done her part by ordering a bunch of cameras and setting them up around the office, but that wasn't enough to satisfy him. Even after she'd assured him that they were hooked up to a private network and that they couldn't be accessed without the proper password, Leipfold had been unconvinced.

"Technology's like a woman," Leipfold had said. "You can't live with it. You can't live without it."

"How old-fashioned."

Cholmondeley had called into the office to deliver an update, explaining that he'd arrived safely in Croydon and that he was in place to protect Constable Groves and her mother if the Boys in Blue made a move. He wasn't armed, despite Leipfold's insistence that he should protect himself somehow, but they were hoping that wouldn't be necessary.

"It's not a bad gaff, you know, James," Cholmondeley said,

when they all gathered at Leipfold's office to catch up over a video call. "Better than my place, at least. And Mrs Groves is lovely, a very generous woman."

"Any sign of the Boys in Blue?"

"Not yet," Cholmondeley said. "But I have news from Constable Richards. She's not very happy with you, James, although she doesn't know it."

"What do you mean?"

"She doesn't know it was you who published the data," Cholmondeley explained. "Although she has her suspicions. You might want to make sure that she never finds out."

"I'll do my best," Leipfold replied. "How did she take it?"

"It's unbelievable, James," Cholmondeley said. "I've never seen anything like it. She's pulled out all the stops and called for a wide-scale internal review. Last I heard, there'd been a whole bunch of raids. Dawn raids, you understand. All over the country."

"She's going to be busy for a while, then," Leipfold said. "Any results?"

"It's too soon to tell," Cholmondeley replied. "But let's just say that we went in hard and fast. We're talking dozens of raids and hundreds of arrests. It's all going to come out in the open, James. They can't hush this up, even if they do have a hold on the newspapers."

"Then it's as good as over," Leipfold said. "And they'll know it just as much as we do."

"Watch yourself, James," Cholmondeley cautioned. "They won't go down without a fight."

"I know," Leipfold said. "That's why you're staying with Constable Groves. You stay safe, Jack. And keep us updated. This is the calm before the storm, you mark my words."

*   *   *

That night, a storm came.

It was a vicious, sapient storm, the kind of tempest that belonged in a Shakespeare play and not on the streets of London. The people ran from doorway to doorway, seeking some kind of shelter against the inclement winds and the angry rain, and a leak sprung up in the ceiling and started pouring water down on to Leipfold's desk.

Ever the pragmatist, he moved his desk six feet to the right and put a bucket there.

He wasn't the only one in the office. Maile was there too, and so was Bram, though Leipfold had told him he could stay at home. Maile and Leipfold were the public faces of the company, and Bram was new enough to stay under the radar…maybe.

"I'd rather take my chances at the office," he said. "You guys need looking after."

"You've brought your nightstick, then," Leipfold said.

Bram nodded.

It was a little after midnight when they heard the noise. The office was just off a side-street, and so even in the middle of London, there wasn't much passing traffic. That meant that when a motor pulled up outside, all three of them picked up on it. They listened in silence as the engine was turned off and then a car door was opened and closed. Leipfold's eyes met Maile's and he saw his own excitement reflected there.

Then the buzzer rang and all three of them almost leapt out of their seats.

Leipfold scooched over to the buzzer and picked up the handset. "Hello?"

"James, it's me," his visitor replied. "Let me in."

"No," Leipfold said. "You're the enemy."

"Yes, well, sort of."

"Are you alone?"

"Yes."

"Then I'll buzz you up."

Leipfold had an uncomfortable feeling in his stomach, but he could also see from the camera setup that Mike Croft was telling the truth and that he was out there alone. That meant that it was three against one.

"Maile," Leipfold said. "Set up the live stream. I want a feed going out from our security cameras, inside and out, by the time that Croft gets up here."

"On it, boss," Maile said.

Leipfold smiled darkly. He'd briefed Bram and Maile on this when they'd first formed their war council. The goal was to make their security cameras public domain, at least if they thought they were under threat. That way, if it was a false alarm, they could cut the feeds. And if it wasn't, they'd leave some sign behind to tell the tale of what had happened.

Leipfold, Maile and Bram gathered around Leipfold's desk, Bram nearly spilling the bucket of rainwater in his haste to get over to the screen. The three of them watched as Mike Croft let himself into the building and climbed the steps towards Leipfold's office. Then he opened the door and let himself in.

He looked like he hadn't slept for months, and he'd been soaked by the storm and resembled a rat who'd fallen down a drain. Leipfold made no move towards him, so he took off his coat and hung it. The rain was still dribbling down its sleeves and pooling on the floor.

"Should I go and get another bucket, boss?"

"No, Maile," Leipfold said. "Let it drip. We've got business to attend to."

He backed away from his desk and stood up to his full, less-than-formidable height, then took a couple of steps towards the centre of the room. Outside, the storm was still howling, and a bolt of lightning lit the room for a split second and was gone, followed shortly afterwards by a roll of thunder that sounded like a harbinger of the apocalypse.

"So, you're here," Leipfold said. "You know what we've done, then."

"Yes," Croft said. "I know. And so do the Boys in Blue."

Leipfold shrugged and said, "They don't scare me."

"Yeah!" Maile exclaimed. "You tell him, boss."

"Do you treat all of your clients like this?"

"Some of them," Leipfold said. "It depends whether I suspect them of working for some shady organisation."

"I won't be working for them much longer, Mr. Leipfold," Croft said. "The shit has hit the proverbial fan."

Leipfold looked at him suspiciously, then glanced back to look at Bram and Maile, who were watching the proceedings with tense faces. Maile flashed him a weak thumbs up and he winked at her. Then he turned back round.

"Okay," Leipfold said, clapping his hands together. "How about you tell me why you're here?"

"I'm here to warn you," Croft said. "You need to get the hell out of here while you still can. They're coming for you. They're coming for me, too. They're coming for all of us."

"Who are you?" Leipfold asked. "I mean, who are you *really*?"

"Wouldn't you like to know?" Croft replied. He shook his head and chuckled to himself. "You'll find out soon enough."

* * *

Mike Croft lurked around at the office for another hour or so, and Bram even made the man a cup of green tea, but he didn't have any new information for them. In fact, Leipfold got the impression that he knew less than they did, although that wasn't saying much. Their dossier was complete.

When he finally left, Leipfold told Maile and Bram to get some sleep. Maile curled up in a sleeping bag on the office floor, while Bram took the sofa. Leipfold spent most of the night at his desk, multitasking by reading a book and watching the security cameras at the same time. He was almost expecting someone to shove a firebomb through the letterbox, but that didn't seem like the enemy's style.

Their retribution, whenever it came, would be subtle and brutal.

When the morning came and Leipfold Investigations opened for business, all three of them were sluggish and grumpy. By 9 AM, Bram had fallen asleep in his chair and Maile had developed the caffeine shakes after drinking three cans of Monster.

There was a buzz at the door at a quarter to ten that woke Bram and sent Maile tumbling from her chair. Leipfold had been expecting it, but even he was surprised. He looked at the camera feed, saw who it was and buzzed them in.

"Ah," Leipfold said, opening the door to his office before they had chance to knock. Behind him, Bram was rubbing the sleep from his eyes and Maile was trying (and failing) to stash their sleeping bags down the back of Leipfold's filing cabinets. "It's good to see you, Constable Cohen. To what do I owe the pleasure?"

"It's an official visit, I'm afraid, Mr. Leipfold," Constable Cohen said, strolling into the office with more confidence than usual. Leipfold guessed that was good news and that the raids on the Boys in Blue had gone as planned. If they hadn't, Cohen would be out of a job, assuming they didn't just take his life instead.

Leipfold watched Cohen as he slipped a sheaf of papers from a plain white envelope and handed them over to him.

"I'm sorry to be the one to tell you this, James," Cohen said. "I'm here to deliver a Bosman warning."

"What's a Bosman warning?" Maile asked.

"It's bad news," Leipfold said. "But nothing that we weren't expecting. He's here to tell me that the police have reason to believe a credible threat against my life."

"Not just your life, actually," Cohen added. "The whole lot of you are at risk."

"We know," Bram said.

"And yet you're all here anyway," Cohen observed. He looked around the room and flashed a wan smile at Leipfold. "Well, I commend your loyalty. Usually, with a Bosman warning, people ask to go under witness protection. But I guess you guys have already discounted that."

"Got it in one," Leipfold said. He nodded at Bram, who wheeled over to the little kitchenette where Leipfold kept the kettle and flicked the switch on. "Cuppa?"

"No thanks, James," Cohen said. "Must dash. You wouldn't catch me dead around here. Let's hope we can say the same about you, eh?"

"Charming."

"Oh," Cohen said, walking back towards the door. There was no need for him to pick his coat up because he hadn't taken it off. "One more thing. Gary Mogford is worried."

"About me?" Leipfold asked, his expression deadpan. "That's kind of him."

"You know what he's like," Cohen said. "It's not you that he's worried about, Mr. Leipfold. He's worried about his career. He reckons we're moving too quickly and that we're going to overstretch ourselves. He makes a good point. If we bust any more bent cops, we're going to run out of policemen."

✴   ✴   ✴

The attack came on Friday night, when half the country was out getting pissed while the other half slumbered on. It was the great dichotomy: to drink or not to drink, that was the question.

Jack Cholmondeley could have quite happily gone for a scotch on the rocks, but he had work to do.

Constable Groves was still convalescing, spending most of her time on the sofa or in her bed, and her mother was old and physically handicapped thanks to obesity and a gammy knee. They'd both been happy to have Cholmondeley around the place, even though they thought the whole thing was unnecessary, and Cholmondeley was happy to be there.

He was even happier to be there when he heard the tell-tale tinkle of broken glass.

It was the sound of trouble and reminded him of barroom brawls and riots. In that particular case, the sound was quiet and subtle, just on the edge of his hearing. It wasn't the sound of a rock being thrown through a window.

It was the sound of someone delicately chiselling a hole in some glass.

Cholmondeley looked around and took stock of the situation. He was on a sofa bed in the living room, smack bang in the middle of the building. The Groveses had been more than happy for him to take one of the spare rooms, but Cholmondeley had insisted on taking the living room so that he was better placed to protect them and to listen out for intruders. Groves and her mother were upstairs in their respective bedrooms. The sound of the glass had come from above him, probably from the bathroom.

He pulled himself wearily up from the sofa bed and picked up his truncheon. A keepsake from the good old days when he'd first joined the force, it was made of solid oak and had seen several years of service before it had been upgraded for a more modern alternative. Cholmondeley had been allowed to keep it as a souvenir. He'd never expected to use it again.

He held it there in his right hand, testing its weight and swinging it casually into his palm. Then he started climbing the stairs in the darkness, dodging the sticky step that always creaked beneath his weight and holding his breath as though it could stop him from exposing himself.

He reached the top of the stairs a little too late, and the intruders—for there were two of them—reached the turning by the banister first. Cholmondeley reacted on instinct, doing the only thing he could think of. He reached out and grabbed one of their legs as they passed, then yanked backwards and sent the trespasser tumbling to the floor. He hit it hard and bounced as he did so, pirouetting in the air and hitting the stairs behind Cholmondeley.

At the same time, Cholmondeley bellowed the first thing that he thought of.

"Right, you horrible little shit-splat, I'll fuckin' 'ave ya!"

It wasn't very Jack Cholmondeley, but it didn't have to be. It was a tactic that he'd borrowed from the SWAT teams, standard shock and awe. He was banking on the fact that whoever he was dealing with would be so surprised by the sudden shout that they wouldn't process what he was saying. He was also banking on it waking up Groves and her mother.

Cholmondeley didn't pause to see what happened to the guy who rolled down the stairs, instead propelling himself forwards and up the rest of the stairs on to the landing. He glanced quickly at the shadow in front of him and saw enough of an outline to lower his head and to charge straight at him, spearing him and driving him against the wall. Both men grunted as they hit it, and then they were at each other with their fists and their feet in the darkness.

A light came on from Groves' room, and it shone out from beneath the door. There wasn't much of it, but there was enough for Cholmondeley to get a better look at what he was dealing with. He'd fallen back, and his opponent was pulling himself to his feet. Cholmondeley whipped his truncheon through the air and made contact with his opponent's knee.

The man went down in a tangle of bruised bone, but there was no respite for Jack Cholmondeley. The first man had picked himself back up and grabbed Cholmondeley's foot. He pulled at it and Cholmondeley hit the deck, but then he lashed out with his foot and heard a grunt as his heavy boot connected with something.

The light grew in intensity as one of the doors opened and Constable Groves stuck her head out into the corridor. Cholmondeley turned and made eye contact with her, and then she slammed the door closed again and pushed her back against it, as Cholmondeley had briefed her to do. He could hear her talking from the other side of the wall and knew that she'd called the cops, though it wouldn't do them much good. By the time that they arrived, the situation would have been resolved, one way or another. And who was to say that the Boys in Blue wouldn't make a move on them?

Cholmondeley kicked out again, though he didn't connect with anything, and then he looked up to the top of the stairs and saw that his other opponent was climbing to his feet. Cholmondeley thought fast and whipped out his nightstick again, catching the other guy in his good foot. Soon, all three men were on the ground, fighting fist to mouth and scrambling desperately for purchase.

Then there was a sound like a coconut being opened with a machete, and one of the men became a dead weight across him. Another coconut was opened and then the other guy was down, too.

Jack Cholmondeley crawled out from beneath them and looked up. Constable Groves' frail-looking, elderly mother was looming above him with a metal poker in her hand.

"I thought you might need some assistance," she said.

"Thanks," Cholmondeley replied. "Let's just hope you didn't hit them too hard. I want to ask them a couple of questions before the police get here."

* * *

Cholmondeley got to ask his questions, but only of one of them. The other guy was still unconscious. When they raised the lights, they saw he was bleeding freely from a deep gash to his eyebrow. Cholmondeley asked Mrs Groves to fetch a cold compress from the bathroom, but that was as far as he dared push it. Sure, there were two men down, but there was a good chance that there were more of them.

The cops took twenty minutes to arrive, and that was plenty of time for Cholmondeley to ask his questions, though he didn't get any answers. It was the old army trick of answering only with name and rank, except that the young man with the cut on his head would only give them the same four words: "They're gonna get you."

"I'm sure they are," Cholmondeley replied. "But not today, Sonny Jim."

Groves had pulled a few strings back at the station and ensured that Sergeant Mogford was overseeing the first responders. As luck would have it, he'd been on duty when the call came in, and he and Constable Cohen had been the first on the scene.

"Fancy seeing you here, Jack," Mogford said, his voice gruff and unperturbed. "A break-in, you say?"

"Aye," Cholmondeley replied. "The Boys in Blue."

They were standing in Mrs Groves' living room, and the place was looking pretty crowded. Coppers were standing shoulder-to-shoulder with paramedics, and any chance at forensics was well and truly shot.

"So what happened?" Mogford asked.

"How long have you got?" Cholmondeley replied. "Perhaps we'd better take this back to the Old Vic?"

"No," Mogford said. "The walls have ears there. I assume you've swept this place for bugs?"

"Something like that," Cholmondeley said. "I had a little look round, at any rate."

"That will have to do," Mogford said, looking cautiously around the room and then making eye contact with Jack Cholmondeley.

"Listen, Jack. We've got Terence Rowbotham in for interviews. He's refusing to talk, but I've seen your files and I'm convinced we've got enough to take the bastard down."

"He'll talk eventually," Cholmondeley said. "He'll do whatever he has to do to save his own neck."

"He did say one thing," Mogford replied, stroking his chin absentmindedly. "He told us that we're making a mistake and that we're pulling the tail of a sleeping tiger."

"Of course," Cholmondeley said. "How else are we supposed to wake it?"

"I hope you know what you're doing, Jack," Mogford said. He had a sour expression on his face and looked as though he was wracked with doubt. "I promise you. We're going to do everything we can to take these bastards down. We've not always seen eye to eye on things, but I think we can agree on this. One rotten apple spoils the bunch, Jack."

"Then we'd better take out the rotten apples," Cholmondeley replied. "You got my list?"

Mogford nodded and said, "Yeah, thanks to Constable Cohen."

"Give that boy a promotion," Cholmondeley said. "He's one of the few good apples you've got left."

Mogford grunted and scowled at the floor.

"We'll have to see if this actually works," he said. "If it doesn't, we're all screwed. A promotion will be the least of anyone's worries."

Chapter Twenty-One:
A Household Name

ON FRIDAY MORNING, THE prime minister hosted a press conference.

He had a habit of doing that, and so the journalists on the scene were the unlucky ones, those who'd drawn the short straw. Since being elected into office, the prime minister had averaged two press conferences a week, mostly to champion his party and to talk about all of the good they were doing. It was all the usual propaganda, but it helped to feed the great content machines behind the tabloid press and to give the illusion of progress, even when the country was just steering itself blindly into the future.

But this press conference was different, in tone as well as in subject matter. The PM was being escorted at either elbow by harsh-looking bodyguards with radios strapped to their belts, and he was making his announcement from inside Downing Street.

Maile O'Hara was watching it all unfold from her office. She had her desk in standing mode and was staring at the live feed as it came through her monitor while holding her hands behind her back. She looked like a judgmental schoolmistress in front of an unruly class, but that suited her just fine. If Bram saw her through the glass partition, he'd know from her posture to leave her in peace.

"…and so it's with a heavy heart that I come to you today," the PM was saying. "Unfortunately, there are enemies of democracy out there who seek to undermine the fundamentals of our society. Honesty. Decency. Compassion. These are what we thrive on."

Maile scoffed into her coffee.

"That's why I'm announcing a new task force," he continued, as Maile watched the feed with a look like thunder across her brow. "It's time for us to take a stand against corruption. My advisors have informed me that a dossier has been released which implicates many senior members of the Metropolitan Police Force, as well as several high-ranking members of the British Army and numerous executives in positions of power within the news media, in a number of crimes ranging from impersonation and petty theft to murder."

Maile scoffed again and checked her pulse, then started pacing backwards and forwards in front of her desk to burn some of the anger out. She'd always had a healthy disdain for authority figures, but the PM took the biscuit. And he looked like a piece of ham that had been left out in the sun.

"It's my pledge to you, the British public, that I'll stamp out this corruption," the prime minister continued. "No longer will our country be run by the so-called Boys in Blue. No longer will elitism rule the roost. No longer will our society by led blindly by greed and nepotism."

"Speak for yourself," Maile murmured. She found herself fighting a sudden urge to book a new tattoo of the Soviet hammer and sickle. "You went to Eton."

"I'd also like to thank a member of the public who was relentless in his pursuit of the truth," the prime minister continued. "James Leipfold, if you're listening, I want you to know that the nation is grateful."

"Holy shit," Maile murmured, muting the feed and scrabbling in her handbag for her phone. She navigated through her contacts list to Leipfold's number and pressed the dial button, then smiled to herself as she heard it vibrating through his desk and down through the floorboards.

"Leipfold," he said.

"Boss, you've got to see this," Maile replied, not wasting any time on pleasantries. "You'd better, uh, step into my office."

* * *

"Christ," Leipfold said, rubbing his chin and staring thoughtfully into space.

"Yeah."

"That's some crazy shit," Bram added, helpfully.

"Do you hear that?" Leipfold asked.

"No," Maile said.

"Exactly," Leipfold replied. "It's quiet out there."

"What's your point?"

"It won't be for long," Leipfold said. "We're at the centre of a shitstorm, Maile. I hope you weren't planning on popping down to the shops."

Leipfold's prediction came true around ten minutes later, when the paparazzi started to arrive. He'd taken the precaution of locking the front door and pulling the blinds over the windows, but it was hard to ignore them. There must have been at least three dozen of them, swarming the office from both sides and making Balcombe Street look more like Oxford Street.

They took the intercom off the hook shortly afterwards, when it quickly became apparent that they weren't going to stop attacking the thing until someone answered. Maile put some music on downstairs and Leipfold locked himself up in his office, but the commotion outside was continuing to grow. When he skived off for ten minutes to dip some ginger biscuits into a cup of tea, he found his own front doors were splashed all over the news sites.

"It's crazy out there, boss," Maile said, when the three of them downed tools for their afternoon update. They'd just heard from Jack Cholmondeley, who was still at the Groves place and who'd been watching the situation unfolding on the news. The cops had arranged for a couple of extra patrols, but Cholmondeley was still worried that the Boys in Blue would return to finish the job. "You're going to have to do something."

"You're probably right," Leipfold said, staring introspectively into his coffee. He sighed and reached a decision, then stood up and strolled over to his jacket, which was folded over the back of one of the chairs in the downstairs reception. "I'd better go out there."

"That's not exactly what I had in mind."

"Don't worry," Leipfold said, flashing his confident grin and looking for all the world like a used car salesman patting the hood of a lemon. "I know what I'm doing."

Inside, he wasn't so sure, but he'd been reading a book on self-actualisation and figured it was time to put it to the test. If he acted confident, perhaps that confidence would rub off. He just needed to not think about the high rooftops and how easy it would be for a trained sniper to put a bullet through his eyes.

When he opened the front door of the office, he was almost knocked back inside by the press of people. He had to push against them to work his way out, and once the door had closed behind him, he was left with an uncomfortable feeling that reminded him of being at the front of a mosh pit at a heavy metal concert. He could smell half a dozen different brands of breath mint.

He held his hands up as an array of microphones was thrust in front of him.

"Let me guess," he said. "You guys want to ask me some questions."

A dozen different sentences were thrown towards him all at once, and even with his aptitude for multi-tasking, he struggled to take it all in. There were dozens of microphones and almost as many cameras, as well as enough journalists to fill out a moderately sized local paper.

"I think—" Leipfold said, and then it happened.

He noticed movement out of the corner of his eye and was already turning when one of the journalists reached into his coat pocket. Leipfold was worried that he had a firearm, and so he was relieved when the hand came out with a knife. It was a twelve-incher, a mean-looking thing that would have looked out of place in a kitchen drawer. The guy was six feet away from Leipfold and there was a press of bodies all around them, but he pushed through and came up by the microphones at the makeshift podium.

His assailant took a swipe at him, but Leipfold moved like a cat in the night and as he fell backwards, the blade tore harmlessly through his leather jacket and was turned away before it met his flesh. At the same time, Leipfold grabbed the guy's arm and bent it backwards, shoving his shoulder into his midriff and sending him tumbling over. Leipfold's leg was behind the knifeman, and he swept him over it, then moved towards him while he was still tumbling through the air. As the attacker threw his arms out to break his fall, Leipfold zeroed in on him and stamped on his hand until the knuckles cracked and the knife went skidding uselessly aside.

While all of this was happening, the crowd had pulled back, but they were soon pushing forwards again and Leipfold was scanning them for further threats. He backed up first behind the podium and then all the way to the door. The journalists surging towards him reminded him of zombies in some 1950s B-movie.

He looked around desperately, knowing that they were too close for him to find his key and slip back inside the office. He didn't know if there were any other would-be assassins in the mass of flesh, but he didn't want to take the chance.

Then a siren pierced the air and the crowd started to scatter, especially after a familiar voice came over a megaphone. Constable Cohen was ordering the crowd to disperse, and while Leipfold couldn't make out where the car was, it was comforting to know that he had an ally, especially one with the full might of the law behind him.

A minute later, when Cohen was finally at Leipfold's side, only a couple dozen journalists were left, at least in the ten square metres outside Leipfold's door. The rest had retreated to a more sensible distance, but they were still watching like hawks in case a story developed, which was looking increasingly likely.

Three of the journalists had joined Leipfold in holding his assailant under citizen's arrest, although it didn't look as though their help was needed. The man was still curled up on the floor in a parody of a maggot, clutching his wounded hand to his chest. If he really was a journalist, he wouldn't be writing any copy for a while.

"What happened?" Cohen asked.

Leipfold eyed him warily, then looked at the copper beside him. She was a youngish woman with fierce eyes. Leipfold had never seen her before, but the fact that she was with Constable Cohen was enough of a recommendation for him.

"Better ask him," Leipfold said, nodding at the man on the floor. "He's the one who pulled the knife on me."

"What happened to his hand?"

"No idea," Leipfold said, innocently. "He's going to need medical attention, though. Can you have him seen to?"

"We can work something out," Cohen said. He had a grim expression on his face that reminded Leipfold of how Jack Cholmondeley had looked when he'd heard about the fates of the women in his building. "I've got a couple of questions to ask him first. We'll start by checking him for ID. Hey, where are you going?"

Leipfold, who'd turned around and who was patting his pockets to find something, smiled to himself and shrugged his shoulders. He answered without bothering to turn around.

"I've got a business to run," he said. "Not to mention a crossword to do and a statement to make to the press. I don't think I'll be answering any of their questions, though."

"What about ours?" Cohen asked.

"You know my number," Leipfold replied, letting himself into the building and being careful to lock and bolt the door behind him.

*   *   *

The phone was ringing off the hook, as it had been all day. Even with both Bram and Maile working the reception, there was only one phone line, and so they took it in turns to field questions from journalists and, on one occasion, to have a lengthy chat with an anonymous source who'd promised further information on the Boys in Blue.

For his part, Leipfold was watching the chaos unfold from his upstairs office, ceaselessly watching the bank of CCTV cameras in case he caught someone trying to set fire to the place. His paranoia had reached new heights, making it worse than it had been back during his drinking days, but this time at least, it felt justified.

True to his word, Leipfold had enlisted Maile to help him film a short video statement, which they'd uploaded to the company's website and which they were directing the journalists to when they called and asked their questions. He wasn't accepting interviews, though.

"But why not?" Maile protested, when he told her about his decision while softening the blow with a lukewarm can of Monster that he'd found inexplicably stashed in one of the filing cabinets. "We should capitalise on this, boss. We should ride the wave of publicity and use it to promote the company."

"Why bother?" Leipfold replied. "We don't need it. We've got more than enough work to go around, and the prime minister's statement gave me the best advertisement I've ever had. The phones haven't stopped ringing."

"Yeah," Maile said. "But that won't last forever. We need to set up some data capture forms and start building a proper mailing list. You should do an AMA or a Q&A, too."

"Stop throwing acronyms at me," Leipfold growled. "You're not helping my headache. Besides, there's a reason why I don't want to answer their questions."

"Because you're a stubborn fool and you insist on doing things your own way?" Maile murmured.

"What was that?"

"Nothing," she said.

"Yes, well," Leipfold continued. "The idea is to preserve an air of mystery and intrigue. It's great for my personal brand, just what the punters like. But there's another idea too, and I think you'll like it."

"Go on."

"I want them to focus on the data," Leipfold said. "If I give interviews and start answering questions, my face will be plastered all over the television but they'll lead with that and not with the information. If I take a back seat now, they'll have no choice. They'll have to tell the full story."

"I wonder," Maile replied. "I think you might be underestimating the press, James. If they don't want to talk about it, they won't."

"Then it's even more important to get the general public on our side," Leipfold said. "Do you know—"

But then the phone rang again, and Maile excused herself to answer it because Bram was in the bathroom. She scooted back over to the reception desk and picked up the phone, then listened to the caller before scribbling something down on a piece of paper and holding her hand over the mouthpiece.

"Boss," Maile said. "You're going to want to take this."

"Who is it?"

"See for yourself," she replied, handing the receiver over to him. Leipfold frowned at her and then held it up to his ear.

"Hello?" he said.

"Ah, James," Cholmondeley replied. "Good of you to take my call. I imagine you're fairly busy. I've got a question for you."

"Fire away," Leipfold said.

"Did I just see you on the telly?" Cholmondeley asked.

*　*　*

The rest of the day passed in a crazy blur. Overnight, James Leipfold had become a household name, but unlike the vacuous celebrities from the reality TV shows who sold their souls for their fifteen minutes, James Leipfold didn't want to be famous. He wanted to be respected, but he also wanted to walk down the street unmolested.

Balcombe Street had been closed off after Jack Cholmondeley had pulled a few strings and arranged for some police protection, but the occasional journalist still slipped through the cordon. The only statement that Leipfold had given was a raised middle finger and something that sounded like it might have been "for coughs."

Meanwhile, the news channels were running the story every hour while political pundits filled in the gaps with their white noise commentary. One of the nationals had announced they'd be releasing a special edition featuring a mixture of Leipfold's data and their own investigations, and after a slight lull in the late morning, the international press picked up on it and Leipfold's name started making its way around Fox News and CNN.

Maile O'Hara was coming under increased scrutiny too, though she'd been expecting it and had locked down her online presence to avoid fuelling the fire. Jack Cholmondeley had been mostly overlooked, which was probably fortunate for his career and his reputation at the Old Vic, while Bram Shakespeare hadn't been mentioned at all.

Leipfold wasn't surprised about that. He'd been at the company for such a short amount of time that they hadn't even added him to the payroll.

The weekend passed in the way that weekends do, though the three of them stayed in the office and survived on delivery pizza and ginger biscuits. Going home was out of the question. There was too much work to do and not enough time to do it in, and besides, there was safety in numbers.

Leipfold didn't tell them about the dead dog he'd found outside the office when he went downstairs on Saturday morning to pick up the paper. Instead, he called Constable Cohen to let him know what he'd found and to draw attention to the gap in their security that had allowed it to happen.

"Sorry, James," Cohen said, his voice sounding lethargic and underscored by horn blasts from impatient drivers as it filtered through Leipfold's smartphone. "We've got a couple of units in your area on standby if anything happens, but we're not a private security firm."

"You told me my life was in danger."

"Exactly," Cohen said. "We served you with a Bosman warning. That's really all we can do unless we catch someone in the act."

"Quite," Leipfold said. "I've always been confused by that. Don't they say that prevention is better than the cure?"

"Yes," Cohen admitted. "I'm not too sure about that myself. Unfortunately, I don't make the rules. Unless a crime is underway or is actively being committed, we're powerless to step in."

"What about attempted murder?"

"You mean the guy with the knife," Cohen said. "He spent the night in the cells and has been in the interrogation room with Sergeant Mogford all morning."

"He won't talk," Leipfold said. "Not if he's with the Boys in Blue."

"We'll see about that," Cohen replied. "Listen, Mr. Leipfold, I've got to go. They've got us all working overtime to cope with the shitstorm. I'm going to send over a list of names for you and your team to take a look at. I'd like you to work your way through them and to provide me with any information you might have that could help our investigation."

"Consider it done," Leipfold said.

That conversation took place on Saturday morning, and it left the rest of the weekend for Bram and Maile to research the names and tie them back to their database of usernames from the dark web. Maile complained at first, but it was half-hearted. She just resented taking time out from the MMORPG she'd been playing. Bram, for his part, was just glad to have something to do.

Without meaning to, the new recruit had found himself taking on a new and improved role at the company, acting more like an agent in the field than as a receptionist or a computer grunt. It helped that the field in question was limited to the 230 square metres that made up their office. The boy had a knack for doxing that put Maile to shame, and he was light years ahead of most journalists. He ended up doing most of the leg work, no pun intended, tracking down new information and forwarding it to *The Tribune* before waiting for the ensuing press coverage.

Seventeen new arrests were made on the Sunday morning, but the headlines were dominated by the home secretary, who'd been officially charged with racketeering and conspiracy to pervert the course of justice. It seemed that no amount of influence was enough to stop the long arm of the law when it was reaching out to embrace him.

But then something else happened that upset the apple cart once more, leaving Leipfold smacking his fist against his desk in desperation and shouting, "I just want to get back to work!"

The leader of the opposition gave a press conference of his own from party headquarters, accusing the prime minister of complicity in what was already being referred to as "the Leipfold case."

He also called for a general election and promised to open up a debate on the floor of the House of Commons.

Chapter Twenty-Two:
The Eyes of the World

MONDAY, MAY 1ST, WAS a bank holiday, but while the rest of the country was soaking up the unusual bank holiday sunshine, Leipfold was pacing up and down in his office and considering making a tinfoil hat.

Jack Cholmondeley had started work again at the Old Vic, and not a moment too soon. Leipfold figured they'd need all the help they could get, and Cholmondeley was the only cop that Leipfold had ever met who seemed impervious to politics, threats and bribery, as though he'd somehow developed an immunity.

Leipfold wasn't worried about Cholmondeley, but he was concerned for Constable Groves and her elderly mother, who no longer had any protection. He would have sent someone round if he'd had the resources, but he didn't. The best he could do was to hope that the Boys in Blue had got the message and that they'd target him instead of her.

It didn't offer much comfort.

Meanwhile, all three members of staff were exhausted, and Maile looked as though she was going to pass out until she drank her third energy drink of the morning and gave herself the heebie jeebies. Her heart rate shot up to 170, and she started shaking harder than a junkie who was craving a fix. Then the sweats started, first the hot sweats and then the cold. She gave Leipfold a running commentary, though she seemed detached and disinterested.

Leipfold guessed that she was so used to them that she'd learned to power through.

He made her drink a glass of water anyway, and she ended up lying down in reception with her laptop in front of her, typing away at it while occasionally checking her wrist to take a look at her heart rate. Leipfold was downstairs with her, ostensibly to give Bram his official onboarding but mainly so he could keep an eye on her.

The three of them were sitting around in the downstairs office, their nervousness and unease bringing them together, when the buzzer rang. At first, they all ignored it because it had been going off almost non-stop ever since the press had descended upon them, but then the office phone rang, followed by Leipfold's mobile. He let it ring and go to voicemail, but then it buzzed back into life again and he answered it reluctantly.

"Hello?"

"Are you going to let me in, Mr. Leipfold?"

"Oh, it's you."

Leipfold sighed and pinched the bridge of his nose, then nodded at Bram, who wheeled over to the intercom and buzzed their visitor in.

Tabitha Swordrock had lost a little weight since the last time he'd seen her, and Leipfold supposed it was from the stress. She'd also developed deep bags beneath her eyes and was twitching nervously and whirling around at the slightest noise. When the kettle boiled and spat steam out into the slightly musty air of the office, she nearly jumped out of her skin.

Maile slipped her a couple of tablets of propranolol and escorted her to a chair while Leipfold poured out their drinks. He'd brewed decaf for Maile and Swordrock. He didn't think their nerves would take anything stronger.

"Mr. Leipfold, you've got to help me," she said, once she'd settled enough to share her story. "They're coming after me. I'm being followed, and I've been getting weird phone calls. When I got home on Saturday, someone had sprayed 'traitor' across my windows. They've poured weed-killer on my begonias, too."

"Have you seen them?" Leipfold asked. "Or spoken to them?"

Swordrock shook her head and took a tentative sip at her coffee before replying. She had the mug cradled in her hands as though its life-giving warmth was the only thing keeping her going.

"Other than 'traitor', I've had nothing," she said. "Even when they call my phone, I can only hear heavy breathing. But it's them, all right. It has to be."

"It's a warning," Leipfold said. "And it bears all their hallmarks."

"There's more," Swordrock continued. "They're deporting my clients. Not just one, you understand. All of them. It's too much to be a coincidence. It's a targeted attack. They've already started proceedings against a number of my clients, and others have been receiving the phone calls. You have to do something, James."

"Like what?"

"You have to stop the Boys in Blue before they do something drastic," she said. "My clients came to the UK looking for freedom from persecution. Many of them are fleeing warzones, and most have already lost friends and family members. They came here to be *safe,* James. Now look."

"Democracy is dead," Leipfold said. "Or at the very least, it's dying. I hate to tell you this, Ms. Swordrock, but our government doesn't give a damn about you or your clients."

"It shows," Swordrock said. "Christ, James. I've always been proud to be British. Churchill, Wordsworth, Shakespeare, all those dead old guys."

"I'm still alive, thanks," Bram interjected.

"It's the living you want to worry about," Leipfold said. "The dead can't kill you."

"You think it'll come to that?"

"I'm not sure," Leipfold said. "The Boys in Blue are powerful, but we've broken their spine and pulled their teeth. They'll retaliate, but I don't think they'll retaliate against you."

"I haven't done anything."

"Not true," Leipfold said. "You helped us, and to the Boys in Blue, that may well be enough. You want my advice?"

"I'm here, aren't I?"

"Get you and your clients out of the country while you still can," Leipfold said. "Jump the gun and flee before they come for you, preferably to a country without extradition. I'd go for the UAE. You can disappear there and still live in comfort."

"And what if I don't want to?" Swordrock asked.

"It'll only be for a month or so," Leipfold said. "Just until we know that the danger has passed."

"And how am I supposed to move my clients there?" she asked. "I'm not exactly made of money. I can't just charter a plane and fly them out of here."

"You can't," Leipfold said. "But maybe I can."

"You have that kind of money?"

Their conversation was interrupted from a bark of laughter from the sofa, where Maile was still lying prone and doing her breathing exercises while typing away at something on her laptop.

"Have you seen our office?" she said.

Leipfold ignored her.

"Think about it," Leipfold said. "The eyes of the world are upon us. We have some powerful enemies, but we also have some powerful allies, all of those who are in favour of truth and democracy."

"So?" Swordrock asked. Her earlier anxiety had disappeared along with her cup of coffee, to be replaced by a look of curiosity, even though her hands were still shaking and her life was at stake.

"We can't charter a plane, but someone else can," Leipfold explained. "All we need to do is to find someone with a big wallet and a desire to raise their middle finger to the government. Leave it with me, Miss Swordrock. I'll see what I can do."

*   *   *

When Swordrock left his office, Leipfold donned his leathers and followed her out. She'd driven there in a lime green Fiat, which made it easier for Leipfold to follow her through the streets. But he wasn't really watching her car. He was trying to spot whether someone was pursuing her.

The ride filled him with adrenaline, and he thrilled at the familiar feel of the streets slipping past beneath his wheels as he wound his way through the city. She was heading south, and Leipfold felt his mind drifting as his senses took over. He wasn't distracted, as such. It was just that he knew the roads well and he had a lot on his mind, fourscore tiny different clues all pricking away at his psyche like ancient blades giving him the death of a thousand knives.

He took his mind off the road for a second, if that. But that was enough.

A black jeep shot over from a busy intersection, making an illegal right turn and swerving across the road in front of him. Leipfold looked up and had just enough time to throw his hands in front of his face, and then his bike smashed into the side of the vehicle.

It wasn't a high-speed collision, but it felt like one. Leipfold went over his handlebars and into the side of the jeep, then tumbled through the air and came down hard on the asphalt. Some half-forgotten instinct from childhood judo classes kicked in, and he brought both of his arms down flat to break his fall. He felt his bones rattle and a white-hot flare of pain seared along his left arm and into the little space inside his skull behind his eyeballs, but he slowed his momentum and instead of bouncing when he hit the floor, he skidded along it.

His leathers saved his life, and he knew it. That was why he wore the things in the first place. His helmet had taken a nasty whack from something and the visor had caved in towards his face, but his head seemed remarkably intact, although his brain felt a bit like his stomach did when he took a steep bridge too quickly and it dropped away beneath him.

Leipfold was medically trained and knew that the best thing to do would be to lie still and wait for an ambulance in case he'd sustained internal bleeding or spinal damage. But he also suspected that this was no normal accident.

He pulled himself shakily to his feet and then leaned against a lamppost. The intersection hadn't been too busy, but the collision had happened in broad daylight and people were flocking out of nearby buildings or getting out of their cars. As he looked on, one of the jeep's windows wound down and there were a couple of muzzle flashes, accompanied by the loud sound of their artificial thunder.

Leipfold ducked instinctively, his mind taking him back to the rough Kuwaiti desert and his time in the British Army, but the bullets weren't meant for him.

They were meant for Tabitha Swordrock.

He raced towards her vehicle, but he knew before he got there that he was too late to do anything. Nevertheless, he took her pulse and pressed his ear to her mouth, but there were no breaths and no final words for him to learn from.

And then he spotted something on the passenger seat.

* * *

Leipfold was treated at the scene by two paramedics, who'd first ascertained that there was nothing they could do for Swordrock, who had two bullets in her head. Her killers had wound back through the streets again before Leipfold could get a good look at them, though he'd noted down the number plate. He didn't think it would be much help, but he had a good idea of who'd been behind the attack.

He didn't tell the cops about the fob he'd taken from the passenger seat of Swordrock's car. He was still trying to make sense of it himself. It was emblazoned with the logo of the Grosvenor House Hotel and bore the number of room 302. The room that Jayne Lipton had died in.

He tried to figure out what it all meant. If it was a message, it wasn't a clear one, and it was hard to tell whether Swordrock had been carrying the key herself or whether it had been thrown through the open window by her killer. Leipfold had been too busy peeling himself back up off the road.

The paramedics had wanted to take him to the hospital to take X-rays, but Leipfold had refused any further treatment once it became clear that he wasn't about to drop down dead. He had a job to do.

Camilla, his motorbike, had fared remarkably well in the crash. Sure, she'd taken a few knocks, but her engine whirred into life on the first attempt and he was soon back on the road again, albeit feeling more shaken than before and with a closer eye on the traffic around him.

He made a mental note to send her in for servicing, but he didn't expect to get to it any time soon. She still ran, and that was enough. The deep scars in her side would have to wait. Still, despite the adrenaline, he kept to the speed limit. The last thing he needed was another accident—or to be stopped by the police.

He wound through the streets towards the Grosvenor House Hotel and parked a block away, trusting the backstreets to be good enough to keep Camilla hidden until he needed to make a getaway. As an extra precaution, he padlocked her to a lamppost opposite a Tesco Express. They had security cameras, and so if anyone had any bright ideas about stealing her or doing further damage, he'd be able to track them down.

Then he walked through Mayfair and marched confidently in through the hotel's opulent double doors.

Leipfold had been there before, including the day that Jayne Lipton's body had been found. He'd been given a lifetime ban, but a little time had passed and he noticed as he walked into the foyer that a different receptionist was working the desk. Still, he kept his cap pulled low over his eyes and walked in with his side toward her so that she couldn't get a good look at his face. She said something as he walked in, but he didn't catch what it was and simply grunted in acknowledgment.

He knew exactly where he was going; room 302 on the third floor. He'd been there before.

Fortunately for Leipfold, he had a near-eidetic memory, and that meant that he could run up the stairs and repeat the route he'd taken on his last visit. When he reached the third floor, he knew exactly which door to go to.

He took a deep breath and then inserted his stolen key fob into the door. It unlocked on the first try. Leipfold pushed it open, though he held back for a moment to wait for a response. When none was forthcoming, he stuck his head through the door and scanned for threats, noticing as he did so that the window was open and a cool breeze was flowing through the room.

He stepped inside the room and looked around, with a cursory glance telling him that it was just a normal hotel room, albeit one that a young woman had once died in. The main room looked clear, and so he turned his attention to the bathroom.

He was just reaching for the door handle when it burst open and crashed against him, the momentum and the weight of the wood driving him backwards into the wall. Leipfold looked up and saw a flash of metal, then reacted on instinct, hooking his head beneath his aggressor's arm and driving him back into the plasterboard.

The man tensed as the air was knocked out of him, and Leipfold used that time to back away towards the door, which was still hanging open. His opponent hunched over for a moment and then hauled himself back up, giving Leipfold a good view of his face. But he didn't recognise it, and Leipfold had a knack for names and faces.

"Who are you?" he asked.

But the knifeman didn't answer, opting instead to rush at Leipfold, who stepped out of the way just in time. Then the two of them were in the hallway. The man lunged again, and Leipfold dodged to the left, the tip of the blade brushing against his jacket and ripping through the stitching. Leipfold reached up automatically as though to stem the flow of blood from a wound that wasn't there.

Then the knifeman was rushing him again, the blade held high in the air in a grim parody of a villain in a slasher movie. Leipfold fell back, realising too late that he'd trapped himself in a corner. The attacker was coming at him from his right, but the path to the left was partially blocked by a potted fern that would have forced him back into the danger zone.

Leipfold's eyes darted automatically around the corridor, looking for an escape route or something he could use to disorient the man. He settled on an emergency button behind a plate of Plexiglas, but it was too far away and the blade was coming towards him and—

The air lit up with the harsh sound of electricity, accompanied by a smell like pork scratchings that made Leipfold drool involuntarily, even though his brain overruled his stomach and told him what he was smelling.

His attacker hit the floor like a piano dropped from a third-floor window and twitched slightly as he curled up into the fetal position. Leipfold looked up and regarded his rescuer with a solemn, unfazed expression.

"Ah," Leipfold said. "Sergeant Mogford. I was wondering when you'd join me."

Chapter Twenty-Three:
National Security

IT HAD BEEN A busy evening for Gary Mogford. It was a Monday night, which was never a good thing, and that jammy bastard James Leipfold had been playing silly buggers and getting him involved in some hare-brained scheme of his. Although he couldn't fault Leipfold's logic.

At first, Mogford had been furious to learn that Leipfold had interfered with evidence at a crime scene, but then he'd thought about it and been forced to grudgingly admit that the detective had a point. Over the last couple of weeks, he'd seen more of the Boys in Blue than he would have liked. To begin with, they'd been little more than a conspiracy theory, an old ghost tale that had worked its way around the police force like a virus. He'd not believed the rumours at first, and Gary Mogford could be stubborn when he wanted to be, but it was a whole lot more difficult to ignore the rumours when the evidence was there right in front of him.

He'd spent his last six shifts working on a team as part of Operation Bourne, an initiative he'd spearheaded after receiving Leipfold's data dump. The goal was to bring down the bad apples without spoiling the bushel, but it was becoming increasingly obvious that the whole damn orchard was corrupt.

"It comes down to something when we can trust James Leipfold more than we can trust our own coppers," Mogford grumbled, as he and Constable Cohen made their way through the corridors towards interview room B.

Constable Cohen just grunted in assent, then led the way into the room and started the recording.

"The date is Monday May 1st," Constable Cohen said. "The time is currently 21:35. Present is myself, Constable Steven Cohen, as well as Sergeant Gary Mogford and the interviewee, uh…"

"Rupert Pritchard," Gary Mogford supplied.

"Fuck you," Pritchard said.

"Right," Cohen said. "Well, with that outburst out of the way, perhaps you could tell us why you were at the Grosvenor House Hotel."

"Perhaps you could tell me why James Leipfold was there," Pritchard replied.

"He's not the one in a police interview room," Mogford said. "In fact, it might interest you to know that shortly before we apprehended you, an attempt was made on Mr. Leipfold's life. Quite the coincidence, wouldn't you say?"

"That's all it is," Pritchard replied. "I'm not a killer. I'm just a messenger."

"A messenger with a knife," Cohen said, leaning forward across the desk and fixing Pritchard with a stare that could have bubbled paint from the walls.

Mogford was proud of Cohen, despite himself. He was a quick learner, and he'd come a long way since he'd first been sequestered from the reception team and brought into active investigations. It was a good job, too. Mogford was rapidly running out of coppers to lean on, except for the young ones, the ones who were keen to make a name for themselves and who hadn't had their ideologies crushed by the sheer scale of human misery that they experienced each day.

"Listen," Pritchard replied, leaning in to face Cohen until the two of them were almost nose-to-nose. "I know why I'm here. You and the lads think I'm one of the Boys in Blue."

"Got it in one," Mogford murmured.

"Well, you couldn't be further from the truth," Pritchard said. "I'm not with the Boys in Blue. I'm with MI5."

"And I'm the Queen of England."

"Look," Pritchard said. "What do you want from me?"

"Information."

"But I'm just a messenger!"

"Yeah?" Mogford said. "And what was your message?"

"It's more than my job's worth to tell you that," Pritchard said.

"You've got more than your job on the line, Sonny Jim," Mogford told him. "You're looking at a charge for attempted murder, and you'll be lucky if we don't throw in perverting the course of justice."

"It doesn't matter," Pritchard replied. "If I tell you anything more than I'm authorised to tell you, I'll be dead within a week."

"So what are you authorised to tell us?" Cohen asked. He'd shifted position again and was sitting upright in his chair like a vulture on a falconer's hand. Mogford flashed him a sideways glance and then looked back at the man on the other side of the interrogation table.

"What he said," Mogford added.

"Sweet Fanny Addams," Pritchard said. "I can give you my name, my rank and my serial number, which as you chaps can confirm, I've already done."

"It checks out, sir," Cohen murmured, although Mogford could hear the reluctance in his voice. "We found his name on the electoral roll and it lines up with what he told us."

"And have you contacted MI5?"

"I put in a freedom of information request," Cohen said. "But we might have to wait a while for them to get back to us."

"Damn it," Mogford growled, smashing his fist into the table and upsetting Cohen's coffee, which spilled over the sides of his Costa cup and trickled across the table. Mogford ignored it and instead stood up from his chair so that he loomed over the suspect like a bad hangover. If Pritchard really was with the secret service, he'd be used to tactics like that, but it was worth a shot regardless. "Now you listen here, you horrible little man. I don't care whether you work for the bloody Pope. If you commit a crime in my city, I'm going to make you pay for it. You were caught red-handed at the scene. I know that for a fact, because I was the one who collared you."

Pritchard sighed and slumped backwards in his chair. He didn't look defeated, but he did look as though he'd crossed the Rubicon.

"Listen," he said, "I like you, and—"

"Hah!" Mogford ejaculated.

"As I was saying," Pritchard continued. "I'm going to level with you. I was sent after James Leipfold for a specific reason. I had orders to silence him by any means possible."

"Including murder?"

"If it came to it," Pritchard said. "It's a case of national security."

"If he's telling the truth, those orders came from the top," Cohen said. "Not many people could authorise that."

"Why would I lie?"

"To save your own skin," Mogford replied. "If that's all you've—"

"Mike Croft," Pritchard said. "He's the man you should be talking to, not me. I was here under orders."

"You said," Mogford murmured.

Pritchard smiled grimly and pushed himself back from the table.

"Who do you think gave me the order?" Pritchard said.

∗   ∗   ∗

It was the following morning, and Mike Croft was a couple of miles away from the Old Vic and inside a dimly lit office on Balcombe Street. James Leipfold was sitting opposite him and frowning beneath his shock of ginger hair. He was haunted by the knowledge that if he hadn't tipped off Jack Cholmondeley about the key fob—and if Cholmondeley hadn't passed the information on to Sergeant Mogford—he might have been a dead man.

His back hurt like a motherfucker, and he'd been popping ibuprofen like there was no tomorrow. Camilla had been more badly-damaged than he'd realised. She still ran, but her engine was making a sound like a caged lion, and he wasn't too sure whether she was road-worthy.

"So," Croft said. "We meet again."

"Yes indeed," Leipfold replied. "Thanks for coming. I think it's about time that we laid our cards on the table."

"Sure," Croft said. "I've got a royal flush. How about you?"

"Five aces," Leipfold replied. "Who are you really, Mr. Croft?"

"I'm your client," Croft said.

"Not anymore," Leipfold said. "I carried out the investigation you asked of me, and I've come to an unavoidable conclusion. You, Mr. Croft, are the enemy."

"I work for the government."

"Exactly," Leipfold said. "I didn't learn a lot from my old man, and in fact he was a bit of a bastard, but he did teach me one thing. Never trust a politician."

"I'm not a politician," Croft replied.

"No, you're more than that," Leipfold said. "You're a glorified criminal, nothing more and nothing less."

"I was just following orders."

"So were the Germans," Leipfold replied.

"I do my job for the greater good," Croft said.

"So did the Germans," Leipfold murmured. He looked moodily around the office. Bram and Maile were still camping out downstairs, but he doubted they'd climbed out of their sleeping bags. Maile rarely woke up before 8 AM, and she wasn't properly conscious until after her first can of Monster.

"Listen, James," Croft said. "I'm on your side, though I'm not surprised you don't believe me. I wouldn't believe me if I was in your shoes."

"Then we're at an impasse."

"Perhaps not," Croft said. He smiled at Leipfold and reached into his jacket pocket, withdrawing a sterling silver cigarette case with six cigarillos inside it. He put one between his lips and flicked open a Zippo lighter. "Do you mind?"

"Yes, I bloody well do."

"Fair enough," Croft said, replacing the cigarillo inside its case. "I can wait a couple of minutes. The thing is, James, I've told you the truth, or at least a version of it. I work for the secret service, but not for MI5. They're as corrupt as they come. I report to a higher authority, and they have…well, shall we say, a vested interest in taking down the Boys in Blue."

"Go on."

"MI5 are the old guard," Croft said. "Ever heard of Captain Kell?"

"Captain Vernon," Leipfold replied, his eidetic memory dredging something up from an old documentary.

"Precisely," Croft said. "He was a founding member, in charge of the army division of the secret services. He graduated from Sandhurst and fought in the Boxer Rebellion."

"Who for?" Leipfold asked. "The Boxers or the Alliance?"

"You know your history," Croft replied. "You should go on *The Chase*."

Leipfold sensed a note of approval in the man's voice, and it gave him a momentary rush of ambivalent pride that quickly developed into ego-shame. He hated himself for feeling flattered, and so he recomposed himself and forced a poker smile onto his pallid face.

"Only if I'm a chaser," Leipfold said. "But you were saying?"

"Officially, Captain Kell was a war hero," Croft explained. "Unofficially, he was a liability who almost lost us the war. Churchill fired him in 1940 for being an old fart who was completely unprepared to deal with the threat of Axis spies in the Second World War."

"Thanks for the history lesson," Leipfold said. "But if you could get to the point sooner rather than later, I'd appreciate it. I haven't had my breakfast."

"Neither have I," Croft replied. "I was woken up by a grizzled private detective who ordered me to come to his office."

Leipfold said nothing. He just fixed the man with one of his inscrutable stares.

"Captain Kell was many things," Croft continued, "but he wasn't incompetent. He just had his hands full with the Boys in Blue."

"He was a member?"

"He was a grandmaster," Croft said. "One of the first leaders they had. He's the reason why the Boys in Blue have infiltrated as much as they have. It was his mission to spread their tendrils as far and wide as he could."

"Looks to me like he succeeded."

"Indeed," Croft said. "He wasn't the first man to lead the Boys in Blue, but he was the reason they spread throughout the military and the emergency services. But Kell has been dead for nearly eighty years, and times have changed. According to the government, the Boys in Blue don't exist."

"I have a binder full of evidence that suggests otherwise."

"James, we both know that the Boys in Blue are a threat to democracy," Croft said. "That's why I hired you in the first place. I represent a new agency, an evolved secret service that has so far flown under the radar. No one knows we exist, not even the Boys in Blue. And that's why we needed someone outside the system, someone who could take those bastards down for good."

"We?" Leipfold asked.

Croft smiled and opened up his cigarette case again.

"Come with me and I'll show you," Croft said. "I'm driving. I'll smoke my cigarillo on the way."

Leipfold paused for a moment, his brow furrowed as his mind raced at a thousand miles an hour. Then he came to a decision.

"I'll get my coat," he said.

*   *   *

Croft's car was idling outside Leipfold's office, the chauffeur in the driver's seat looking up and down the street as though he expected a parking warden to show up at any minute and give him a ticket.

Privately, Leipfold thought that was unlikely. Balcombe Street was a backwater, despite being in the middle of the city. The coppers tended to focus on Marylebone and Baker Street. While the wardens occasionally showed their faces, it was once or twice per week at most.

Croft and Leipfold climbed into the back of the black sedan and the chauffeur took off, winding skilfully through the streets towards Westminster.

"We're taking you to a secret location," Croft said.

"And you didn't blindfold me?"

"I didn't see the need to," Croft replied. "In case you haven't noticed, the windows are blacked out. No one can see in or out, and that's just how I like it."

"Fair enough," Leipfold said. He didn't see much point in reminding Croft of his eidetic memory. The detective knew the city like the back of his hand. Even with the windows blacked out, he could tell which direction they were moving in by the pitch and yaw of the vehicle.

Slowly, methodically, Leipfold committed the turns they took to his memory. Far from taxing him, it scratched a metaphorical itch. He knew the city's streets better than any cab driver, and he didn't need the Knowledge to know where he was. There was one point at which he wasn't sure whether they'd taken the first or second left at a roundabout, but then he figured it out a couple of streets later. Then he sensed them crossing the river and heading south past Waterloo towards Hammersmith.

"Champagne?" Croft asked, withdrawing a bottle of Dom Perignon from a small refrigerator that was hidden discretely within the vehicle's upholstery. He popped the cork off the bottle and poured out a glass, then held it out for Leipfold to take it.

James Leipfold fixed him with a look that suggested he'd just smelled a sewage refinery.

"It's eight o'clock in the morning," Leipfold said. "And I don't drink."

"Suit yourself."

A stilted silence descended upon the two of them, and for the next five minutes or so, the vehicle continued to meander through the streets. Leipfold counted twelve left turns in a row and came to a disturbing realisation.

"Why are you driving us around in circles?" Leipfold asked.

"Standard protocol."

"Standard protocol is for other people," Leipfold said. "Whoever dreamt it up has obviously never met me. I think it's about time that you told me the truth, Mr. Croft, if that's your real name. Who are you taking me to see?"

Mike Croft sighed and said, "I'm taking you to see the home secretary."

*   *   *

Leipfold had assumed that Croft was joking, but his assumption was quickly proven wrong. He also found out that he was wrong about the vehicle's purpose. He wasn't being taken somewhere specific. The vehicle itself was the meeting point.

He realised that when the chauffeur slowed the vehicle to a stop somewhere in White City. The car's door opened, and a man stooped and climbed in to sit opposite Leipfold and Croft on one of the vehicle's plush seats. It was a big car that had been heavily modified, but it wasn't a TARDIS and so its overpaid designers had only been able to do so much. The two rows of chairs faced each other and there was ample legroom, but it was still cosy. Up close and personal, there was no mistaking who the man was.

His name was Roger Gough, and he was a remarkably dour-looking man in his mid-fifties, though stress and politics had made him look older. His hair had once been brown, but it had turned a salt-and-pepper grey and started to fall out in places, resulting in a toupee that had been brutally mocked in the tabloid papers. He was in good shape for his age and was regularly photographed riding his bicycle or striding sweaty-faced up and down one of the hills in his constituency, but he still retained an unhealthy pallor, as though he spent too much time in front of a computer screen.

But Leipfold thought that was unlikely. Gough was a regular face on TV and in the newspapers, and he seemed to spend half his political career on some field trip or other trying to win the favour of the general public. He had a cool, calm and collected vibe that hid a ruthless streak that was occasionally revealed through his actions.

When he entered the vehicle, he grunted as he bent down and then wheezed as he reached over to strap himself in. He walked with a cane, and Leipfold cast his mind back to an article he'd read that had talked about how Gough had been elected in the first place. He'd been working a more junior governmental role when he'd been involved in a near-fatal traffic accident that had left him with a limp. Somehow, it had also boosted his popularity amongst the public, and he'd been at the top of the political pecking order ever since.

"It's good to meet you at last, Mr. Leipfold," Gough said, his voice rasping as though he was just getting over a cold. "I've heard a lot about you."

"And I've heard a lot about you too," Leipfold replied.

"Naturally," Gough said, dismissively. He produced a monogrammed handkerchief from an inside pocket of his jacket and blew his nose into it, then theatrically folded it back up and returned it.

"I still don't understand," Leipfold said, after the silence hung in the air like the aftermath of a bad fart. "Are you the good guys or the bad guys?"

"It doesn't matter," Gough replied. "There is no good and bad in this game. There's only power and those who seek it."

"I have no interest in power."

"Just the truth," Gough said. "I know. I've done my homework, Mr. Leipfold. I'm here to ask you to do what's best for the country, and it just so happens that it's also what's best for you. You've done the job that we hired you for. Now I'm asking you, I'm begging you, for your own sake. Quit while you're ahead. Don't dig any further."

"You brought me all the way over here to tell me that?" Leipfold asked, incredulously. "Why didn't you just send one of your lackeys?"

"I've tried," Gough replied. "The problem is that you never listen to them."

*   *   *

Gough and his chauffeur dropped Leipfold back at his office. He was just brewing himself his first cup of coffee when his phone pinged with an update. He looked down at it, swearing to himself as he fiddled with the touchscreen and tried to remember what Maile had said when she'd shown him how to use it. There'd been a notification from one of the exterior cameras. When he finally figured out how to open it, he was surprised to see that a copper was standing on his doorstep. The intercom buzzed a couple of seconds later.

Leipfold slid over to the buzzer without getting up from his chair, then pressed the button to let his visitor in. It was only Jack Cholmondeley, and he was there in uniform. He didn't waste any time with preamble, cutting to the chase before Leipfold had a chance to offer him a drink.

"I'm troubled, James," Cholmondeley said. "So many cops have been accused of corruption that before long, we won't have anyone left. Taking out the bad apples is one thing, but what are you supposed to do when the whole damn orchard's gone rotten?"

"You're the best person there is to clean things up," Leipfold replied. "If anyone can do the job, you can."

"If it doesn't get me killed first," Cholmondeley said. He sighed and sat down on Leipfold's sofa. "Well, if it does then at least I'll die doing what I love. I'll die in the pursuit of justice."

"You won't die at all, old man," Leipfold said. "At least, not for a while."

"Perhaps you're right," Cholmondeley said, the sombre expression on his face lightening as though the years were dropping away from him. "Time has a wonderful way of sorting these things out."

"Have we had any results?"

"Too early to tell," Cholmondeley said. "I think the ringleaders will go down, but as for the others? Your guess is as good as mine, but I have a horrible feeling they'll walk."

"So why did you stop by?"

"I just wanted to say hello," Cholmondeley replied. "I enjoyed working with you, James. And I learned a lot."

"You have Maile to thank for that."

"I was also hoping that you'd have some more information for me."

"Nothing yet," Leipfold said. "But we're working on it. And in the meantime, if you can press corruption charges on the leaders and make it stick, the world is going to start demanding answers. Think of the Boys in Blue as like a hydra. You cut off all the heads."

"Indeed," Cholmondeley replied, gloomily. "But we don't have any fire."

"Not yet," Leipfold said. "You worry too much, Jack. You can purge the rest of them over time, and without leadership, the body will die. Besides, I'm worried about something else entirely."

Chapter Twenty-Four:
Not Dead Yet

IT WAS WEDNESDAY, AND Leipfold and the gang were talking ethics.

Work on the investigation had stalled to a halt, mostly because it was out of their hands. There was a feeling in the air that they'd done all of the hard work and that the cops were just picking up the pieces, but at least Jack Cholmondeley was reporting back to them.

"It's because we're different generations," Maile said. "If I was in Stanley Millgram's experiments, I would have told him to go fuck himself."

"That's as may be," Leipfold replied. "But if a train was approaching two babies and you could pull a switch to kill an old man instead, would you do it?"

"That depends," Maile said. "If it was Rupert Murdoch then yeah. If it was Jack Cholmondeley, probably not."

"Murdoch's been taken in for interviews," Leipfold said, grinning at her from across the top of a fresh cup of coffee. "I hope they nail the bastard. We've done our bit. Now we can move on with our lives."

"Oh, hell no," Maile said. "We can't leave it like this. The story isn't over. I need to know what happens next."

"That's not a good enough reason to put our lives at risk."

"Who says we're still at risk?" Bram said. "Seems to me like the enemy's been defeated."

"It's when an opponent looks defeated that they're at their most dangerous," Leipfold reminded them.

*   *   *

But there were no more attempts on their lives, and Jack Cholmondeley's presence at the Groves residence had become something of a nuisance for all involved. Groves herself was getting better, but it was still early on in her rehabilitation and she was under orders to spend as much time as she could lying down, although she was able to hobble around the house with the help of a walking stick.

Leipfold still insisted on the office being manned around the clock, but that didn't pose a problem. Cholmondeley stayed over from time to time when he got lonely, and Leipfold himself was sleeping there each evening on the basis that it was safer and more comfortable anyway.

Bram and Maile just commuted to and from the office and slept at home, like normal people.

On the following Tuesday, James Leipfold made his first TV appearance, not counting a piece that had aired on the evening news when he'd disappeared and been taken for dead during the first Gulf War.

He'd been booked for a late-night talk show with a Z-list celebrity and spent most of the interview sweating uncomfortably in the chair and staring straight down the camera lens as though he was daring it to swing a fist at him. But still, he got his point across. When the interviewer, a young comedian by the name of Libby Lopez, asked him about the Boys in Blue, he came alive.

"I'm going to be honest with you, Ms. Lopez," Leipfold said. "By this point, everyone knows who the Boys in Blue are, and I didn't come here to rehash definitions or to tell people what they already know."

"So what did you come here for, Mr. Leipfold?" she asked.

"I'm here with a warning," Leipfold said. "The Boys in Blue may be crippled, but they're not dead yet. They also have their greasy fingers in a whole bunch of pies, from MI5 to the media. I want people to be on their guard. I want them to call out bullshit when—"

Then the broadcast cut to a message from the show's sponsors.

* * *

May moved slowly into June, and life returned almost to normal. Bram had settled into life at Leipfold Investigations, and Maile had adapted to middle management with surprising ease. Business was booming, mostly thanks to Leipfold's newfound notoriety, and they were able to reinvest some of the money into sprucing up the office. Leipfold had been thinking about taking on a fourth employee, but his mind rebelled against the idea on the basis that three was two too many. He knew they'd have to take on someone new eventually, but he'd rather stall the moment for as long as he could. And besides, he'd rather be more selective about his cases than to work for any old Tom, Dick or Harry.

The lowest point came at Tabitha Swordrock's funeral.

The ceremony took place at a crematorium in Richmond, and the whole of Leipfold Investigations showed up to pay its respects. Leipfold was wearing his only suit, while Maile was wearing a black dress that made her look like a ghost from a low-budget horror movie. Bram was looking particularly sharp, and he'd even polished his wheelchair. Camilla was in the shop being serviced and so the gang had booked a black cab and travelled there together.

Jack Cholmondeley was there too, and so were Constable Cohen and Constable Groves, although Sergeant Mogford was conspicuously absent. Groves was pale and she moved slowly, but some of her strength had come back and she seemed remarkably composed given that she could just as easily have had a funeral of her own.

The priest spoke movingly about Swordrock's life and the work she'd done for the community, and he called up several friends and family members as well as a colleague or two to share memories of their own. Nearly two hundred people had turned out to pay their respects, a testament to her impact and influence amongst the local community.

When it was time to sing hymns, Bram burst into tears and sobbed uncontrollably. Maile rested an arm on his shoulder and murmured something into his ear.

As they emerged from the service, the rain pelting down and soaking through their clothes, there was a screech of rubber, and Leipfold turned his head towards the sound. It reminded him of the first case he'd worked after Maile joined the team, and that reminded him of all the corpses they'd encountered along the way. The vehicle was a nondescript Citroën, and Leipfold committed the number plate to his incorruptible memory.

Then the car's window rolled down, and a long black barrel poked out of it.

"Down!" Leipfold shouted, throwing himself at Maile before she had a chance to react and bearing her down to the asphalt. Bram ducked and rolled forwards, finding a 4x4 to hide behind for some cover, and all three of them were faster than the bullets, which rang out a second after they hit the ground and which buried themselves uselessly amidst the foliage surrounding the graveyard.

Leipfold peered cautiously out from around a dark green electricity box and saw that the vehicle was already picking up speed and heading away from them.

"Stay down!" he shouted, simultaneously reaching into his pocket to place a call. His first call was to Jack Cholmondeley. His second was to 999.

But the vehicle had disappeared into the city, and the next time it surfaced, it was in a Surrey suburb and some inconsiderate bastard had set fire to it. Cholmondeley handed the crime scene over to a forensics unit, but he had little hope that they'd recover anything.

Worse, the attack had been meticulously planned. The CCTV cameras along the street had been taken out with a heavy object, and while some peripheral cameras had caught sight of the vehicle as it made its escape, it looked like they'd mapped out their getaway in advance to take side routes and avoid the traffic.

The gunman was never identified, and no trace of the attackers was ever found. But it weighed heavily on Leipfold's mind.

More time passed, and June rolled into July. The Boys in Blue had disappeared from the public eye again, although the blogosphere was still abuzz with conspiracy theories and independent investigations. A well-known YouTuber had gone viral with a story linking the Boys in Blue with several prominent American businessmen in the oil and gas industry, but otherwise, the organisation seemed dormant.

Leipfold suspected that was because half of their members were either out on bail awaiting trial or locked up in a cell somewhere.

The case had taken an unusual turn, and Leipfold had never seen anything quite like it. After their dossier went live, it was pored over by media organisations and the general public alike. The media had quickly moved on to the next big story, but the public had stuck with it and continued to investigate. Suddenly, it seemed as though everyone was a PI, and Leipfold and his team had watched as the keyboard warriors had done their work for them, augmenting the original dossier with more and more reports of corruption, human trafficking, drug dealing and even murder. It turned out that the long arms of the Boys in Blue stretched even further than they'd previously thought.

Then all of a sudden, Leipfold Investigations hit the news again after the leader of the opposition delivered an impassioned speech in the House of Commons. Leipfold never heard the speech, not being a fan of the televised news channels, but he did read a transcript.

Most of it was the usual political bluster, but he did put forward a motion to call in the ombudsmen to carry out an investigation of the true extent of corruption within the British political system. Leipfold suspected they'd be there for quite a while, whether they found ties to the Boys in Blue or not. But he also suspected that the plan would get shot down before it could ever happen.

Still, he entered the latter half of the month with a smile on his face. Whether the investigation happened or not was immaterial. The fact that the Boys in Blue were being openly discussed in the Houses of Parliament was enough for him. It was over.

He'd won.

* * *

Richard Corbett, the leader of the opposition, was a reasonably good-looking man in his mid-forties. There was a lightness to his eyes and a friendliness to his expression that gave him a certain warmth, and that was what had taken him to the top to begin with.

That hadn't stopped the press from pillorying him and nicknaming him the Bulldog, though it hadn't caught on amongst the voters. Leipfold also suspected that was why he'd spoken out against the Boys in Blue in the first place. They represented the establishment, and the establishment was whoever was currently in power. As the leader of the opposition, he had a vested interest in uncovering any corruption, especially if it reflected badly upon the prime minister.

He was also standing in James Leipfold's office, looking curiously around as though he'd never seen anything quite so quaint before.

"You wanted to see me," Leipfold said.

"I did indeed," Corbett replied. "Perhaps you heard the speech I gave in the Houses of Parliament."

"You'll forgive me, I'm sure, if I missed it," Leipfold said. "No offence, Mr. Corbett. I'm sure you have wonderful policies."

"Some would say so," Corbett replied. He smiled and looked around again. Leipfold followed his eyes, noticing as he did so that his office was descending back into chaos. He made a mental note to ask the cleaner to give the place a makeover.

"What do you want?" Leipfold asked.

"I'd like to offer you a deal," Corbett replied.

Leipfold sighed.

"The problem is, Mr. Corbett," Leipfold began, "I've been offered a lot of deals of late and I'm starting to get sick of the things. I don't do politics."

"I've heard as much," Corbett admitted, still smiling from beneath his shapely beard. "The thing is, Mr. Leipfold, only a fool would turn away an ally, and you're no fool."

Leipfold sighed again and said nothing. He could sense Corbett's eyes on him, but that didn't mean much. He shrugged them off and took a sip from his coffee.

"I'm not asking you to do much, Mr. Leipfold," Corbett said. "Just keep on doing what you do best. Keep on being provocative."

"I see," Leipfold murmured. "I'm to be the worm on the end of the hook."

* * *

Maile and Bram were keeping themselves busy at the office in Leipfold's absence. He'd been out of the office for most of the week before, and he'd finally caved and had a spare set of keys cut so that Maile could let herself in and lock up without him.

"Sometimes, I wonder," Maile said, as she took a swig from a can of Monster and glanced over at Bram in his wheelchair.

"About what?" Bram asked.

"About Leipfold," she said. "How the hell did he ever turn a profit in this place before we came along? He's never here."

"I'm sure he has his reasons."

Maile scoffed. "Yeah, right," she said. "Speaking out against secret societies and stoking the fires of the conspiracy theorists."

"Someone's got to do it."

"Have they?"

"I guess."

The buzzer sounded throughout the office, and Maile stood up to answer it before being waved back down again by Bram, who wheeled across to the intercom and pressed the button. He didn't bother to ask who it was. That had gone out the window a couple of weeks ago when the drama around the Boys in Blue had died down and Leipfold had started spending less of his time in the office.

When the visitor entered, Maile barely looked up. She was sitting on the sofa while Bram worked the reception desk, and her eyes were glued to her laptop, at least to begin with. She listened in as she continued to type away.

"Can I help?" Bram asked.

"Yes," their visitor said. "I'm looking for James Leipfold."

"I'm afraid he's not here at the moment," Bram said, putting on his best customer service voice and sounding vaguely like a disembodied voice on a voicemail machine. "He's been kept a little busy by some of our cases. Can I take a message?"

"Yes, please," the man said. There was an audible click, one that Maile recognised but only from the movies. "I want you to tell him to clear his schedule."

Maile looked up from her laptop screen at last and saw exactly what she'd been hoping not to see.

Their visitor, a pretty normal-looking guy by most standards, had a six-shot revolver in his hand and he was pointing it at Bram's head.

Chapter Twenty-Five:
Silky

JAMES LEIPFOLD HAD BEEN taking a break from his caseload to enjoy a lemonade at the Rose and Crown when his mobile phone rang. He looked down at it, saw that it was the office number and immediately answered the call, just in case it was urgent.

It was.

He raced back to the office as quickly as he could, thankful that he no longer drank and that he was always able to hop behind the handlebars at a moment's notice.

Bram hadn't said much on the phone, but he'd said enough. It seemed as though whoever the gunman was, he wasn't worried about secrecy. Bram had flat out told him that there was a gun to his head, and Leipfold had believed him. And if their goal was to use his employees as bait, it had worked.

He parked Camilla on the street outside his office, chained her securely to the railings and then let himself into the building. He wasn't in a hurry.

Leipfold twisted the key in the lock of the building and let himself into the foyer, which was unlit except for the last rays of the trailing afternoon sun. It was a pleasant day outside, but there was an oppressive air to the office.

When he opened the door to the downstairs office, he found himself looking at one of the builders, the same man who'd sparked something somewhere in Leipfold's memory. He focused in on the distinctive mole where his sideburns met his five o'clock shadow.

"I know you," Leipfold said.

"Well yeah," the man said. "I was your builder."

"I know *that*," Leipfold said. "But I've met you before somewhere."

"No funny business please, Mr. Leipfold."

"Silky!" Leipfold exclaimed, delighted to put a name to the face despite the imminent danger he was in. "I haven't seen you for years."

Silky looked at Leipfold and raised an eyebrow, but he didn't say anything.

"I'm sorry," Maile said. "My pepper spray and Bram's nightstick can't do much against a pistol."

Leipfold looked over and smiled softly at her.

"Okay, Silky," Leipfold said. "I'm here. What do you want?"

"Siddown," he said, waving the gun vaguely in Maile's direction. Leipfold sighed and walked over to sit on the sofa beside her. "And shuddup. I don't want to kill you, James."

"Then put the gun down."

"I can't do that," Silky said. "I've got a job to do."

"Oh yeah?" Leipfold replied. "And what's that? What are you trying to achieve here?"

"I've always wanted to get my own back on you, James," Silky said. "And I've never liked you, ever since I first set eyes on you in that godforsaken hellhole of a jail. So when someone offered me three grand to come and wave a gun around, I took them up on it. I'm here to give you a warning."

"Another one?"

"I don't know anything about that," Silky said. "I just got told to come in here and to do this."

Suddenly, before anyone could react, Silky pointed the gun towards the ceiling and pulled the trigger, discharging a round into the overhead lighting. Leipfold felt Maile flinch beside him, and he himself had awful flashbacks to his time in the desert when he'd come under heavy fire from the enemy.

"That's your warning, Mr. Leipfold," Silky said. "As for the message, you're to stop talking about the Boys in Blue and to let things lie."

"You have no idea what you're involved in, Silky," Leipfold replied. "If you're not careful, you'll end up with a bullet in your head for your troubles. The people that you're dealing with aren't the type to leave loose ends flapping in the wind. And besides, if I stop investigating, someone else will take up the trail."

Silky discharged another round into the ceiling, and Leipfold frowned at the man as he thought about how much it was going to cost to get the damage repaired.

"Stop it!" Maile shouted, and Silky shifted position slightly to point the gun at her.

"Be quiet, little girl," Silky growled. "If you're not careful, I'll fuckin' shoot you."

Then he took a couple of steps backwards and turned to look at Bram, although he still held the gun on Maile and Leipfold.

"Then again, perhaps I should shoot the cripple," he said.

"All right, all right," Leipfold said. "We get the picture, Silky. Now point that gun at me. I'm the one you want. Leave my employees out of this."

"Fair enough," Silky said. He switched his aim and pointed the firearm at Leipfold, then his fingers twitched as he pulled the trigger. A hunk of plaster exploded from the impact, sending dust and chips of paint raining down on the back of Leipfold's head. Something had cut his ear and it was bleeding, but although the wound stung, he didn't think it was serious.

Three shots left, he thought.

"I'm going to be a national hero," the man said. "I'm going to be on the front of all the papers. Everyone's going to know my name."

"Is that what they told you?" Leipfold asked.

"They told me a lot more than that," Silky said. He raised the pistol momentarily and used the barrel to scratch his eyebrow.

Bram saw his chance and took it, spinning the wheels of his chair to propel himself towards the door. Leipfold had left the door open and he was only fifteen feet away, but he was also at a significant disadvantage. He was only halfway there when the room was filled by another report. This time, the bullet pinged off the bottom of Bram's wheelchair and buried itself in the carpet.

"Hey," Bram protested. "Watch it. These things don't come cheap."

"Cheaper than a funeral," Silky said. He backed away towards one of the windows, swinging the barrel of the gun between Bram, Leipfold and Maile. "Sit back down."

"I'm in a wheelchair."

"You know what I mean."

Bram scowled, but he also backed away from the doorway and returned to his spot at the reception desk.

"People like me are needed," Silky continued.

"What?" Leipfold murmured. "Nutters with guns who come into the story at the end of the third act?"

Silky didn't seem to hear him.

"You disgusting, wishy-washy liberals sicken me," Silky continued. "The secret service is needed, the coppers are needed and from what I've heard, so are the Boys in Blue. People can't be trusted to govern themselves."

"You don't get to make that decision," Leipfold said.

"And neither do you, Mr. Leipfold," Silky replied. "My bosses do. They're saving lives and stopping terrorists. What are you doing, Mr. Leipfold? Boosting the divorce rate by helping paranoid lovers to spy on their spouses?"

"It's a living," Leipfold said. "And it's a more honest way of making a living than what you do. I can sleep at night, Silky. Well, mostly. How about you?"

"I don't sleep," Silky replied. "I mostly—"

That was as far as he got because there was an almighty bang and the office door swung open. All four heads spun around to look at the intruder, and Silky fired off another shot, which whizzed within a foot of Jack Cholmondeley, who'd fortunately pushed the door open with a foot instead of an arm.

"Put the gun down, lad," Cholmondeley said. "Someone's likely to get hurt."

"Yeah," Silky said. "You, if you're not careful."

"We've got the place surrounded," Cholmondeley continued. "And James, I do wish you'd taken the Bosman warning more seriously."

"What do—"

But Silky was cut off again as one of the windows smashed and a canister hit the plush carpet about ten feet in front of Bram's desk. It made an unusual sound and then started spitting tear gas into the room, and while Silky's attention was distracted, Leipfold launched himself up from the sofa. Silky raised the gun and squeezed off his final shot, which this time buried itself in the sofa where Leipfold had been sitting just a second or two before, narrowly missing Maile and her laptop.

Silky squeezed the trigger again and then a third time, pointing the barrel at Leipfold's skull, but the red-headed detective didn't flinch. He just continued along on his trajectory, bearing towards Silky's legs and taking him down in a rugby tackle that hit the carpet with a satisfying whumph.

Before anyone could do anything else, the coughing started, and then a half dozen rapid response troops were rushing into the room with their weapons raised.

*   *   *

Maile O'Hara had a smile on her face because Leipfold had given her a pay rise. She supposed it was his way of making up for the psychological trauma that came from having a firearm discharged at close quarters.

Jack Cholmondeley had stopped by the office on Leipfold's instructions, and the boss was still insisting that no one had ever been in any danger. He'd even impressed Maile by logging into the camera network and scouting out the office before his arrival.

"As soon as I saw it was Silky," Leipfold told her, "I knew we'd come out safely on the other side. Silky is many things, but he's not a killer."

"He's an idiot," Maile replied. "An idiot without a plan."

When Silky had been cuffed and escorted out of Leipfold's office, he'd shown no regret or remorse. He'd acted as though it was all part of the job he'd been given, and perhaps it was. Maile had a horrible feeling that he expected to be released almost as soon as he was detained, and she had an even worse feeling that he was right.

As the boss liked to say, someone was playing silly buggers.

Silky's arrest flew under the radar at first, but then some of the conspiracy sites picked up on it and pretty soon, the online hive mind was taken over by gossip and speculation, most of it so ill-informed that Leipfold had trouble keeping a straight face when Maile told him what people were saying.

But one of those rumours turned out to be true, as Leipfold and Maile found out on Wednesday 5th July, which was the scheduled date for the initial hearings for the ringleaders of the Boys in Blue. Leipfold and his team had been expecting something to happen, but they'd been expecting it to come in the form of an envelope of ricin being pushed through the letterbox or another visit from one of Leipfold's old enemies.

Instead, they were greeted by a wave of suicides that started to come in during the breakfast news. The deaths, it seemed, were a message. Eight men were dead in maximum security jail cells, and all eight of them had hanged themselves with a variety of makeshift nooses, constructed out of shoelaces and bedsheets.

One other man had attempted it, but he'd been unsuccessful. The guards had caught him in the middle of the act during one of their regular patrols and rushed him off to hospital.

Leipfold guessed that they were the only guards who weren't on the take. It seemed too much of a coincidence that the other eight men could have gone unchecked for long enough for them to shuffle off their mortal coils.

Perhaps they hadn't even been suicides. He supposed that only time and the subsequent inquiries would settle the matter for sure.

As the news broke, the gossip around the Boys in Blue began again, and the prime minister had announced a news conference outside 10 Downing Street at one-thirty in the afternoon. Leipfold waited impatiently for the conference to start, killing time as he did so by playing chess on his phone and filing some of the paperwork that had been hanging over him for the last few weeks.

He got so absorbed in the game that he didn't look up again until he'd got the black queen checkmated, and by that time the PM had already made his announcement. Leipfold unmuted the TV and then quickly muted it again once he realized that the so-called experts on the news channel were just regurgitating what was being shown in the ticker along the bottom.

Prime Minister Arnold Floyd announces his resignation. Deputy Prime Minister and Home Secretary Roger Gough to assume leadership role.

He was blaming it on Brexit, but Leipfold wasn't so sure. If the rumours were true, he'd been a stooge to begin with, a puppet that the Boys in Blue had manipulated to do their bidding. Even if that wasn't the case, he'd been the one in charge of the country when the scandal had hit the news. It was his country, and thus his responsibility.

But Leipfold wasn't convinced that replacing Floyd with Gough would make a difference.

*   *   *

The surprise announcement had half the country in uproar, and within three hours of the news breaking, the stock markets had tanked and there was talk of the banks collapsing again, though Leipfold didn't think it likely.

That evening, Gough held a press conference of his own in which he said that the prime minister's decision had "come out of the blue" and that it was "a surprise to everyone." Leipfold had jotted both of those quotes down with a big question mark beside them.

Gough had also called for a national election, arguing that the British people deserved to be ruled by a prime minister who'd been elected into office. But he didn't have the power to order such an election, at least not in any hurry, and Leipfold doubted that he'd follow through. If it went to the vote, he'd probably win anyway, but then there was always the leader of the opposition...

Leipfold shook his head to clear it and muttered something about all politicians being the offspring of female dogs.

More worryingly still, the backlash against the political mainstream had led to a rise in the far right, with one prominent politician using the drama at Downing Street to peddle his own unique brand of bigotry.

What a time to be alive, Leipfold thought. Then he wondered whether he'd pinched that expression from Maile and, if so, how his employee had managed to rewire the way that he thought.

She'd certainly been a big influence on him. Since she'd joined the team, he'd had to get used to being in the spotlight, and his investigation into the Boys in Blue had catapulted him into some sort of Z-list limbo. He wasn't quite a household name anymore, but he was the answer to a question on a television quiz show, and that was still more fame than he'd bargained for.

The television interviews had dried up, but *The Tribune* had started asking him for comments from time to time and he'd been invited to talk to the BBC on a late-night radio show that aired around the world. To Leipfold, that was the biggest sign yet that the age of the Boys in Blue was over. The BBC had been just as corrupt as any of the Murdoch media, but it looked as though they were trying to make amends.

They even asked him if he had any plans to run for the prime minister's job if Gough went ahead and called a new election. He'd said no, of course. He had his work to focus on, his company to build, and the constant, burning desire to pursue the truth.

*   *   *

Jack Cholmondeley was back at his poky little flat. He'd stayed there for longer than he'd ever imagined, but it was finally time for him to move out and into a place of his own.

It wasn't with Mary, but that would have to do.

His marriage was dead, not dying, and its fetid corpse was buried six feet beneath the surface of the soil. Mary Cholmondeley had switched back to using her maiden name, and he could hardly fault her. He'd gone from worrying about how he'd ever live without her to wondering why they'd stayed together so long. There was a lot of truth to her accusations that he was married to the job. It didn't leave much time for a mistress.

It was Cholmondeley's last night in the flat, and he'd spent the evening packing his belongings, ready to pick up the keys for his new place the following morning. It wasn't much, but it was an upgrade.

He whistled while he worked, but he was off-key and he knew it. His mind wasn't on it. While he kept his hands busy working through the detritus that had gathered since he'd first moved out of the house he'd shared with Mary, his mind drifted and settled on the Old Vic.

Constable Groves was back, though she was on desk duty and still had to walk around with the aid of a cane, despite being on the younger side of thirty. Constable Cohen had been nominated for a commendation by Sergeant Mogford, who apparently *did* have a heart, and was the first in line for a pay rise once the politicians signed off on a funding boost. Mogford himself was doing some solid work, and it looked as though he'd kept things ticking over just fine in Cholmondeley's absence. All the same, the old man had a feeling that he was glad to see him back.

But all that thinking had pushed him to think about something else. He had to keep an eye on his own future, and he had a feeling that everything was going to be fine.

He realised that he hadn't thought about Mary for over a week, and even then the last time had been to idly wonder whether he'd be receiving divorce papers any time soon. He hoped he would be. It wasn't as though he was in a rush, but it would be nice to get the damned thing out of the way.

Maybe Mary was right after all, Cholmondeley thought. *Perhaps we both need to move on with our lives. I always loved my job more than her. I just wouldn't admit it. I can't hate the old girl for opening up my eyes.*

Jack Cholmondeley was a copper, and so he approached the problem like a copper would. He looked at it practically, and he'd arrived at a single, inescapable conclusion. The best thing that Mary had ever done for him was that she'd paid her half of the mortgage thanks to some old bail bonds and the inheritance she'd been left by her father.

Now that there was no Mary, he needed to find himself a roommate to keep the costs down. And as luck would have it, he knew just the man.

He grinned to himself and made a call to James Leipfold.

Chapter Twenty-Six:
Recruitment Drive

JULY PASSED, AND SO did August.

James Leipfold and Jack Cholmondeley were officially housemates, and the two of them were living in a fairly spacious two-bedroomed apartment above a Tesco Express. The apartment was in decent shape and it was homely enough, although it was never going to pass a fire safety audit. If a fire broke out at Tesco, they'd just have to hope that they weren't at home.

Bram and Kat had started dating, although they hadn't made it official. If anyone asked, they said they were "seeing each other." Maile took a not-so-secret guilty pleasure in it, feeling like a cross between Paddy McGuinness and Victor Frankenstein.

Business was booming at Leipfold Investigations, to the point at which Maile and Bram were struggling to keep up with their workloads. They'd both ended up taking on a ton of overtime, for which Leipfold was paying them time and a half. The system worked, but it wasn't ideal.

"Maybe we'll hire someone else," Leipfold said, following his train of thought to its final destination by talking to himself, as he often did.

"Yeah?" said Bram, who was sitting within earshot at the reception desk. "Like who?"

"I have no idea," Leipfold replied. "I thought that perhaps you could write up a job description and get it shared online. You'd better run it past Maile first, though."

"Damn right," Maile said. She was in her office, but she had the door open, and Leipfold presumed that she wasn't wearing her headphones. "You know the rules, boys. Nothing written leaves this office until I've taken a look at it, and that includes emails to clients. We've got a certain amount of professionalism to maintain, and Bram uses commas like I use caffeine. James, your spelling's okay, but you use too many dangling modifiers."

"Duly noted," Leipfold said, tipping a wink at Bram, who grinned but said nothing.

"Anyway," Maile continued. "We might not need to look too far. I think I know the perfect person."

"Kat Cotteril?"

"You read my mind," Maile said. "She's been looking for a new challenge, and I think she's got a lot to offer the company."

"Like what?"

"Well, she can take care of herself for a start," Maile said. "We've been taking self-defence classes. Plus, she seems to be getting on pretty well with Bram, if you know what I mean."

"I'm not convinced that's a good enough reason to hire her."

"Well, we've got to hire someone," Maile said. "Kat's good with people, so she can run reception while Bram and I focus on the tech stuff. Besides, you saw what she can do with a little makeup."

"That's true."

"And she's not just good backstage, making actors look like corpses," Maile continued. "She's not a bad actress, either. I'm sure she'd be more than happy to go undercover if we needed her. Plus, half of our clients are jealous spouses hiring us to follow their husbands."

"So?"

"Have you ever heard of a honey trap?"

"Isn't that from *Winnie the Pooh*?"

"No," Maile replied. "But nice try. A honey trap is when you use an attractive woman to lure a cheater into cheating. Kat can slide into people's DMs or get chatting to them at clubs. We'll soon find out whether people are loyal or not."

"And Kat's an attractive woman?" Leipfold said. "I always thought she was…well, average."

"You're not exactly a looker yourself, James," Maile replied. "Anyway, Bram seems to think so. She's a normie, you know? Well, more normal than any of us."

"Hmm," Leipfold replied. "Well, we'll see about that. Arrange for her to come in for an interview. I'd like to talk to her."

*   *   *

There'd been a recruitment drive at the Old Vic, too. The problem was that with so many bad cops rooted out and placed under the spotlight, the police force was in desperate need of some fresh meat.

Constables Groves and Cohen had been put in charge of the process under supervision from Jack Cholmondeley. Mogford was still busy working on the Boys in Blue cases, many of which were going to court. But there were many more of them where the suspects had been released without charge, though those in positions of power had been placed on gardening leave with an irony that kept Cholmondeley smiling from dawn to dusk.

Then came the evenings, which were more difficult. It was rare for James and Jack to both be home at the same time, but they were already starting to bicker like an old married couple whenever one of them failed to do the washing up or to take the bins out when it was collection day. The arrangement worked as much as it could, but they were two grumpy old loners who appreciated their personal space. It was lucky that Leipfold spent half of his nights at the office, while Cholmondeley was taking on a bunch of overtime to refill his dwindling retirement fund.

Meanwhile, the world was changing around them. Promises had been kept and the country had gone to the polls in a general election, leading to a landslide victory for the leader of the opposition. During their election campaign, they'd promised to uphold and maintain individual freedoms by reminiscing about the glory days of the British Empire, whatever those were.

To Jack Cholmondeley, it sounded suspiciously like the views of an old colonialist, of the type that made up the majority of the Boys in Blue. It was a worrying development.

But that wasn't what was on Jack Cholmondeley's mind. Like Mary had always said, he was married to his job, and that was why the recruitment drive was dominating his every waking moment. And he'd learned something from working with Leipfold, especially with cybercrime on the rise.

He'd learned the importance of having a Maile.

*   *   *

"You need to come and look at this," Bram said.

He was speaking into the smartphone app that Maile had hooked them all up with that acted like an encrypted walkie talkie. Leipfold had resisted it at first, until he'd started to see its merits. Now, barely a month after its adoption, it was hard to get him off the thing, and they talked to him more over the app than they did in person.

Maile had been in her office and so she was the first to join Bram, but he insisted on waiting for the boss before he told her what was up. When Leipfold came down, Bram told Maile to put the kettle on and asked the boss to take a seat.

"You're not going to believe this," Bram said. "But it's all over the news."

"Cut to the chase, kid," Leipfold said, his pulse racing the way it always did when he felt like he was wasting time. Bram had a good heart, but he wasn't so hot at knowing his boss' little quirks, and Maile often had to steer him in the right direction.

"The prime minister," Bram replied. "That is, I mean, the former prime minister. Ah, screw it, just see for yourself."

He twisted his laptop around in a neat 180, and Leipfold started reading the screen. Bram had booted up the BBC News website, and they were in the middle of a breaking news report.

Leipfold read the ticker as it scrolled across the screen:

Former Prime Minister Kidnapped.

"Turn the volume up, would you?" Leipfold said.

Bram grunted and did as he was told, unmuting the video player until the newsreader's voice filtered its way out of his speakers and into Leipfold's reception office.

"...official statement has no word on what the kidnappers want," the newsreader was explaining. "But sources have told the BBC that 10 Downing Street has received a short letter with a simple demand..."

"Here we go," Leipfold murmured.

"...which read, 'Bring us the head of James Leipfold.'"

"Shit," Leipfold said.

Acknowledgments

THANKS ARE DUE AS always to the usual crew: Donna Woodings, Carl Woodings, Alan Woodings, and Heather and Dave Clarke.

The Leipfold books wouldn't exist in their current form without the constant support and hard work from my publishing team, and to my long-term editor and partner-in-crime Pam Elise Harris in particular. We've worked on eleven books together, which Pam says might be the most books she's ever edited for one author.

The Leipfold series also owes a lot to the encouragement and support of the team at Encircle Publications, who took a chance with the republication of *Driven* and have been instrumental in its further development. Thanks to Eddie Vincent, Cynthia Brackett-Vincent, Christopher Wait, and Deirdre Wait.

Many of my constant readers, to borrow the term from Stephen King, have been asking me for updates and supporting me on my journey as I work on this series, and so if you're been one of the people who've reached out to me over the years, thanks are due to you as well. On the bad days, it's you guys who keep me going.

And of course, even if I haven't mentioned you by name, I want to thank you for picking up my books in the first place. I hope you had as much fun reading this as I had writing it.

Until next time…

Join the Conversation

THANKS FOR JOINING JAMES Leipfold, Jack Cholmondeley, Maile O'Hara and more in the latest instalment in the Leipfold series.

James, Jack, Maile, and I would love to hear what you think. Whether you loved or hated the book, please let us know by tweeting @DaneCobain or by leaving a review on Amazon and Goodreads.

Reviews help indie authors to sell their books, so please do take the time to share your thoughts. I link to my favourite reviews on Facebook and Twitter, so be sure to follow me there and to check out my site for further info. I'll see you soon!

danecobain.com
facebook.com/danecobainmusic
instagram.com/danecobain
youtube.com/danecobain
twitter.com/danecobain
tiktok.com/@danejohncobain

About the Author

DANE COBAIN IS A published author, freelance writer, poet, and musician. His releases include *No Rest for the Wicked* (supernatural thriller), *Former.ly* (literary fiction), *Come On Up to the House* (horror), and *Meat* (horror), as well as The Leipfold Mysteries, *Driven* (Encircle Publications, March 2019), *The Tower Hill Terror* (April 2020), *The Leipfold Files* (June 2022), and the newest, *Boys in Blue*, published in June 2024. For the latest news, follow Dane on social media (@Dane Cobain) and visit www.danecobain.com.

MORE GREAT READS
FROM DANE COBAIN

Driven (*Detective*) A car strikes in the middle of the night and a young actress lies dead in the road. The police force thinks it's an accident, but Maile and Leipfold aren't so sure. Putting their differences aside, and brought together by a shared love of crosswords and busting bad guys, Maile and Leipfold investigate. But not all is as it seems, as they soon find out to their peril.

The Tower Hill Terror (*Detective*) James Leipfold and Maile O'Hara are back with a brand-new case. The Tower Hill Terror is on the loose, a serial killer with a grisly M.O., and Maile and Leipfold must work fast to take him down before another body is found. Meanwhile, Leipfold's cop friend Jack Cholmondeley finds himself working on the same investigation, but the killer is always one step ahead.

The Leipfold Files (*Detective*) Join a young James Leipfold as he discovers his knack for uncovering the truth and takes the early steps towards forming his detective agency, Leipfold Investigations. This collection brings together twenty-four James Leipfold short stories, including three shorts that take place between *Driven* and *The Tower Hill Terror*. It's a must for all fans of the Leipfold series and any serious reader of quirky detective novels and cosy mysteries.

If you enjoyed this book,
please consider writing a review
and sharing it with other readers.

Many of our authors are happy to participate in
book club and reader group discussions.
For more information, contact us at info@encirclepub.com.

Thank you,
Encircle Publications

For news about more exciting new fiction, join us at:

Facebook: www.facebook.com/encirclepub

Instagram: www.instagram.com/encirclepublications

Sign up for the Encircle Publications newsletter:
eepurl.com/cs8taP